*The Kindness of
Terrible People*

and Other Stories

The Kindness of Terrible People

and Other Stories

Stephanie Dupal

Published in the United States by Swan Abbey Press

Swan Abbey Press and the Swan colophon are trademarks
of Swan Abbey Press, LLC.

The following stories in this collection have been previously published, in slightly different form: "To Lie Engulfed in the Waves of the Sea" in *Maryland Literary Review*; "The Ethics of Keeping Company with Strangers" in the anthology *Muddy Backroads: Stories from Off the Beaten Path* (MadVille Publishing, 2022); "Madeleine Bouletier, She-Wolf of Crozon" in *Orca: A Literary Journal*; "Love Among the Orange Groves of Old Hollywood," "The Boy and the Bear," "Over the Mountain Steep," "Godfrey Green," and "The Beast Who Knew the Songs of Billie Holiday" in *The Northern Virginia Review*; "A Baby of the Ganges" in *Fiction International*; "The Kindness of Terrible People" in *Griffel*; "What Came After the Harvest" in *Broad River Review*; "Olympic Hopeful, 19, Dies After Winning U.S. Figure Skating Championships" in *Cerasus Magazine*; "The Words of All Our Fires" in *Storgy Magazine*; and "Boys and Girls Swimming Like Dolphins" in *Stonecoast Review*.

LIBRARY OF CONGRESS CATALOGING-IN-PUBLICATION DATA
Names: Dupal, Stephanie, author.
Title: The Kindness of Terrible People and Other Stories / Stephanie Dupal.
Description: Sister Bay: Swan Abbey Press, [2025]
Identifiers: LCCN 2025908012 | ISBN 978-0-9965103-1-8 |
ISBN 979-8-9909292-1-0 (ebook)
Classification:
LC record available at https://lccn.loc.gov/2025908012

Printed in the United States of America on acid-free paper

*For my mother, my sisters,
and my daughter*

Contents

CONTENTS

To Lie Engulfed in the Waves of the Sea

Whenever Manon awoke from dreams in which she still played for l'Orchèstre Symphonique de Montréal, the feel of the cello lingered between her knees, and the whitecaps of her life—the echoing arcs of *before*, *during*, and *after* the accident—came crashing in her thoughts once more. The instrument remained with her throughout the day like a phantom limb. It was still pressed against her during her solitary breakfast when, among a stack of bills on the counter, she opened a letter from the town of Matane. She knew this part of the Lower St. Lawrence well, having vacationed there as a child. She imagined the smell of the sea imbuing the envelope.

She pulled out a note written in decisive penmanship that explained the drawings accompanying the letter. In one drawing, three stick figures stood on a hill of white. Two tall women, with aggressive fingers pointing in all directions like the branches of brambles, flanked a little girl dressed in a red snowsuit, with tears in her eyes, great big drops of blue as big as the women's ski boots.

In another drawing, a multitude of misshapen hearts floated around the words *Je t'aime*.

Manon had received several other letters like this one, but she hadn't replied to the little girl who made the drawings. She'd shut out so many people from her life and lost interest in so many things already. She'd become difficult, even refusing to wear the wrist brace she received from the hospital. What was the point of wearing it if it couldn't cure her handicap? Whatever chores Manon performed, the clinicians' prognosis rang clear in her ears, words that thrummed her heartbreak: she would never play again.

She couldn't accept her fate when she ricocheted through a series of daily appointments and self-selected tasks: *read for one hour, walk outside if the weather allows, cross the street to the dépanneur to buy little Vachon cakes, meet with the physical therapist or the psychologist—or, better yet, the psychic.* When speaking to her therapists, Manon complained of being a case assigned to a 'government-issued' social worker, a woman who insisted on dressing like a medical professional with her cheery scrubs and sturdy rubber shoes, even though her only purpose was to investigate Manon's request for welfare after it was denied. The worker, Catherine—she could never remember her last name: Lévesque or Lavallée or Larivière—told her she was not without options. She should at least try to teach music.

*   *   *

Months before at Mont-Tremblant, in the queue to the chairlift, Manon had listened to a mother pushing her daughter ahead. "Marie-Soleil, grouille-toi!" she said. The girl wore a red snowsuit and she appeared a glossy tomato gliding along a white plate. She skittered her feet back and forth and made little progress. She was learning to ski without the aid of poles. The mother turned to Manon and said, "Scuse ben," and, fearing she might be an American or an Anglophone from a neighboring province, mouthed a loud exaggeration of words: "So sorry! My daughter is new."

"Y'a pas de quoi," said Manon. She helped the mother by scooting on the other side of Marie-Soleil, and together they pushed the girl into the mouth of the lift cabin. At once, they sat in the chair, which scooped them up with an accelerating sweep, and the mother pulled down the bar over their thighs. Manon and the mother arranged their poles while Marie-Soleil wiggled her bottom between the women. She took off her insulated mitten and handed it to her mother so she could wipe her nose with the back of her hand.

The mother said, "Véronique Turcotte. On vient de Matane."

There are places to ski around Matane, said Manon in French.

"Val-Neigette, oui," she said, waving Marie-Soleil's mitten as though swatting a fly, *"but it's not the same as this."*

"Manon Tremblay." She held out her hand.

Marie-Soleil whimpered. She dangled her short skis and the chairlift shook. *"What if I can't get off? What if I fall?"*

"It's her first time here."

Marie-Soleil said, *"At Val-Neigette, you put a stick between your legs and it pulls you up the bunny slope."* She had the earnestness of a five-year-old facing certain death. Her brown eyes stared at Manon with rabbity fear. Her body reminded Manon of her cousin Amélie at that age, yet Marie-Soleil exuded warmth and charisma when Amélie had been moody and calculating.

Manon tried to soothe the girl. "Voyons donc, Marie-Soleil, ta maman et moi, *we're going to hold you and you'll be sandwiched between the two of us when we get off. You'll just ski along. I promise, it'll be all right in the end."*

The women talked of nothing: of the weather, gray and cold over the Laurentian Mountains, of Montreal and Matane, of their careers. Véronique worked in finance, one of those jobs she described as eternal bureaucracy. She took interest in Manon's status as a cellist.

"Wow," she said, "une musicienne comme ça! T'es quelqu'un, toi."

You are somebody.

The chair climbed up the mountain and slowed, dipping before a hollow of snow where those who had already gotten off the lift assembled to wait for friends or adjust their goggles or position their poles. Marie-Soleil put on her mittens and pawed at her face with those great lobster-claw puffs. She said she was afraid of the teenagers sitting in a semi-circle, their snowboards a short wall toward which they would careen. When the time came to disembark, the red heft of Marie-Soleil squirmed and fell forward. Manon reached out to catch her, slipping an arm around her waist. The girl was solid and heavy, a soup can tipped forward, and she took down Manon with her. Véronique, holding her daughter's shoulders, toppled over them.

Manon heard the fracture of her ulna and screamed.

*　　*　　*

Mont-Tremblant. The irony of this name, the *trembling mountain*, in addition to her common last name, Tremblay, foreshadowed that accidental moment of losing her abilities. Her bones mended but her tendons did not. Halting movements accompanied by a staccato of pain replaced the dexterity of years of practice. When she tried to hold her bow, her hand shook, and music became a series of scratching sounds on the strings.

Now here she was, Manon Tremblay, sitting on a hard chair in the corridor of a dusty school for the performing arts in Westmount, on the Anglophone end of the island of Montreal, awaiting her turn, a folder of papers in her lap. She closed the brief on the boy with whom she would be auditioning. She'd met him once before, seated like this in a different yet identical hallway, and they played a game of listing all the peculiar things they loved to varying degrees of strangeness. He confessed to liking the smell of strangers, while she revealed she loved to lie.

She wiped her palms on her pencil skirt. She could wear fitted clothing that entrapped her legs now, though she found no comfort in this freedom. Heat gathered under her collar, her long hair blanketing her body. She should have tied the strands in a knot, the way she used to when she played in the orchestra.

A woman in a tweed blazer, neither unkind nor enthusiastic, greeted and led Manon through a maze of turns to the auditorium. They passed the door to a swimming pool, and Manon heard the squeals of children within. The smell of chlorine assailed her. "The students are swimming?"

"We rent out the pool on weekends. We had an athletic program, but no more. There's no money for the arts now, and the budget is even worse for athletics," said the woman. On the opposite end of the long hall, she opened double doors, and they walked down a narrow aisle separating rows of folding seats covered in burgundy velvet.

At the evaluators' table, three figures sat without moving. They would not smile at Manon. The man in the middle held her resume to his face, as if he needed the illumination of paper to understand why she was auditioning for this job.

"Manon Tremblay? Of the OSM?"

"Yes."

He said, "Why are you applying to this secondary school? The money is—" He did not continue.

"I would like to teach." Her French accent was unforgiving.

"Someone like you could do better."

She thought, *I am nobody now and nobody wants me.* She said instead, "It has always been my dream to teach children music."

"I see."

She was afraid they would dismiss her. They might even say they couldn't afford her, though it was she who couldn't afford not to work. She'd been turned down elsewhere already. This was her second interview with this school, and she faced the impossible task of turning pages of sheet music written in a cypher she couldn't read. What stories she told the previous hiring committee to charm them! She once heard that to lie convincingly, she should practice by telling a story backward. Life was a trail on which she could walk in any direction, but she thought of her stories as waves, and she modeled their variations to the ebb and flow of her desires. She managed to convince her interviewers that, along with her parents, she learned Braille as a child to teach a younger sibling who was born blind.

She hoped the languor of music would transport her through portals of knowledge and offer her the instincts necessary to accomplish miracles. She inhaled deeply to fill her lungs with what bravery she could muster, and she turned to face the stage, where Christophe, the teenaged boy she met previously, shifted on a long bench, a keyboard before him. *Un clavier.* She expected the enormity of a grand piano, its keys yellowed with age. She could not hide behind a keyboard, and they would see her falter.

She approached him. Christophe Michel was thirteen years old. She'd read his brief fully. He was born in Haiti, near the capital, and in 2013 during an explosion in the center of Marché Hyppolite, his body was thrown some distance against the wall of a building. He had been walking to school, just five years old. His family immigrated to Montreal soon after. Now he stared ahead and waited for her instructions.

"Christophe," she said. "C'est Manon. Tu te souviens?" *Do you remember?* She touched his shoulder. "J'ai un peu peur, tu sais." *I'm a little afraid, you know.* She wanted to say something profound and moving so he would come to her aid, but she opted for truth. *"I need your help. I know it's you who's playing, but it's me they're judging."* She remembered what he said about strangers and she told him she liked the scent of his shampoo, which reminded her of green apples. She regretted this detail, the mention of the apple's color.

He smiled and told her she smelled of vanilla mixed with the warmth of a winter fire. Her hair, which fell to her waist, brushed him. He touched the strands, and so she moved to let him trace the long scar on her wrist.

He asked, *"Does it hurt?"*

She whispered so only he could hear, *"I need this job and I would like to teach you and the other students. I'm lonely without the music."*

With a curt movement of his head, he let her know he understood.

"They're waiting."

"I know."

She hesitated and said, *"I have a secret: I lied about the sheet music. I can't read it. And I don't understand the experiment. When you play, you're not reading the partition with your finger. So why this page-turning?"*

"Sometimes I need to find my way through the music and there's a pause, so you'd put my hand in the right place, but this piece I know by heart. Assieds-toi, tout près." *Sit closer.* He added in French, *"Turn your body so they won't see us."* He traced a treble clef on her thigh. "Manon-la-vanille."

"Perfumes have notes and accords, like music," she said. "J'aime l'odeur des instruments. Et l'odeur des pages de partition."

"Moi aussi," said Christophe. "Et j'aime l'odeur du chlore." *I love the smell of chlorine.* He whispered, "Regarde mon pied." *Watch my foot.*

"When you're ready, Christophe!" yelled the evaluator.

"One moment!" he yelled back. He said to Manon so only she could hear, *"There's something I want. I'll cover for you and you'll get the job, but you have to promise to help me."* He told her what he most desired from any teacher at this school. For practical reasons, they denied his request every time.

"If they find out, I'll never get the job or they'll fire me before I can even begin."

"They won't." He waited. *"Promise me,"* he said.

Instead of annoyance, a familiar happiness overtook her. Her heart beat faster just thinking of it. *"When?"*

"They'll invite you again to meet the other teachers and their students in two weeks, on the day of Open House. Come one hour early and meet me on this stage. I don't have big enough shorts and I can't ask my parents or they'll know I'm up to something."

"I'll take care of it. C'est promis."

"On commence!" announced Christophe to the evaluators, who shook their heads at his sudden use of French.

How strict and proper those Anglos always are, thought Manon.

Christophe splayed his fingers on the keyboard and exhaled. He played Gabriel Fauré as if guided by the stars of the nocturnes, and she wanted to close her eyes and join him in the music; to feel the sound of his notes filling the air in concert with the remaining sharpness of the swimming pool; to value the talent of this boy beside her who conjured the purest adagio from such a terrible instrument. He played so well, she believed she sat next to the great Évelyne Crochet.

Manon traced the sheet music, too quickly or not quickly enough, she didn't know. She could not decipher the raised dots on the paper. They lined before her in full mystery, and she wondered at the boy's tenacity, the hours spent reading notes followed by a transposition to piano keys.

If she passed this audition, she would learn Braille because her fingertips could still feel. She would learn a new language for a boy like Christophe, a boy who could play to the rhythm of an old auditorium's fragrant mustiness and the notes of her perfume. Christophe tapped his foot on top of hers while he continued to play. She understood he'd given her the signal to turn the page.

*   *   *

The previous fall, just before Manon's accident, the director of l'Orchèstre Symphonique de Montréal had commissioned new advertisement for the upcoming season, and the musicians arrived early for the photo shoot. There was talk of making classical music sexier and more accessible to the public. Manon watched, unfazed, as Gilles Nadeau, who vied for Manon's position as first chair and principal cellist, volunteered to unbutton his shirt. His bleached teeth dazzled, just as his semi-permanent tan enchanted both the men and women with whom he slept. Manon rarely listened to his stories of sexual conquest and, to punish her, he tried to convince the other cellists she was nothing more than a bitch and a diva.

The photographer ignored Gilles and asked Manon to move her cello to center stage. She ordered a stylist to undo Manon's hair, and she begged her to play Saint-Saëns's *Swan* because she was a fan of Yo-Yo Ma's rendition and she wanted to hear her version. The photographer stepped from side to side and then stopped, having found something at last, and she positioned the umbrella lights so their reflection fell on the length of Manon's body.

When Manon played, the swath of her hair draped the side of her cello. The musicians gathered to the side of the stage and watched her transformation. The director clapped and moaned, while bending his knees like a child, "Oui, oui, oui! C'est parfait, Manon. C'est parfait!"

This photograph of Manon—her face and body half-bathed in light, arms bent to receive the world—graced billboards all around Montreal. She was suspended above *L'Autoroute* Décarie; among terrible ads for sex shops and La Ronde amusement park and the casino; on Boulevard Taschereau in Longueil and Brossard; on the outside wall of Place des Arts; and in metro station after metro station, where, when the compartments moved at terrifying speeds, she became nothing more than a blur.

*   *   *

At the department store, Manon rode the escalators with her bad wrist trembling on the black rubber handrail that advanced upward to the floor above. She thought of the chairlift and being with Véronique and Marie-Soleil. Sunlight pierced the clouds, casting a momentary, yet scintillating, glow on the snow. Marie-Soleil chanted, "C'est tout brillant, partout, partout." The sun had disappeared when the chair slowed its ascent.

Manon perused rows of books until she found a manual for learning Braille. After buying the book and another titled *Pedagogical Practices for the Effective Teaching of Disabled Children,* she rode two more escalators to reach the top floor. She asked a salesperson where she could find clothes for teenagers. The woman told her to round the corner where a mannequin wearing a Hawaiian party shirt stood guard. Manon saw him, his arms bent against his chest, his head turned to the side. He surveyed women's vacation clothing across the aisle like a neighbor peering over his fence in a beer commercial. He seemed almost human and in a state of perpetual fulfillment. She envied his detachment from the world.

Two older women, short and round and wearing felt hats atop their heads, walked behind Manon. One said of the mannequin, "Y'a une tête de Gino celui-là." *He looks like a Gino, that one.* They moved on to the vacation racks.

Manon said aloud, "Y'a une tête de Gilles." She looked about her, combing her hair from her face and over her shoulder. The two women, some distance away, slid hangers on a circular rack, which squeaked with every push of too-large blouses. They were arguing about each item's size and color and suitability to Fort Lauderdale's climate. "Doux Seigneur, Thérèse!" said one of the women in supplicant exasperation, and Manon smiled to herself. She took three steps forward. The mannequin's feet were screwed to a plinth. She couldn't resist reaching for his hand. No one saw her pull at his wrist, where the hinge popped out as easily as quartering Barbie dolls of their movable limbs, which she'd done often as a child.

Manon put the hand in her purse. If she second-guessed herself, she would run out the store and throw the hand in the nearest bin, afraid to be caught stealing something of such questionable value. Would they make her pay for the entire mannequin? For a replacement hand? Would a judge punish her for the nightmares Thérèse and her companion would claim to have when they were interviewed by police as witnesses who had actually seen nothing at all? Manon felt alive and exhilarated at the prospect of either being apprehended or being invisible, a heroine taking home a perfect man's stolen hand.

Once among racks of boys' clothing, she inspected fabrics and patterns. She wanted the right shorts for Christophe, even if he couldn't see himself wearing them. She slid her own set of hangers, repeating the *couic-couic* of metal-on-metal other customers made. It sounded to her like the tuning of strange instruments, but the scent in the air was altogether different than in the spaces of auditoriums. She smelled something artificial and manufactured she supposed pleased buyers.

There on the rack, in a glorious hue of flamingo pink and striped in teal and orange, was the thing she rode two metro lines in the dead of winter to find. She took the hanger to the register and, when the cashier asked if she was making a purchase for her son, Manon said yes while pushing the mannequin's hand to the bottom of her purse.

Someone tapped her shoulder. "C'est vous, la dame sur toutes les affiches?" *Are you the woman on all the posters?*

Manon recognized the two women from before, women who had enough imagination to name a mannequin Gino. She liked them for being capable of invention. "Oui," she said. She'd started to tell strangers who stopped her during long walks in her neighborhood that her identical twin had been separated from her at birth in a freakish hospital mishap, swapped with another child who was raised as her sister, and *she* was the woman on the posters. *Haven't you seen the story in the papers? My twin is quite famous. She plays the cello like a dream.*

One of the two women produced a cellphone from her purse and asked if she could take a picture with Manon.

"Voyons, Lucette!"

"Bon sang, Thérèse!" said Lucette, and to Manon, "Ça vous dérange pas, Mademoiselle?" *You don't mind, Miss?*

"Non, bien sûr."

The cashier gave Manon her bag and offered to take the photo. Together, the three women smiled.

Manon went home to her apartment and put the mannequin's hand on the counter next to Marie-Soleil's drawings. She lifted the pages, smelled the waxy odor of crayons and phantom sea breezes from Matane. On the refrigerator, she placed the drawings, held by magnets in the shape of semiquavers.

She tore paper from a ledger and retrieved a pen from a drawer. She put on her brace to hold her wrist while she sat at the counter, pushing the plastic hand with the tip of her pen. It was like a congenial friend or a toy animal—a crab or an octopus—or a volleyball on a deserted island to keep her company. Manon wrote the date in the corner, and she addressed her letter with the words,

Ma belle Marie-Soleil,

Je te remercie fortement pour tes bon voeux. ...

...

...

...

Ton amie,

Manon.

*   *   *

She named the hand Gillou. When she went walking, she stuffed him in her large coat pocket, their fingers pressed like forks in a utensil drawer. She put Gillou next to her when she watched television and read books on her living room couch, where afternoon rays warmed her through icy windowpanes. She carried him from room to room and she thought of buying him a leash, yet she didn't want to scar him the way her own hand had been scarred, so she carried him everywhere instead.

Once, she opened the large case of her cello. The case had gathered a thin film of dust, which she wiped off with the help of Gillou, a polishing cloth balled in his palm. She traced the white horsehair of her bow and pinched the strings on the cello's neck. She liked to hear the little plinking sound, alive and wanting.

She perched Gillou on the lip of her kitchen sink when she washed dishes. Before bed, she laid the hand on her nightstand where, in its palm, she placed her earrings. While he was there beside her, fingers straight but curled at their tips like a cup begging to receive alms, she no longer dreamt of playing in the orchestra as she did before. She believed Gillou was a dreamcatcher. Already he inspired her to give her physical therapy sessions the dedication she previously denied them. She considered calling friends to ask them to come over for dinner, even the musicians with whom she no longer played.

*   *   *

In a dream made from her memories, Manon, five years old, wearing a purple bathing suit covered with stars, sat in a slight channel of seawater, hitting hills of sand with a red plastic shovel. She was surrounded by a set of excavation tools. She raked and ploughed furrows through which rivulets sluiced down to the hole she'd dug so deep that water seeped up and filled the bottom. She could put her legs in the hole and she half disappeared.

She fished for silver minnows swimming in schools near the shoreline. She'd caught seven, scooping them out with her hands. She liked the tickling of their little fishtails and the way the sun refracted on their bodies like tinfoil. She carried them in her orange pail to her hole, where she hoped they would go about their business so she could observe them. Her cousin Amélie stood above her with her fists on her hips, chubby legs splayed. She was knock-kneed and her potbelly stretched out her Strawberry Shortcake swimsuit.

"C'est quoi ça?" she asked. She was just three months older than Manon, yet already six and not still five, so she thought herself the manager of whatever enterprise Manon undertook. *"They're going to die,"* she said in French. She reached down to eddy the water. The fish darted away.

"They're not," said Manon, hoping to dismiss her. She despised Amélie, who was already so much taller and bigger than she was.

"Oh, they are. They can't live in sand."

"I'm taking them home and putting them in a bowl." Manon had already named two of the minnows: Justin had a nick near its eye and Josiane was marked with a dark spot by its fin.

Amélie stomped her foot too close to the opening and sand fell in a landslide on the minnows. Enraged, Manon grabbed Amélie's leg and bit her calf. She was quick and efficient, leaving two red arcs of teeth prints on her cousin, who howled and ran off to her mother.

"Manon! Ma petite malcommode!" yelled her aunt Lynne from her beach chair. She got up and ran to Manon, who looked at her with a quizzical expression. *"What do you have to say for yourself?"*

Manon feigned innocence and repaired Amélie's damage by cementing the wall with wet sand and tapping it into place with her shovel. "Quoi?"

"You bit Amélie."

"I didn't. It was the dog."

"What dog? There are no dogs here." Tante Lynne pointed to the leg of Amélie, who sobbed. *"Those aren't fang marks. They're your teeth."*

"They're not."

Snot collected under Amélie's nose and her mother pinched her nostrils and wiped her fingers in the sand. Amélie pointed at Manon. She was crying and hiccupping and coughing all at once, and her face was red and wet. "C'est elle, la menteuse!"

"I know, mon amour. *There's a special place for* achalantes *like Manon.* Oui, les petites menteuses seront toujours des petites perdantes." *Little liars will always be little losers.*

Manon thought she herself would accomplish great things and become somebody even if Tante Lynne didn't believe it. Tante Lynne was such a *cow* anyway. Une vraie vache, she heard her mother say after she and her sister had an argument on the phone.

Both Tante Lynne and Amélie left her to go summon Manon's mother, who'd fallen asleep on her beach towel some hours before. Manon stomped off toward the waves. The sun was setting and there was a pretty glow on the sea. Shells and sea urchins littered the beach and among them she saw a dead jellyfish. It danced with the motion of the waves. She found a piece of driftwood and pulled the jellyfish ashore. She loved its translucence tinged with pink. She poked it a few times and it wobbled.

Manon's mother approached her and said, *"You'll have to say sorry."*

Manon wanted to lie to her about the dog, yet she loved her mother, so she told the truth.

Her mother stroked her hair and asked her to make amends. *"It's time for supper,"* she said. *"Come. I've brought sandwiches and potato salad and cubes of Jello."*

"What color of Jello?" asked Manon. When her mother told her cherry red, she was disappointed.

They ate on the beach from a cooler filled with ice. The two girls faced each other. Every so often, Amélie would mewl and complain about the throbbing in her leg. Manon ignored her and asked for more Jello. She took the bowl of cubes, which had begun to lose their shape, and she walked over to her hole. The water was so murky from the landslide she could no longer see Justin or Josiane or the other minnows she hadn't yet named. With her bowl still in hand, she lifted her shovel and went to inspect the jellyfish. She prodded the mound to find the right place to carve out a small piece. She tried to cut a compact cube and she put it in her bowl. She returned to the hole and waited.

Amélie arrived, as Manon planned, announcing, *"I told you they would die."*

"You did." She turned her body so Amélie wouldn't see the Jello.

"What's that?"

"Extra Jello. My mother didn't tell you, but there was cream soda Jello with the cherry Jello. She just didn't want to share it with you."

"Cream soda Jello? That exists?"

"It's the best," said Manon. *"It tastes like real cream soda. It's my super-favorite."*

"Oh."

"I'm sorry," said Manon, ready for what would come next. *"I'm sorry I bit you."*

Amélie crossed her arms in front of her chest, covering the eyes of Strawberry Shortcake's face. *"Give me your cream soda Jello, then."*

"It's the last piece."

"You owe me," said Amélie. She knelt next to Manon and turned her face to the sky. She opened her mouth.

Manon held her hand high above Amélie's face so she would see the color of the sample she pulled from the bowl, so creamy and delectable-looking. Then she released the little gobbet and watched it drop into the gaping hole of Amélie's mouth.

*　　*　　*

On the day of the Open House, Manon packed a small duffel bag with clothing for Christophe and herself. She added two new towels, and a nylon cap for her hair, and she tucked Gillou in her bag. She thought of all the ways this experiment could go wrong, yet she was unafraid. She entered the school building and listened for echoes of people's movements. She heard the scraping of chair legs against the floor somewhere in a room to her right. When she peered through the small windows of the double doors, she saw administrators and teachers putting tablecloths on rectangular tables and decorating the space with balloons and signs. She remembered the way ahead to the auditorium. No one saw her push through those doors.

Christophe sat on the stage, legs dangling. "Manon?" he said.

"C'est moi."

He hopped off the ledge and gripped his cane. *I know the way to the changing rooms,* he said.

Christophe guided her to a small alcove with a drinking fountain. On each opposite end, a door led to a locker room. Even in the corridor, they could hear the sound of splashing water, the shrill blow of a whistle, and children talking and laughing. They smelled pungent chlorine. Manon unzipped her duffel bag and gave Christophe the swimming trunks she bought for him at the store. She had wanted these trunks to match the colors of her swimsuit. She described the flamingo pink and mango stripes, while putting a big towel in his arms. She knew she could not help him change out of his clothing, so she spared him the embarrassment of asking if he could manage it on his own. She squeezed Gillou and said to Christophe, *"I'll wait for you on the other side."*

He nodded and went through the door to the left. Manon went in the other direction and changed into her swimsuit. She pinned her hair back and donned the nylon cap, tucking loose strands underneath the elastic band. She took out the remaining towel from her duffel and stuffed the bag at the bottom of a locker. Before closing the metal door, she pulled out Gillou.

When she entered the open space of the pool, Christophe was waiting for her, his towel draped over his shoulders. She took it from him and placed both their towels on one of the plastic chairs lining the wall. The pool was long and wide. Children from a church group took little notice of Christophe and Manon, though she saw the puzzled looks exchanged among a few mothers. Their leader, a woman in a modest black bathing suit adorned with the frill of a little skirt, waded toward them, so Manon took Christophe's hand. She held Gillou in the other. She didn't care if these mothers saw. Together, they went down the steps and submerged their bodies to their waists.

The water was cold. Christophe shivered. The mother in the skirted suit swam closer. She seemed angry, and her eyebrows furrowed. She looked like Tante Lynne. Before she could speak, Manon held up Gillou to stop her and mouthed in English that Christophe was blind and needed therapy. She said, hoping these women were Anglicans or Presbyterians or whatever form of Christianity possessed them, "I'm part of the volunteer group with the foundation. Did the pastor text you? He told me he would."

The mother said, "What foundation?"

Christophe tugged on Manon's arm, a pained look on his face she perceived as theatrical exaggeration. "Is she a racist? Is it happening again?"

The woman put a hand to her chest and inhaled as though struck by an arrow to her heart.

Manon cooed, "Non, non, mon garçon."

The woman nodded and said with disdain, "Ok. Stay." She waded back to her children, the smallest of whom, a redheaded boy, waved to Manon. She used Gillou to wave back. The boy laughed. He was missing three front teeth on top.

Manon pulled Christophe to her but only touched his shoulders. She tipped him backward, and explained how to float. He did what he was told, his arms at his side. When he got the hang of it and his body settled in plank position, she joined him. Her hearing tunneled surrounding sounds, through water and the mat of her hair against her ears.

She held Christophe and Gillou. They were starfish with sunrays for fingers, stick figures of an enclosed sea. Christophe whispered, "C'était mon rêve. En Haïti, tout petit, je voulais nager dans la mer." *It was my dream. When I was little, in Haiti, I wanted to swim in the sea.*

Manon said, *"My parents took me to Sainte-Luce-sur-Mer when we couldn't go to New Brunswick, which my aunt's family preferred. Sainte-Luce is between Rimouski and Matane on the Saint-Lawrence, where it's a gulf and no longer a river."*

"In Haiti, Port-au-Prince is on the Golfe de la Gonâve. I remember the smell of brine mixed with seaweed on the wind."

She played along. *"I remember the smell of sea urchins on the sand."*

"I remember the color of waves and trees and birds."

"I remember the transparency of jellyfish moored on the beach."

"I remember my father promising to teach me to ride a bicycle and my mother promising to teach me to swim in the sea if I practiced my scales."

"I remember playing the cello."

He turned his head to her, even if he could not see her. *"Teach me to swim."*

Manon imagined the notes of the second movement of Gabriel Fauré's "Sonata no. 2 in G minor, opus 117," and she dreamt of the two of them playing together on the small stage of this school's auditorium, she with her cello and he with a proper grand piano.

She said, *"They'll fire me, you know, if they find out I brought you to the pool without your parents' or the school's consent. And I haven't even worked my first day."*

Christophe said, *"My parents think I'm practicing and helping out with the Open House. People meet me and think this school is so wonderful."* He asked with some hesitation, *"But wouldn't it be worth it, even if they did fire you?"*

She turned her face to him and answered, "Oui." She pulled him toward her gently and said, "Merci, Christophe."

Through this motion, Gillou slipped, tumbling like a dying polyp to the bottom of the pool. The redheaded child, splashing near her, fetched it. He surfaced and asked if he could keep it. Longing for Gillou tugged at Manon, yet the behavior of this little boy's mother bloomed in her mind, so she whispered, "Go hide it in your towel and take it home. Later tonight, surprise your mother by putting it under her pillow. She's always wanted a hand. She told me. That's why she tells everybody in the family, 'Won't anyone give me a hand?'" The child brightened with understanding. He tucked Gillou in his swimming trunks so his mother wouldn't see.

Manon followed the boy's progress to the chair where his mother had dropped his things. She saw him bury the hand in his towel. She moved her arms back and forth and her body skimmed the surface. There were ripples around her like the swaying of currents. She studied

Christophe next to her and the contentment on his face. She wanted to ask him if he could smell seawater in this pool, as he had smelled the Golfe de la Gonâve, so far away, but she didn't want to disturb his waking dreams. Instead, amid the cries and laughter of church children, she listened to the music she and Christophe made on the stage of her mind. She heard the echo of Marie-Soleil chanting about the brilliance of snow, and the rhythm of that song accompanied the piano and the cello. She imagined a symphony. She kept on floating.

The Ethics of Keeping Company with Strangers

I'm listening for your signal. When you knock twice, I turn off the engine. I hear our truck puff a long, final scrawl of exhaust, the dying breath of an old friend banged on the passenger side, its hood soldered in three distinct patches where rain iced through rust two winters ago. In the cab, the smell of Tangerine Arbre Magique wafts when the little cardboard air freshener sways from the rearview mirror like a forlorn Christmas tree. I lean as far as I can and roll down your window. We're somewhere in the Utah desert, on our way to Lunar Crater in Nevada's Pancake Range, to celebrate the start of my senior year in high school. Just before the truck's engine started to putter and we pulled over, you said, "Class of '87, can you believe it, Liz? It all went by so fast."

And now, Dad, I can hear you cussing outside, in the September morning heat, as you bend over the intricate mess of wires, pipes, and parts, though all I see is smoke and the propped hood's rust flaking in interesting patterns on what was once a hearty tomato red. The sun's burnt the glaze off—the varnish, the veneer—whatever it's called, and in the center the metal has turned a dark orange, like autumn leaves.

I'd like to turn the keys a notch to hear if frequency can be picked up in the desert, but I'm afraid you're tinkering with the battery and I don't know if it's possible to get shocked from a battery. What would people listen to out here on Labor Day weekend? A local station probably plays nonstop country honky-tonk. There's always better entertainment on our Citizens Band Radio.

You taught me the CB codes and regulations, the ethics, as you say, of keeping company with strangers, on the New Year's Eve to New Year's Day drive we did from Denver to Green River on I-70. Buddha Boy was telling us about his wife's custard cream pie waiting for him at home, asked if we'd tasted custard cream pie, and, after you replied, "Negatory, Buddha Boy," you handed me the device and said, "How about you, Hot Wheels? You ever tasted custard cream pie?" That's my handle: Hot Wheels. We don't see the people we're talking to. They don't see me in my wheelchair. They don't get the joke.

I take the CB receiver and outline the toy car you glued on top of it. It's a black muscle car with shooting flames on the sides. You lower the hood, pop it down twice with your hip. I sway back with the motion, holding on to the window frame. You look worn out, yet you smile.

"Hey, I think we're going to see some desert up close,"

you say. You come around to the driver's side wiping your hands on your thighs. "Remember last time we came through here, you said you wanted to poke around and find new ant specimens. Well, looks like we're going to do just that. You up to it?"

"Might as well. Before or after we get this thing fixed?"

"After. If it weren't for the damn truck, I tell you." You always do this, say 'I tell you,' when you just don't know how to explain what's going on. And if you wipe your forehead when you say it, which you do just now, then I know you're worried.

"It's not like it hasn't happened before," I say. I don't want to emphasize that we're gas station latchkeys, and this time our escape to safety will be harder, considering we're in the middle of nowhere and the temperature is rising. There's a good breeze, though in an hour or two the road will shimmer with long mirages.

"First, we need to find the You-Are-Here spot." You wink at me, rubbing your chin a little with your fingertips. "We need to go in the direction of the nearest town."

I open the glove compartment, hand you our tattered *Utah, the Beehive State* map, and you unfold it on the seat. I scoot, so I'm not sitting on southeastern Idaho, on weird-named towns like Soda Springs and Malad City. Your finger traces the line of Highway 6, tapping along the places we've already passed.

"Jericho. About two or three miles down. We're right outside Little Sahara."

"I'm taking my notebook." I pull it out from under my seat, pressing down the curled paper edge of eleven years of ant observation. It's as thick as a ream of paper and heavy as a small puppy.

You walk to the back of the truck and open the tailgate. I can hear you slide my wheelchair on the flatbed. I pat the cover of my notebook before opening the passenger door. You unfold the chair and I hold on to the armrests, with my back facing the seat. It's a smooth motion until my feet hit the ground with an awkward thump. I reach up and grab my notebook from the seat. You push me around to the front of the pickup, and my wheels hit the asphalt of the road. I open my notebook to the first page, written in blue ballpoint ink, your block letters large enough so I could read the entries on my own. I had just turned six. You never corrected my sentences.

The ants walk crazy. One ant walks around in a big circle one way and then the other way. Ants carry things bigger than their bodies. I haven't seen an ant eat. All they do is walk in circles and carry things. If you kill an ant, if an ant gets killed by accident, another ant will get another ant, and they carry the body down to the place where they have the funerals. Their antennas move around their head a lot. I think that's how they talk to each other. They send signals. We can't hear them. They're very small signals.

You look over my shoulder. "Never knew a kid who wanted to know so much." You wipe your brow with your sleeve and take off your yellow Mack cap. You graze the stubble on your chin with its plastic snap-on straps and it sounds like a cat's tongue on skin. It must be 85 degrees already. You rest your left arm on the rubber window seals of the opened driver-side door. "I'd find you poking through the grass with the telescope's magnifier. I think you even unscrewed the bottom plate to make it easier." You lean against the door and cross your arms in front of your chest. "Look at this sky over the land. Blues and oranges and pinks as far as the eye can see. You need to make me a description like that McCarthy fellow you were reading. What would he say about this lonely road and these here mountains of the desert?"

"It's not too gory for me anymore? You made me skip pages, but I imagine he'd paint this scenery in a way that feels real" I say. "The way life is. We could die of thirst even in the most beautiful place on earth."

"Well, bet your bottom dollar there'll be no blood and guts on this meridian road."

I groan. You're such a dud of a dad sometimes with your rambling commentary. "I'm going to read you some Willa Cather when we get home. I think you'll like her better and the way she saw the West, only not the Archbishop book. I still can't finish it. I fall asleep every time I try."

"You'll have to get our trucking crew in on it, but not when they're driving." You look worried, watching the horizon. "That's all we need is to kill them with boring books about Catholics."

I shift my wheels to the left to follow grooves in the road and the herringbone of old tire marks.

When you and I travel together, like this, I read out loud and over the CB. I have six regular listeners from base unit, plus whoever tunes in to our channel. As Foxy Lady says, it's better than a book on tape. You can ask questions and you don't have to fool around with the tape deck if you've missed something. Her husband, Haywire, always agrees. "That's right, Foxy Lady, that's right." He doesn't say Big Ten-four because she's sitting next to him. Big Ten-four is code. Although its meaning will change according to the situation, it means, I hear you—I know what you're saying—I agree.

Foxy Lady made Haywire drive two straight shifts when I read *Pale Horse, Pale Rider* on our way to Reno in June. We kept up with their rig as best we could. When I read the part about Miranda getting the letter that said Adam was dead, Foxy Lady cried. "Hot Wheels," Haywire said, "no more of them crazy romantic stories. Next time, we're reading some Louis L'Amour. He'd do justice to a title like *Pale Horse, Pale Rider*."

Haywire doesn't like it when Foxy Lady has her bleed-ing-heart moments, as he calls them. More than eighteen months after the Challenger burst in the air like a fire-cracker gone wrong, she still talks of the schoolteacher who died with the crew. For some reason, this woman pulls at her. She never speaks to us of the long lines of pinkish smoke, the contrails of cotton candy we saw night after night on television, but she talks about this schoolteacher, and Haywire just says, "Hush now, darling, hush. She's teaching all the baby angels in heaven now. Believe you me, lady." When he calms her down like that, I imagine her leaning on his shoulder while he drives.

"Let's get this show rolling," you say.

In the distance, a buzzard perches on a tree. He is a silhouette against the dust and the sky's dry white that encircles a blinding sun. On the other side of the road, the Rockies block the horizon far off to the east. What I like about being here is the long quiet. The long quiet is a different kind of silence than not hearing anything, because it's the sound of things you can't see. Everywhere has its own long quiet.

The buzzard sits still. I need a wingspan. I've always wanted to start ornithology, however difficult this kind of research would be for me. The shots from *Mutual of Omaha's Wild Kingdom* are always the same: scruffy-looking bird lovers wearing thigh-high rubber boots wade deep in marshlands, with various sets of binoculars hanging round their necks. *Look at that Great Heron*, the man with the beard whispers to the camera. *It's a beauty*.

I open my notebook to a blank page and write:

Saturday, September 5, 1986. Highway 6. Three miles north of Jericho. (Find nomenclature.) Buzzard: most likely male, rich brown plumage. Could be mottled, not able to tell from the distance, about 250 ft. Light underside. Perched at top of bush. Does not move. Watches. Calculates.

I can hear you behind me fussing with the keys and the ignition, trying to get the CB to work. I flip through pages of my notebook, looking up at intervals to see the buzzard. In my handwriting, I read an entry for my first ant farm.

Carpenter Ant Farm of Elizabeth Fraser

Day One

The ants are beginning to branch out west. They are larger than the backyard ants. Six years of backyard research isn't like this slice of glass. I need a cross-section of the backyard.

I'm tempted to cross out some minor mistakes in many of these pages, yet it would mislead foundation work. It took me a few years to get their rituals down. During the third year of the carpenter colony, the queen died. This is, by far, the most critical event for any colony. Authoritative transference.

Year 3, Month 10, Day 5

The queen has died. The workers came within minutes and they held a council. The worker I marked with a yellow paint dot is taking the lead. She's tapped the others with her antennae and she even redirected one with her mandible. I observed them for four consecutive hours. The yellow-dot ant pressed the others to move the queen to the refuse chamber. The dead queen lay among the tiny droppings of her people. Three princesses are waiting to shed their wings, to see who will be next, who will be queen.

Year 3, Month 10, Day 6

The queen's body has disappeared. I can't see the yellow-dot ant. One of the princesses removed her wings. She must have been fertilized. I missed the mating, probably happened last night while I was sleeping. Just like that: new monarchy. It's 11:35 p.m. and I can't stay up any longer. I've just come back from the fair and I missed the queen's burial.

Year 3, Month 10, Day 7

The yellow-dot ant resurfaced. A few soldiers are circling the colony's entry. By order of the yellow-dot ant? The new queen selected her quarters. I can't see her. She's covered the glass with dust while nesting. It's only a matter of time before one of her workers cleans her quarters. It's only a matter of time before the yellow-dot ant takes over the colony.

"Breaker One-nine, does anyone have a copy for this here Sandman?"

"Ten-four, Sandman. This is Card Dealer, good buddy." His voice crackles with static.

"What's your Ten-twenty, Car Dealer?"

"Northbound on 6, about to pass Jericho Junction."

You turn up the squelch and we can still hear Card Dealer, without the static. "Car Dealer, my girl and I are stuck southbound with a pickup that quit on us. Can you mark time from Jericho to where we're at?"

"I think he's saying Card Dealer, Dad."

"Ten-four, good buddy. You want me to send a Ten-two-hundred, Sandman?"

"Negatory. My girl and I are going back to Jericho and getting some lunch. You know if there's a mechanic down there?"

"Passing Jericho, Sandman, starting the count. Don't know about a mechanic. Big Texaco and diner though."

I look up to see my buzzard, and he takes flight.

Flight: swoops down, four measured beats of wings and picks up speed, height. Slows down flapping. A nice span, even breadth, nice regular rhythm.

I sketch his outline. I have to be fast. With my left hand on the rubber, I turn as best I can to follow him, and with my right, I fill out his silhouette. On the horizon, I see the metal of an 18-wheeler coming toward us. The sun flicks on the wheeler until it's about three hundred feet away, and then the truck starts to slow down. The steamy hoot of brakes simmers down, stops.

Card Dealer's wheeler has custom airbrushing on the cab, a painting of a straight flush. Card Dealer opens the door and drops his legs and the rest of his body from his seat. He has to use the footrest. He's a fifty-something trucker with a belt buckle the size of my fist. There's an eagle head on his buckle, a full-bodied eagle tattooed on his left arm, and an ace of spades on his right forearm. The ink's old and blue.

"Sandman," Card Dealer says, looking back and forth between the two of us. "Let me turn my baby around and get you folks back to the Texaco." He pulls on his right earlobe, no longer looking at me. "Happy to help."

"Thanks, buddy, but turning that thing around on this road might get you stuck in the process. There's no place to do it right. My girl and I are going to make it on our own." You nod to me and raise your left eyebrow twice, which I understand as a sign not to argue with you. "What's the count?"

"About 2.8 miles from here. You know, it'd be my pleasure to take you there."

"That's all right. It'll take us fifty minutes to an hour."

You pat Card Dealer on the shoulder and he does the same, like two chiefs leaving for war.

Card Dealer gets back in his rig. He pokes his head out the window and tells us to take care. You thank him. I wave. When he starts up the road, he honks three times.

"Why'd you say no to him?"

"You're a pretty girl, just like your mother."

I sigh. The ghost of the great Cynthia makes her appearance yet again. "What's that supposed to mean?"

"He offered to help a little too quick. You can't trust nobody, even if you think they're good people. Nothing's what it seems sometimes."

I trace the stitching on my armrest. "He saw a poor girl in a wheelchair. He felt sorry for us."

"Well, we aren't taking a chance on sorry."

We don't say anything else for a while. The small of my back is damp and my shirt sticks to my skin. I can feel sweat pearl on my forehead. The temperature keeps rising. The buzzard reappears. He's circling overhead. "Push me, will you?" I start tracing circles. How does the circle work? Does it move along, forming an invisible spiral? I scribble a few notes here and there on the flight diagram.

"What you're doing there?"

"Buzzard." I point.

"Did you know I had a hawk when I was a kid?"

"You said your mom kept finches in a cage, but nothing about hawks."

"Little buzzard, kind of looked like that one, smaller though. Wasn't really mine, you know. I just picked him up on a deer hunt. He had a broken wing. I got a book from the library and I started to feed him."

"Good for you." There's no cheer or encouragement in my voice. You don't notice, pushing me along this long road to nowhere.

"Kept him in a big moving box with a blanket inside. In the garage. You know grandma."

"And you killed it."

You stop pushing. "Why do you think I would? It didn't die. I took him to wildlife rescue. Somebody had to fix his wing. You think I'd be able to keep it? He only stayed with us for a week."

I want to say the course of nature isn't always so kind, but I don't, so you don't return to the subject of my mother and her accidental death because once you start, there's no end to your longing. I turn the pages of the notebook. How many times have I seen the cruelty of nature in my own life and in the lives of my ants?

Year 3, Month 12, Day 20

I introduced the larvae of the same species into the colony. Within an hour, they have been transported down. I can't see anything.

Year 3, Month 12, Day 21

Soldier ants are making reconnaissance. They divide into files and explore the top of a container they should know by heart. The workers are busy readjusting a tunnel. They clear up an area of glass. Yesterday's larvae are dead. I will not introduce new ants to the colony. Their chemical composition must be different. The larvae were of the same species but of a different colony. Each colony has its own smells, its own signals, its own ways of protecting its interests. Some of the soldiers file back down. What were they looking for? More alien-smelling larvae?

"You know, there's a place around here near Delta with trilobites hidden all over," you say. "It's called Trilobite Mountain. I hear Topaz Mountain is nearby and you can pick topaz bits on the trail."

Here, cruelty: microscopic, quick. Places I can't go.

"We'll go there sometime. We'll get ourselves some trilobites and some topaz. I've been there a while back. I must have been your age. We hiked Notch Peak. You walk up a trail for about three fourths of the way, and then you hit rock formation and you climb. At the top, it's a sheer drop on one side. You can see the Sevier for miles and salt deposits shine like crazy. It's real pretty. You'd like it good."

"Notch Peak. Never heard of it." I'll never go there. Sometimes I think you forget, though I know it's probably always on your mind: the things we can't do. And just when I think I'm about to start crying over a dumb mountain I can't climb, you make the ghost of my mother appear again.

"You know what your mother did at the wedding?"

I don't know why you think her memory soothes me when, in fact, it soothes only you. "You told me already."

"If you don't want to hear it."

Now you're hurt. You'll go quiet on me for hours. You know I can't stand that, so I'll humor you. It's the only thing I can do when you and I are like this, when everything we've built over the years is being pulled from us because she's still on the tip of your tongue. "Go ahead."

"Your mother looks mighty fine and I'm nervous as hell. I've got a crazy shirt on with frilly ruffles and sideburns groomed and sharp as the devil. I think I cleaned up good."

"You looked like Robert Redford in *Butch Cassidy and the Sundance Kid*."

"That's what everybody said."

"I know." How many times have you asked, 'Don't you think I kind of looked like good old Bob Redford in *Butch Cassidy and the Sundance Kid*?' Can't you hear in my voice that I don't want to hear this? You have the look of someone walking through a fog. You're the ornithologist on *Wildlife Kingdom* and my mother is the rarest of birds. You advance slowly through the cadence of the story, afraid she might take flight.

"I can't remember what the minister says, but he says it. I've said my 'I do' part and it's your mother's turn. From the second row behind us, Uncle Gerald gets up and slides to center aisle looking like he's about to croak. He's choking. He scrambles up the aisle and he keels over."

"Oh, he *keels over*."

"Don't poke fun. Uncle Gerald is heaving with his mouth open and awry like it's been taken off its hinge. He's not doing anything except trying to put all his fingers down his own throat. Somebody yelled 'Heimlich!' but your mother just kneeled down next to him, holding his head back, and she reached in and tugged out his lower bridge. Uncle Gerald had swallowed part of his bridge. That's the thing that replaces a couple of teeth, not the whole mouthful."

"Disgusting." I don't want to hear this story anymore. I'll have to think about how much you miss her. I'll have to think about how little I remember from back when there were three of us. You can't expect me to miss the woman who got herself killed and put me in this chair. All the trouble we've had because she fell asleep and drove off the road.

"Your mother, she just stands up, and she waves the bridge in front of the crowd, like she's saying, *Ah ha, dentures!* And everybody starts clapping. We're not married yet and the guests are cheering. Uncle Gerald gives everybody a gummy smile and takes the bridge from her and slides it right back in his mouth. Cynthia and Uncle

Gerald are taking a bow at our wedding. I tell you, your mother was a funny woman."

On the breeze, there's a weird, campy smell of wet earth and gasoline though there's nothing but a shack further down the road. From here, it looks like a shanty made of slats and metal.

"Stay back," you say before you start to run. Your boots clop like hooves, from a steady trot to a soft canter. I start pushing, trying to keep pace with the diminishing outline of your body.

"Dad!" I yell. My breath is cut short from pushing. I see you open a small door on what is now a roof. You help a man out, pulling him out by his arms, then holding him up by his waist. The shack turns out to be an overturned hitched trailer with a makeshift hatch made of wooden slats, like a human-sized crate of fruit. I'm half a football field away, and I hear pigs, squealing high somewhere in there. You both jump off and you sit the guy down against the back of the trailer. He's only a kid my age, maybe a few years older, wearing a gray Alice Cooper t-shirt and ripped jeans, speckled in blood. He looks up at the sky, and says something I can't hear. Then he folds his legs close to his body, putting his forehead on his knees.

"You all right?" I ask him.

He stares at my legs before saying no. "My old man's gonna kill me when he finds out." He rubs the back of his head and growls.

I roll to the side of the trailer, putting my fingers between the horizontal slats. I feel the short, humid breath of a piglet on my knuckles. He can barely wedge the tip of his snout in the opening. It quivers in and out with each breath.

"My dad will get you out. Don't worry, you'll be all right," I tell the pig.

"I tried to get some of them out, honest to God I did, but they got all frenzied and started trampling me down." The kid is talking more to himself than to me.

"Dad, what the hell are you doing?" I watch you pull a rifle from the cab of this kid's truck.

"You should've stayed back," you say, dangling the rifle. "Now go, you can't watch." You climb to the top of the hatch and open the door. "Go, I'll catch up with you." You are a different man, one capable of violence. "Wave in distress if, by the grace of the Almighty, you see a car coming." Your tone hardens. "Don't waste time."

The kid stands next to me. He touches the back of my chair and leans in. "I was supposed to make two trips. Take them twenty at a time for a delivery to Santaquin. Didn't want to take the whole day. I packed them all in there. All of them."

"How many?" you ask the kid.

The pigs' squealing is sickening. They shriek, some of them like newborn babies.

"Thirty-eight. I was making the bend. Next thing I know the trailer's pulling the truck off the road. I couldn't do nothing once the trailer kicked off." He makes a snaking motion with his palm, flat and ready for an invisible handshake. His skin looks thick and dirty, his wrist bloodied raw.

"Boy, you're a dumb shit." You place the butt of the rifle against the hollow of your shoulder. I look between the slats. The piglet is gone.

"Dad, there was a little one on top. Get him out." I see the mass of their bodies, wriggling.

"They're all little. They're pushing and gouging each other on the broken planks. They're suffering." I hear you cock the rifle. "They'll bleed themselves to death one goddamn gash at a time."

From behind, I grab the kid's shirt. "Get on top and pull them out."

He looks at me in panic. "It's a mess. I tried. He's got to."

The squealing dies down. As if they know what kind of man you are, there above them, holding the gun. "Dad," I plead, "wait. There's got to be something we can do."

You ignore me and ask the kid if he has more cartridges. He rummages through the cab and brings you a brown cardboard box. The kid doesn't look at me. He hands you the box.

You take off your Mack cap and watch me with a cold stare. Your mind is made up. The wind lifts a few strands of your hair, ringed by the band of your cap, a halo around your head. I turn to face the road and I start to cry. I feel like I'm four again, unable to do anything on my own, with the heft of dead legs weighing me down.

I turn to see you on top of the hatch and the sun blazes. You are radiant. My body shivers from fear or sadness or the tremor of my weeping. The kid pats my shoulder, but I hardly feel it.

You yell, "They're killing themselves. You can't see the blood. You can't see anything from down there."

"We can thank Mom for that!" I yell back. "You think I give a shit about your wedding?"

"Now's not the time."

"You let her drive because she always had to get her way."

"Shut your mouth, Liz."

"She screwed up our lives."

"Shut up now." You're full of anger. "I'm not going to tell you again."

"Are you going to point that thing at me like I'm a pig?"

In answer, you aim the rifle at the squealing darkness and shoot. There's an ugliness to your face, an unnamed horror turning down the corners of your mouth. I cover my ears. They ring with each shot. The air fills with the tang of gunpowder and new blood. You pause to wipe your brow.

"Fuck that bitch!" I holler in the now-blank quiet. "Fuck that goddamn, fucking bitch! I'm glad she's dead!" And then I deliver the coup de grâce: "She deserved to die."

"I was driving!" you scream. "You don't remember any of it! We switched midway. I killed her and put you in a goddamn wheelchair because I fell asleep driving." Your shoulders fall and you whimper an incantation: "I loved her so much. Oh Cindy, my Cindy." Your face is a shadow.

Nothing is as it seems, you said hours ago. Your expression softens, and I don't want to witness the tumbling of your grief and lamentation. I'd like to think you're about to jump down to reach for me, yet I doubt you will, so I push off and leave the scene as you wanted me to do.

The wheels turn for what feels like the longest time, until my arms ache and my muscles spasm. You, with your Custer-like knowhow of life and death, you wait until you can no longer see me before you pull the trigger again.

In the distance, I see the tall pole of the Texaco sign. The buzzard never followed. He'll watch you walk to Jericho, your fists buried deep in your pockets, while words you thought would never leave your mouth ring in your ears louder than the firing of a rifle.

I've hated my mother all these years. My vision is now blurred, and I can't see all the ways you and I existed in this family of two. Yet the more I think of it, the more I know you are lying. Even now, you want to protect her memory, so you take the blame. I can clear the dust of our memories and know I won't find your version of our story refracted in the mirages of this burning road.

I try not to think of the pigs. I open my notebook to the progress of the yellow-dot ant, before I started the harvester ant colony, before we caught three queens during their nuptial flight in the mating season. It happens every year around Labor Day with the harvester ants. We watched them fly, a cloud of insects, their little winged bodies pullulating the sky. Pullulating. That's what they did.

I wanted the yellow-dot ant to succeed. I wanted it so badly I moved some of the soldiers around, to give her space. I tampered the project.

Year 4, Month 1, Day 2

The yellow-dot ant has taken over the northwest tunnels. She's been tapping and signaling for the past two days. She's rallied two workers and they've displaced the queen to a new chamber. Dragging the queen was a difficult process. Her abdomen didn't pass through her chamber door. Perhaps the message of relocation wasn't relayed properly.

Bees send out scouts to map the territory around their hives. The scouts return and perform a pattern dance that tells the workers exactly where to find food, down to the nearest inch. A scientist once sent out scouts whose wings he had pulled out. They actually walked. They walked all the way to the food and in their pattern dance they expressed the time it had taken them to walk in flight time. It took hours and hours before the workers returned. They had passed the food source, unable to interpret even the slightest of signals.

It must be noon. The sun is at its zenith. The pigs could be dead by now. I'm like you with your awful lies and I'm like the Santaquin kid who had somebody else put those pigs out of their misery.

The yellow-dot ant died. She never took over the colony. And maybe she would have if I hadn't touched her and fooled around with the soldiers. She wouldn't have moved the queen to another chamber and I wouldn't have witnessed her demise.

My notebook, worn and sick in its uneven green, sits on my lap, evidence of a cold case, of an unresolved crime. It's not just me. This notebook is tired, too, injured all these years by the scribblings of my stupid notes. We are part of an insignificant world, refusing to change. I hold the notebook against my chest where it hurts most, and I toss it like a Frisbee far from me. Its pages open, flapping with the soft whoosh of waltzing paper, like it has wings and the sudden gift of flight. It hits the crackled dirt with a dull, hollow thud.

Then there's nothing left but the long quiet. Far in the distance, haze rises from the desert and dances ghostly against the sun. Even when things are hazy and out of reach, we find comfort in the stories we tell each other to keep our hearts beating. There is beauty in that, at least.

I'll get to the Texaco, tap on the glass door of the diner, look in until someone offers to help me. I'll tell the waitress behind the counter about our pickup, about Card Dealer, about a dumb teenager on his way to Santaquin.

I'll start with the pigs. She'll make a phone call. A few truckers will listen and they'll tell stories about the time they saw turkeys running around a highway after an accident. One will say their feathers flew up over his windshield like snow. The waitress will get off the phone, give me something to drink, for free. I will wait for you.

The Santaquin kid will offer you a ride, but you'll refuse.

I'll order custard cream pie if they have it. While I eat the pie, you'll walk in the diner. You'll come over to my table and reveal my notebook behind your back. You'll put it in front of me, knocking on the cover. You'll say, "Don't ever pull a goddamn stunt like this one again, Liz." There will be sadness and fear in your eyes. We won't speak of my mother, at least for a good long while. And we'll forget the ways this story could have played out if I believed what you said.

As we sit there, you'll tell me you felt foolish for not shooting the trailer apart earlier to let the piglets spill out on the ground, their pink bodies rolling in the dust. You'll say less than half of them died. And I'll tell you, finally, about the yellow-dot ant. You'll say everything else in the project is real. You'll say sometimes I'm just off my rocker. And we'll both laugh, yet not in the same way we used to.

After we've eaten, you and I are going to observe the diner patrons with slow and deliberate attention. You'll invite two or three of the friendly ones to join in on our next book reading, but since they work a different trucking route, they'll turn down your offer. We will give the rest of them names—Turkey Feathers, Lonesome Pine, Old Sagebrush Mustache—western names as hardy as desert bones, blanched crisp as the napkins and paper placemats on which I'll take notes. You'll tug your ear or scratch your nose, which we understand as signals. The diner patrons won't notice. They never do. And we'll go on speaking to each other in code.

Madeleine Bouletier, She-Wolf of Crozon

The village of Gretons-sur-Mer commemorated the birth of Madeleine Bouletier, Napoleonic heroine, by erecting a large obelisk in the churchyard. Madeleine was born with an infant body covered in dark hair, which, as the years passed and the girl grew, lightened to a down of reddish-brown fur. On the Crozon peninsula of Brittany, she was the only such animal-baby at the turn of the century. Years before, there had been rumors of a bird-boy who could hover over the sea, buoyed by an enclave of wind against the coastline. Evidence of the bird-boy's existence proved dubious: here a relic feather snatched from a merchant purse, there the hollow bone of a keel-shaped sternum, large enough to hold a human heart, encased in a glass box in Grosbras-Marie's bakery. She used his sternum as a dough paddle and her breads had risen and multiplied in a miracle of golden crusts since. Villagers said she sold his furcula—his wishbone—to a sailor who had nightmare after nightmare while on land. And yet he drowned at sea on his next voyage.

Le pauvre petit.

The Gretoniers stopped believing in the bird-boy because what kind of living thing could have a wishbone and not bring immense luck to its surroundings? There had been in those years insufferable drought that dried children's lips and gave the elderly nosebleeds. A scourging blight of mold spoiled harvests of stored wheat. People went hungry. When their bellies sounded hollow like gourds, they no longer waged their survival on half-breed fortunes. Prayers to saints returned, fulsome at first, and they vigorously ushered an age of penitence among the faithful.

And then Madeleine was born.

Madeleine's mother had been pregnant for nearly ten months. This sometimes happened in villages: babies stayed past their welcome, dozing in amniotic fluid, swimming in their own meconium. Madeleine's father had no money for the midwife, so when his beloved Sidonie writhed in pain on their straw bedding, he called on his neighbors from nearby farms, men and women who pulled out goats from breech positions and calves born in twos. Mère Anselme suggested they push down the swollen belly all at once, but her daughter Clothilde said it was a terrible idea because the moon was not yet full. It would be better to bathe the mother's vulva in a solution of sugar water, to tempt the baby out, she said. While the neighbors argued about the correct method of extraction, Pouilleux-Jambe-de-Bois sat in a corner sharpening a long knife on a leather scrap, slowly forming a burr on the edge of his blade. Every so often, he brushed off the splintered swarf, which fell from his lap to the dirt floor. In the end, it was Pouilleux-Jambe-de-Bois who cut into Sidonie and released the wolf cries of Madeleine.

Qu'est-ce que c'est? they whispered to one another, their heads forming a circle above the dying mother. *Regardez, un chaton! A kitten!* said Clothilde, who scooped the little body in her arms, petting its wet fur while drying the baby in the folds of her skirt. Sidonie, on the hay, moaned for her husband. *Non, ma chérie,* you will not die, he lied. She held out her arms: *Mon bébé!* Clothilde hesitated, but she was an optimist, so she lowered the furry bundle onto Sidonie's chest. When Sidonie saw her baby girl, there was not enough strength left in her lungs for her to scream. Clothilde picked up the child and took her out into the sunlight of a spring morning. Narcissus flowers poked their yellow heads through the grass of a nearby field. The baby stirred against her breast, her little mouth suckling at her skin.

Inside the house, Sidonie died, the rictus of revulsion petrified on her face.

Thibault Bouletier could have hated his child, in a lancing of blame for her deformity and her mother's death, but he loved her fiercely instead. These were the years after the Revolution, years burned in a crucible of change. The peasantry, not knowing which farming calendar to follow, the Julian month of May or the Republican month of Prairial, came to see the country as a halved melon about to rot. Thibault Bouletier, on the morning of his daughter's birth, saw miraculous seeds in the pulp of that fruit.

He named her Madeleine, a weeper at Christ's feet, a purveyor of succor, a protector of the people.

Thibault liked to run a comb through his daughter's hair, and he sometimes amused himself by arranging and tying with velvet bows little tufts and wisps. He could see underneath her pelt that his little girl, now a toddler, had fine features: her eyes were the color of honey, her lips two summer berries. He married Clothilde, who, though only sixteen, loved his child as her own. She made her dresses and embroidered slippers. She sat by the fire, the girl balled up in her lap, while knitting bonnets for Madeleine and her own baby, swelling in her belly. Madeleine heard her parents whisper in the cold of night. They feared for their children, their girl-beast and their moonless-boy. Clothilde believed he would be born into the darkness of a new moon and she apprehended the fate of his soul. In raising Madeleine, she became even more superstitious. They were of pagan blood on this Armorican peninsula, yet she birthed the boy and he did not die. Clothilde thanked what remained of a waning moon, and believed he lived because of that sliver lighting the sky. They named him Luc-le-Lunaire.

Over many years, village boys, born of ordinary, idiotic parents, kicked Madeleine whenever they saw her. Even Pouilleux's son, Jules-le-Boiteux, whose own father had helped usher Madeleine into the world, and who was himself gimpy-legged and not-at-all flawless, taunted her cruelly. The village boys of Gretons took turns calling out the names of female mammals: *chienne!* and *vache!* and *guenon!*, the latter of which, of course, they only learned about from sailors who had gone to Africa and seen monkeys and gorillas through the long lenses of their telescopes. It was the way of these coastal people to believe a history of the world inscribed in the wind of passing sails.

The entire village shunned the Bouletiers, who were left to their own devices in those times of war and famine.

Clothilde, wanting to see her teenaged daughter happy, tried to shave her fur so she could run errands without the leers of other children. She trembled as she clipped the soft hairs. She only completed the task up to the girl's wrist when she noticed that where her hair fell, the grass died. Life went out of the earth, worms shriveling through channels of dirt while clover tri-folded and wasted flat on the ground. Even the soil charred to a crisp. And Clothilde's right hand, which held the shears, withered with age in an instant, dark spots clustering on her skin, her nails yellowing into claws. Luc, now fourteen, stood nearby and, watching the surprise on his mother's face as she beheld her palm, saw fortune in this singular gift. He believed in magic. Ever so resourceful like his mother, he gathered with his father's nippers the shaven bits into a pouch, which he tightened with several knots. Clothilde kissed him and Madeleine, who was crying because she dreamt of hairless skin and because she hurt her mother, though hairless skin was foremost on her mind. The mother said, *c'est rien, no matter,* though she wondered if there could be any future for her wolf-girl.

Thibault came home from the fields in the evening. He took the little pouch and peered into it, his daughter's nestled hairs glistening like the fur of a red fox. *We will try again tomorrow,* he said. He bathed his wife's whole arm in brine and applied a poultice of nettles wrapped in linen.

In the morning, before roosters crowed from the hen-house, alarm bells rang throughout the village. A fleet of British ships was sailing for the nearby beach of Morgat. Luc, already up with his father eating breakfast, said he knew what to do. He explained his plan to his father, who, with his mouth full of scrambled eggs, paused to consider his son's proposal. He put his fork down and placed his elbows on the wooden slab of their kitchen table. He seemed to pray. Looking through the steeple of his outstretched fingers, Thibault gave his blessing. He had faith in his selenic boy.

Luc took the pouch of hairs and rode the old plowing horse to Morgat. He directed her slowly down the cliff with its hairpin turns and steep passage to the beach. The sun rose on the horizon and, before him, six ships towered from the sea. He saw the men on the deck and the men in the rowboats, advancing upon the shore. Luc poured his sister's hairs into the sea, which turned the waters a phosphorescent green. A great serpentine line of this light formed in the water around the enemy. Luc watched them as they sank, the little rowboats and the large ships, swallowed like they hadn't been there before. He watched this just as he watched his porridge grow cold in a bowl that morning, just as he sometimes gazed upon the sheen of his sister's lupine hair, just as he saw his parents, through many seasons, prepare the fields of their farm, hoping for a prodigious harvest.

When the green in the water receded to the dull luster of slate among the white-capped waves of Brittany, Luc turned the plowing horse to crest the cliff toward home. There, holding the door in a wide-open arc while his frame filled the entryway, he announced to his family what he'd done with all the hubris of his youth.

Thibault stood in a corner and listened, pipe dangling from his slackened mouth. Clothilde had stopped wiping breadcrumbs from the kitchen table. Madeleine leaned the broom she used to sweep the crumbs fallen from the table. She stroked the fur of her left arm, which was her habit whenever a bout of melancholy hit her. The family believed in the properties of her fur and, if she had survived this long in that village of benighted fools, they would surely hang her now as a witch. She saw herself dangling from the noose tied to the oak tree in the square.

She would be hanged in a long nightgown painted with the cross of Christ.

She wondered if her hairs would catch fire upon her death or if her body would lose its fur, the ground below receiving their wisps and becoming barren. Or perhaps the hairs would sway in the wind, killing all in their passage. There should have been comfort in this ravage, but Madeleine found none, thinking her little wooden *sabots* would come loose from her feet when she dangled from the rope. How they would laugh at her, as she turned gently under the branches of her gallows, with one foot shod and the other dropping its *sabot*. Damn that Jules-le-Boiteux who would find a way of calling her by the name of a hoofed animal.

Clothilde filled a tub with water from the well and dropped a large square of soap that sank to the bottom. Madeleine and Clothilde plunged their hands to retrieve it. The spot where Madeleine's wrist was shaven touched her mother's claw—the monstrous shape of her fingers—and changed the leathery scales of her skin back to its normal form. Clothilde withdrew her hand in surprise.

Nom de Dieu!

Madeleine held her mother's hand and inspected it. The nails were rosy again, the palm warm and pale. The curse had been lifted, though they both couldn't justify what influences had claimed her limb in the first place. Madeleine had been born shrouded in a cloth of mystery. They completed the wash, the miraculous transformation already fading from their minds. Clothilde lathered the suds while whistling a joyful tune Madeleine recognized as the song of poor Jeannette. She always felt such pity for Jeannette, who, offered in marriage to the son of a prince and then to the son of a baron, chose to be hanged with her useless Pierre instead. When the villagers would hang Madeleine as a witch, they might turn her legend into a song, even if she didn't have a beau.

So, she whistled along with her mother, gladdened by the happy tiding of her future fame.

Thibault and Luc returned from the fields that evening to find Clothilde fully restored. *Oh, oh!* exclaimed Thibault. He lifted the tub of dirty soap water and placed it at the center of the table. Then, withdrawing the remnants of fur from the pouch of his belt, he plunged them and his forearm in the tub. They watched, heads bowed above the ablutions, as the water turned green and transformed his arm into a sagging tentacle. Thibault was pleased, Clothilde horrified, Luc impressed, and Madeleine defeated. With the fastidiousness of a butcher approaching a suckling pig, Thibault took Madeleine's wrist and rubbed his tentacle, which lay writhing on the table. And just like his wife's hand, his limb was renewed. He gave the small pair of silvery shears to Madeleine and asked her to cut her own hair. She obeyed, distributing the clippings to her family, which they pocketed for safekeeping.

Madeleine sulked in the hovel for a few weeks while outside summer burgeoned. The month of July—Napoleon on his steed had brandished his sword and shredded to *lambeaux* Thermidor and Fervidor along with the rest of the Republican calendar—brought a sweltering heat to Gretons-sur-Mer and warmed the waters of the peninsula. The villagers were flattened, *écrasés.* The British, presumably kept home because of the woolen layers of their uniforms, had retreated to their teatime endeavors, while Lord Grenville dreamt of skewering on a spit the little Corsican rat.

Oh, the heat, the heat, how it reduced the men of these wars to dream of ice for themselves and pyres for their enemies!

For Madeleine, of course, these weeks were the worst of the year when she panted herself to sleep. She wanted a barber's blade to ratchet up her fur in great clumps released to the wind, though there was not the slightest breeze to be blown through the acres of their land. She felt accursed, and she dreamt of hovering over the sea like the great black-backed gulls come fishing over Morgat, like the bird-boy himself.

Clothilde, fecund by way of incubating heat, was once again with child, though no one, including herself, knew of this small marvel germinating in her belly. Every day she fetched water from the well and doused her daughter to refresh her. She performed rituals taught by her mother Mère Anselme to bring luck to their door. After Luc's defeat of the British, she grew restless and bored, wishing her children's extraordinary talents—her daughter's magical hairs and her son's precocious courage—be understood by the nation, if not at least by the village. There would be joy in this recognition, perhaps even compensation. Clothilde was not one to waste her wishes on frivolity without a rigorous application of common sense. The British would return—she was calling them back with a collection of fox fur, rook feathers, and dried toadstools. She added to her mash, for good measure, the fat rind of a goose liver pâté gone rancid. Her mother's recipe called for the springtime larvae of frogs, yet, no matter, the incantation would be good enough without.

With a finger slicked in the tallow of her concoction, Clothilde drew words all over the village: *famine* on Grosbras Marie's bakery; *feu* on Pouilleux-Jambe-de-Bois's workshop; *foutaise* on the banns of the town hall; *fièvre* on the wooden doors of the church. She was running out of words beginning with the letter F, and she retreated home after the expenditure of her vocabulary. In the days after Clothilde spread her spell, an infestation of weevils spoiled the village's wheat stores. When the weevils grew fat and their little horned noses snuffed out their supply, Pouilleux's workshop burned to the ground, a strike of lightning without rain igniting the thatching of his roof. And so on with the rest of the village, pillaged by the unknown forces of a bored woman bothered to distraction by the cravings of her pregnancy. No one was dying from the pangs of their hunger or the fevers wracking their bodies, yet the village gathered one evening to discuss exactly what was befalling them. To add insult to the fury of their injury, a traveler from Cap-de-la-Chèvre announced broadly that British sails had been spotted by a troupe of peripatetic nuns gone to pray by way of the cliffs. The villagers, prone as the French are to sulk, did so in stubborn unison.

And yet Clothilde frothed with trepidation.

After the priest sprinkled holy water on his parishioners with the rounded end of his *goupillon*, the aspergillum of his faith, Clothilde raised herself upon the dais erected for the occasion. She brought Thibault and the children with her to show them her thoughtfulness. She was ruining the village so they would more readily accept the gifts of Madeleine, who herself hardly listened to her mother's explanations. The oak tree stood in sight, and she imagined herself once more hanging there. *Un don de la lune! A gift from the moon!* cried Clothilde. Her connection to the asters was tenuous, but she captured the attention of the village, especially as the moon glowed full above them.

It was the unfortunate Jules-le-Boiteux who clamored for proof. And so Clothilde invited the gimpy boy and helped him up the dais. There, she anointed his head with a wisp of her daughter's hairs. His arrogant smile turned to convulsion while the bones of his back cracked with a deafening noise. He changed, transformed by the powers of night and a few strands of a girl's fur. He put his hands down on the dais, hunching on all fours like a wild beast. Tusks appeared growing from the corners of his mouth, great swerving arcs of ivory pointing skyward. Jules was a boar.

There were cries of outrage and the fainting of a freckled girl among the crowd.

The priest signed himself of the cross and shook his *goupillon* with the fervor of a man confronting Satan. Clothilde captured the gaze of her audience with a brilliant opening of her arms, taken by rapture, and this gesture roused her patriotism. *Liberté, égalité, fraternité!* she shouted. *My son and my daughter defeated the British.* Clothilde told the story well and subdued these villagers she'd known all her life. *You who spat on Madeleine, kicked her shins when she was small*—and here she punctuated her speech by kicking the back legs of Jules-le-Boiteux-le-Sanglier who fell back on his haunches—*tortured her with senseless names and unkindness. You who stopped believing in the purpose of her birth—repentez-vous! Your hunger and fevers, the burning of your homes, and the restlessness of your wheat mites are of your making. Weevils for the devils you are!*—there was a great murmuring of shame as they recalled those instances when their cruelty had been so easily dispensed—*And your parents and grandparents killed the bird-boy, he whose innocent feathers had once brought us luck!*—Grosbras-Marie foraged her nostrils thinking of his sternum, which she used that morning to elasticize a batch of bad dough—*you would have killed my daughter, too, if given the chance!*—Madeleine eyed the tree, wondering if this was the moment of her hanging.

Thibault filled a small gourd with water from the well in the square and Luc led Madeleine by the hand. They climbed the dais next to Clothilde and Jules, who whimpered. Luc declared, *I am Luc-le-Lunaire*, while improvising, pointing to the roundness of the moon. *I am the emissary of my sister, the she-wolf of Crozon. You have been cursed, and now we will deliver you through hers.*

A curse for a curse! proclaimed Thibault.

If any of the villagers had thought this through, they would have detected a lack of logic in the words of the Bouletiers. And yet in their growing sense of culpability, they filed nicely before Clothilde, awaiting a sprinkling of Madeleine's fur to transform them into beasts. The change, said Clothilde, would terrorize the British. The Gretoniers might repent of their cruelty and appreciate what a fine girl Madeleine really was—and perhaps when the ordeal of shipping an entire Navy fleet back across the Channel would be over, the village might remember the Bouletiers and all they had done to safeguard their comforts.

And so it was.

The British came and left, cries of supplication escaping their horror-stricken mouths all the way to Plymouth or Dover or wherever hence they hailed. Such bad teeth, the British, and how they mewled! The image of talking beasts soiled their dreams for years. Imagine them landing on the pretty beach of Morgat, sailors and soldiers advancing with black boots through moving sands. Imagine them threatened by a hoard of boars, jackals, and oxen speaking with the words of men. Twice the size of farm animals, the villagers howled and brayed with the rage of their passions. They brandished bayonets and pitchforks, and the British, gone mad with hallucination, flailed their arms, searching these countenances for a sign of mercy.

Madeleine, leading the charge, pointed to their ships, and away they sailed.

In Gretons-sur-Mer, the villagers, through the auspicious care of the Bouletiers, returned to their human form. Sometimes they wondered, looking at their reflection on the surface of water or on the rounded shine of a pewter pitcher, if a part of them had remained beastly, if the whiskers atop their lips had been there before. They wondered, stroking the spot, and mused on their transformation, to that time of war when the fabric of life was briefly woven with magic.

They accepted Madeleine now. As they did so, she seemed more and more like an ordinary girl born of ordinary parents. The Bouletiers made a pretty *sou* returning the villagers to their human shapes, as grotesque as they were. Clothilde had a baby girl, hairless as a mole rat, an animal a sailor had described while on a pilgrimage through Crozon. Luc took over the farm, now trebled in size, and worked alongside his father, who was always wont to tell a story of beasts and wars and all the things people imagine when hunger has hollowed them out.

Some say after the Gretoniers erected the obelisk in the churchyard, Madeleine left the village and married, not to Jules-le-Boiteux as you would expect, but to a boy come flying from the sky, a seagull hovering over their lives throughout times of pestilence, waiting for the land to call him home. Some say Madeleine Bouletier was nothing more than a myth invented by the French, assailed as they were by a succession of tyrannical despots who were beheaded, betrayed, and bemoaned.

War and hunger and a hunger for war, how it changes people.

Century after century, how we grow in the comforts of our appetites and vices in equal measure, awaiting the cycles of the moon as harbingers of our own transformation, yet when we succumb to our beastliness, are we not made in the image of our predecessors, echoing the misfortune of their histories?

There will always be villagers like the Gretoniers, capricious dullards who must be pushed and shoved toward absolution. And there will always be fathers like Thibault and mothers like Clothilde inhabiting stories of goodness, stories in which invention and ingenuity are the hallmarks of our humanity. So, if you had a baby girl born covered with the fur of a predator, would you cradle her in your arms and soothe her with gentle song, knowing how this splendid, cruel world would receive her? Would you sink her body to the bottom of the sea to drown her, knowing how much pain you could spare her, how much love you wouldn't need to give her? Would you? Could you?

Love Among the Orange Groves of Old Hollywood

There are little things nobody warns you about when you're waiting your turn to die: how you'll miss a heavy homemade quilt, stitched just right, covering two bodies; how you'll wait for evening light to fall on the painted walls of a shared bedroom; how you'll hear the song of finches and a woman's voice cluster in your head long after they're gone; how you'll remember the taste of Southern honest-to-God good cooking shared between two bowls and two plates and two sets of spoons, forks, and knives; how you'll forget the way the air smells when there's nothing but love pouring out your lungs because there's no one left to breathe in all that love. Nobody will tell you any of it because nobody feels the way you do. And nobody can understand these things because that's how my life was with my Mary, and how it always was between us: she was mine and I was hers.

I miss my Mary stirring the pot on the stove of our little house, making what she called hot-weather soup. Mind you, it's hot out here in California, hot without that Tennessee bug stillness, swarming around your head like a fog. California was good for the two of us, and we left Nashville weeks before the war. Mary worked in the shoe department at Haggarty's because she was pretty as a button and light as curdled cream, and I started out cleaning house for Mr. Arnstein, a picture producer, till he tried to get fresh with me. I was in the kitchen drying dishes when he came from behind and started to feel his way to my chest, but I was quick. I put a knife so close to his throat, I could've nicked him if I wanted. Goddamn devil just laughed and told me he liked his women real spunky. But he didn't bother me no more after and he gave me a better job. I told Mary what he'd done when we were cozying up for the night in our bed and she laughed just the same he did. "He don't know what you like," Mary said. She put her hand down my belly and between my legs and made it all right.

As Mr. Arnstein's personal assistant, I got to run errands in the car he gave me. Learning to drive with Mary nearly killed us a few times, but we settled in our seats and put the hats back on our heads and just laughed as the car sputtered and stalled. All that driving was a real blessing when I'd see actors on the movie lot and ask them for autographs for Mary. She put Hedy Lamarr's and Tommy Dorsey's in a frame by her side of the bed. Mr. Arnstein had a good Austin 8 for me to go around the MGM studio and deliver all manner of things, even reels. They're most precious of all, so I knew I did good when he let me handle them. I kept the reels in the seat next to me stacked so neat and put a little tea towel on top so the sun wouldn't heat up the cans and melt the film. Mr. Arnstein told me he fired a boy for doing just that. The poor sap piled the cans on the back of his bicycle and parked out in the open. The boy had to go back to Utah, which was a shame because Mr. Arnstein reckoned he'd become one of them farming polygamists.

Mr. Arnstein turned out to be a good kind of devil, if there's such a thing. I worked with him for thirty-some years till he died of lung cancer in 1971. Mary followed six years later from her own cancer that took first her right breast and then her left. She was only sixty-five. Good Lord Almighty, I miss my Mary. To think the whole time we were together in our tiny house.

We'd saved enough money in Nashville tending other people's homes to put down a payment for a mortgage and buy ourselves a house in West Hollywood. There was a porch and a dirt patch out back for Mary's garden. In the early years we could still walk down to the orange groves, and from the porch the smell would be strong as punch in late summer. By the time my Mary'd gone, the groves were long cut down for homes and restaurants and shops. That smell in the air left with her, like the song of all the birds she put seed out for in her garden. She'd make tiny suet balls with scraps of lard and heaping spoonfuls of peanut butter. I can see her rolling out those suet balls and covering them in millet and sunflowers seeds. I kept some pieces of chipped porcelain from Mr. Arnstein. He never married, but he sure liked his things pretty. Sandringham Blue that pattern was, fancy flowers from all the way in England, and she put out those plates in the garden for her birds. "Quit your yapping, Jude," she'd say. "Those sweet fellows over there are called Lesser Goldfinches and that's why I give them gold plates to peck on—ain't nobody telling us who's lesser or greater in the kingdom of our house." She'd talk about the birds she'd seen and which ones she liked best.

My Mary kept a diary of her garden and her birds. She wrote about our life, those things we said and did to pass the days. When we moved here, we told everybody that wanted to know we were sisters and Mary lost her husband. Sometimes she said he coughed blood to death and sometimes I said he died in the war. We settled on telling people he died of tuberculosis on his way to war. People feel a kinship with a widow and a good sister that tries to help. They felt sorry for us, but we felt even more sorry for them for believing anything we said. We had our little lies, me and my Mary.

And now I'm selling the house of our life together for more money than I can count. They don't want the house or the garden or our footprints in cement slabs that go from the porch steps to the street. They don't want to know about the life of two women like us. They want to put our house down like a dying dog. They'll bulldoze it and it'll be gone, but that's fine by me. It hurts too much to think of somebody else planting flowers in the garden or painting new colors on the walls. The life we had is buried in a plot nearby under a pretty headstone with Mary's name on it. I had the carving man put my name next to hers, where it says, "Jude Hardin, Who Loves Her Always." Years from now, those that visit the cemetery and walk by our stone will think Jude was a man, a man dying on his way to war or of some old disease that don't exist no more. But me and my Mary will be cozy in our plot of earth, knowing the good times we had in the safety of all our secrets.

The Boy and the Bear

Sylvie observed the photograph on her laptop and traced the little boy's shoes. She remembered her own son Ollie, a toddler of two or three years, peeling back Velcro straps on similar rubber-soled sneakers. He took a good minute to enjoy the sound of tiny loops releasing even tinier hooks when he undressed, just as he popped bubble wrap when padded envelopes arrived on the doorstep of their small, rundown bungalow in northwestern Virginia. She thought of those years when her boy loved these sounds. Ollie was now seventeen and loop-and-hook closures fastened his corduroy wallet, not his footwear. She still thought of him as Ollie, though he now asked everyone, including her, to call him Oliver.

She had woken at three in the morning from nightmares in which Ollie, the baby Ollie whose features were softening in her mind unless she saw pictures, had fallen in a well and drowned. His body had been fished up and dropped at her feet like an ossified egg. She wasn't able to sleep after restless hours, and she toyed with the notion of not doing any work. She was self-employed at home as a legal consultant, filing immigration and naturalization paperwork for modest fees. She could earn more, but the plight of those who sought her advice troubled her. After years of this work, she could be worn down to file a request for an I-590 visa in exchange for a catering platter of *pupusas* or an embroidered Turkish tablecloth. Money was becoming harder to come by.

Two decades ago, before she peed on a testing strip that revealed she was pregnant, she had been a corporate lawyer in Washington, D.C. This job lasted five years, and at the end she had Ollie. Sometimes she couldn't remember the nature of the work she did. Sometimes she remembered those years in flashes. Even after night terrors, she liked to stay in bed and read the news or catch up on email while her son got ready for school. She was tired, and her back tightened while she waited for him to take his shower. He used her bathroom because the pipes in his were old and rusted and trickled orange water.

"Did you see this?" she asked Ollie when he entered her bedroom. She held up her laptop.

He angled the screen to see the image. He saw a boy belly-deep in wet sand, swollen with sleep.

Ollie studied the photograph. "It happens," he said. He plonked the laptop back on her bed and went to take his shower.

"It happens?" she asked without cynicism.

This was Ollie at seventeen: someone who could look at the photograph of a small child washed up on foreign shores and feel next to nothing. She stared at the boy and his little shoes again, at his red shirt and soggy navy shorts. One more refugee was dead. This boy's photo circled the globe from screen to screen in a bid for allies' mercy.

Sylvie knew too well the plight of refugees, their stories of hardship and loss. She knew the laws and the requirements of her country. She still hoped to distance herself from her clients, but she found the passage of time did nothing to lessen her compassion.

Ollie, who was now over six feet tall and precocious in all the ways she feared, paraded his detachment ever so coolly. She didn't understand why he was turning into such a lout. Her boy—this child she raised on her own, in whom she placed her purest faith, to whom she read on countless evenings books he loved, which she found dull, for whom she baked special birthday cakes in the shapes of superheroes, and with whom she whooped and hollered around the backyard while pointing cowboy sticks against darkening skies—was no longer her ally. *Bang, bang.*

That morning, Sylvie couldn't let go of the image of the refugee boy. It formed itself behind her eyelids in negative, much like letters and words floated mid-space if she read on an electronic device for too long. And against her grief for the death of the Syrian child, she knew she was mourning all the changes in her son and in her life.

Ollie stepped out of the bathroom wearing a towel around his waist. His skin was tanned from a summer of fulltime lifeguarding at the pool. He saved enough money from this job to buy himself a beat-up pickup truck from an elderly widow. The woman explained the truck belonged to her husband, but now, with him gone, she was glad to see it go to a nice young man.

When Ollie drove home in his new truck, Sylvie noticed he had already removed the couple's political stickers. One pasty quote remained:

"Kind words can be short and easy to speak, but their echoes are truly endless."

—Mother Teresa

That old hag, Sylvie thought. Her best friend Grace once said this to her when she praised the nun for her labors among the leprous poor.

"Are you still looking at the dead kid?" Ollie asked his mother. He pushed back his hair, which dripped onto the worn wood of her bedroom floor.

Sylvie watched her son. "Oliver—can't you understand?"

"When you give a shit about the poor or the tortured, it's our money that always runs out," he said.

"There's more to life than money."

"There's more to life than goddamn refugees." He looked at her with the stoned-faced indifference of his youth.

"Why are you in my mug this morning?" she said.

He took a breath and exhaled like an exasperated father. "You don't get it."

"Not if you don't explain yourself," she said.

They measured each other with words, and she was often sidetracked by her son's arrogance. Had she been like this as a teenager? Ollie tapped his toe in the water pooling by his foot and traced the woodgrain. "I'm going to the football game tonight. We're away in Sperryville. I'll leave right after school, so don't bother with dinner." He said this and walked out, shutting her bedroom door behind him.

It amazed her he thought her food preparation hinged on his presence. She heard him rummage through his closet. He enjoyed the rituals of Friday night football and followed the team as often as he could. His best friends were players and they rode the bus, so he tagged along alone in his truck. He was a star runner and swimmer at his high school, and the only reason he wasn't varsity quarterback or point guard was because she had sheltered him from those sports. She'd watched the concussion preparedness video shown in the school gym on back-to-school nights too many times.

Ollie was popular and, until recently, got good grades. Now, he claimed to be burned out and tired of school. He suffered from an acute case of senioritis, he said. Sylvie hoped he would muster the energy to plough through the year with renewed fervor. She didn't look forward to losing him to college, and she was worried about paying tuition. She raised him to be worthy of academic grants. Now that he slacked off his studies, she wished he would earn an athletic scholarship in either of his sports.

At his swim meets, she sometimes forgot to cheer him on. She counted the seconds separating his performance from the state record. And every time she caught herself wishing for scholarship money instead of joining the three-syllable chant—*O-li-ver, O-li-ver, O-li-ver*—the crowd hollered in the hot, echoing sports complex, she experienced the deepest shame.

After Ollie left for school, she drank a cup of tea and waited for Grace to come pick her up for their morning walk. Grace stormed through the front door into the living room wearing around her waist a gray contraption piped with reflective tape.

"Look," she told Sylvie. "Check this out." She drew a water bottle from a holster at her back.

"What? A smartass's fanny pack?" Sylvie said.

"Hydration belt. You can carry a whole lot of water in the bottle, and keep your keys, snacks, and phone in the front pocket." Grace was a woman who knew all the functions of her beloved gadgets. Like Sylvie, she was in her early forties, but, unlike her, she kept up with the latest technology and social media platforms. She was still pretty, and she took such pleasure in being stopped and carded at the supermarket self-checkout area for buying alcohol.

It was Grace who showed her how to Snapchat.

"Why does the message disappear?" Sylvie had asked her friend.

"That's the magic of it," Grace told her. "You can send all sorts of junk and the message goes away. It's kind of like sending the funniest or the worst of you into the abyss."

"What abyss?"

Grace combed her auburn hair back to indicate an airy space in the living room. "The abyss of the binary, I guess."

Sylvie resolved to avoid as much as she could social media, which left her baffled. Her friends—the majority of whom were mere acquaintances or people she knew before she had Ollie—vacillated between personal and political propaganda with kittenish joy. The pace of their confessions and clever comments alienated her.

And there was Grace, a woman she loved and admired, demonstrating the beguiling features of her belt. For all her social flair, she hadn't noticed the shadows underneath her friend's eyes. She was pulling on zippers and talking like a shopping network host. "Check out this pocket-within-a-pocket. It's going to come in real handy when I go out with Abraham."

Abraham was Grace's dog. She named her children Nashiel, Crimson, and Thisbe, but the Newfoundland was a lumbering old fellow named Abraham. It was a turgid choice to foil the offbeat christening of her offspring.

"I want to show you something," Sylvie told her friend. She gave Grace a printed photo of the refugee boy.

"I saw that picture on the news yesterday. It's so sad," she said. "Are you working for his relatives?" The question was improbable, but not impossible.

"No, but plenty of parents with boys like him. Just this year, I helped three Syrian families."

"But the real question is, did they pay you? I swear I'll manage your finances one of these days. I'll turn you into the tax attorney you should be. You'll move into the house next to mine and charge half a grand an hour." Grace was always plotting ways to raise Sylvie's standard of living. She wanted her to start a new career filing the tax return forms of her husband Daniel's medical practice. She wrangled the subject of taxes in loose conversations. She even bought big fiscal books whose weight was on par with their content, but Sylvie had hauled them to the back porch, where they propped up the leg of a broken table.

"Are you ready to go?" Grace said.

"I don't know. I'm utterly beat and I've done nothing today. Do you want a cup of tea instead?"

"I'm in a wee hurry." Grace was always on the move. She managed her two daughters' seasonal middle school fundraisers and did clerical work at Daniel's clinic, which is how she came up with the tax idea.

"I just don't know what I'm doing anymore." Sylvie planted her elbows on her knees and held her head.

"Hey, what's wrong, Syl?" Grace said in her honeyed drawl.

"I don't know how to say this. I feel like everything is slipping from under me."

"That's not your kind of talk. Come on, Syl. What happened?"

Sylvie couldn't fully articulate her aching. "I saw the

picture of the boy, and it just unlocked something in me. I feel like I've been shucked with an oyster knife. Now everything's exposed and I don't recognize what I see inside."

"What do you see, Sylvie?" Grace asked. She sounded like a shrink.

"Nothing. That's the problem. There's nothing inside. Just the grit of sand."

"You know you're a pearl, Syl."

Grace sat next to her friend, thigh against thigh, and wrapped her arm around her shoulder. They both reclined and let their heads fall back on the cushions. They stayed like this for some time, with Grace's arm pinned behind Sylvie's back.

Sylvie wanted to cry and thought about the boy in the picture again. She thought of Ollie and no longer calling him this nickname openly.

"I really do have to go," Grace said. She freed her arm from Sylvie's weight and rose from the couch. "This belt's great, but I guess I'm not supposed to sit against it." She rubbed her back and stretched from side to side.

"I'm sorry we didn't go on our walk," Sylvie said.

"There's always tomorrow. We'll lap the joggers with our power walking."

Sylvie smiled. "Yes."

"I'm the one who's sorry I have to leave you like this." Grace bent down and squeezed Sylvie's knee. "Are you sure you'll be all right?"

"I'm fine. Thanks for being a pal."

Sylvie watched Grace leave. Her gait had a particular elfish cadence like that of a schoolgirl. Their friendship was the product of a public conversation, a kind of Socratic Circle book talk sponsored by the public library. When the dowager of the group huffed that Sylvie didn't understand the allegories of *The Alchemist*, Grace had said, "I'm with you, Syl. I think this book is a crock of shit." Sylvie found in Grace the friend she'd looked for her entire life. She was her Diana Barry, her non-consumptive Helen Burns, her Huckleberry Finn. At first, they met for typical lunch dates, but soon they found themselves going on what they considered real adventures. After a charity dinner at the country club—Sylvie attended in Daniel's place because he had torn his shoulder playing golf—Grace squatted over the ninth hole of the course and peed. She told Sylvie she'd always wanted to do this and she didn't know why.

Years later, to surprise her friend, Sylvie searched in vain for the Abingdon farmer's market where Barbara Kingsolver, Grace's favorite author, sold surplus vegetables. Certain they would find her, Sylvie imagined asking Kingsolver for a few pounds of zucchini, an autograph in a well-worn book, and maybe, with luck, an outing to a restaurant, so they could continue to discuss her work. "It's my best friend's birthday this week and no one loves your work as much as she does," she would have said, sounding like Annie Wilkes, the villain in *Misery*, but no matter. Sylvie's plans flopped: the writer was nowhere to be found.

In retribution for the Unsolved Kingsolver Trip, Grace drove Sylvie to Foamhenge. They both enjoyed the monumental sacrilege of this fake pile of rocks. They packed Nash, Crimson, Thisbe, and Ollie in Grace's minivan. The children played around the hollow stones. Ollie, at eleven, was the eldest. He had hair the color of corn, a smile bright as daylight. He ran to Sylvie and wrapped his arms around her middle. "You're the best mommy in the whole entire world," he said, before running off to tag Nash. She didn't regret denying him a father when he said such things, and her decision not to tell James about Oliver had felt right. In her mind, James, a man she slept with in September 1999 after a Def Leppard concert at an inter-state fair in York, Pennsylvania, was a dreamer and not a doer. For a few weeks they talked on the phone and he visited her in D.C., but he spoke in abstractions, meandering through tangents about the significance of words in the context of time and space, and she dreaded the possibility of being saddled with a headcase. They both lost interest in each other in unison, before her body started to show, as though the last song of the concert setlist, "Let It Go," doomed them to go their separate ways.

At nine o'clock, after hours of binge watching a hit reality series about survival skills in the wilderness, Sylvie opened a bottle of South American Shiraz. She rarely drank, though at times alcohol soothed her nerves. She liked to play music or read a book with a glass of wine, yet tonight, she planned to tank the whole bottle. This was Sylvie at forty-three: a woman who could experience the gamut of teetotaling and lushery and feel everything in between.

She took the bottle to the living room and turned on her record player. She put on an old vinyl of Joan Baez, and she lay down on the carpet. She loved the needle's sound as it scratched its circles and hallowed Joan's voice. The Shiraz was dry and tannic. It left an aftertaste in her mouth she didn't consider unpleasant. Grace and Daniel were the sommeliers of her life. Daniel told her not to buy this kind of wine and promised to provide her with, as he said, the good stuff.

Once, a client had given her a beautiful, vintage bottle of pinot along with a prorated payment for a service she couldn't recall performing. The wine's delicacy taught her she'd drunk cheap piss all her life. She pondered the number of life's wonders awaiting her discovery. *Maybe someday*, which is what she told everyone, including Ollie, when speaking of her dreams.

Sylvie drank slowly as Joan sang about things that mattered to her. Across the room, she could see a crescendo of baby and school portraits lining the hallway. These were milestones of Ollie's youth.

She remembered one specific morning years ago when she dropped off Ollie at daycare, knowing he wasn't feeling well. He'd fussed the day before and whimpered in her arms while scrunching the fabric of her blouse. His grip was strong for a baby of nine months. She was weaning him by pumping her milk at home and at work, and he nuzzled against her chest, the top of his head fuzzy with down, so soft under her chin.

At the office during her team meeting, a coworker played a video of a crying baby as a joke—she couldn't remember why—and her breasts swelled and leaked at the sound. She excused herself and went to the bathroom to clean up her blouse as best she could.

She thought of the fluorescent glare of that bathroom and how she saw the ghost of herself in the mirror. She was no more than a stack of bones with rock-hard breasts.

Her baby was a demanding lump of colic and sometimes she doubted if she loved him the way a mother should. She waited for a sign of love's measure like a yardstick she could hold out to count the sacrifices she was making, sacrifices she'd someday present him at the altar of adulthood. *See these things: they were for you.*

She justified her decision to leave him at daycare even though she knew he was coming down with a bug. His survival—his basic needs—depended on her income.

Later that long-ago day, she picked up her baby and took him home to the pretty one-bedroom apartment she rented near Glover Park in the capital. She fed him from a bottle and gave him a quick bath. He looked the part of a Victorian cupid, sleeping in his ivory footie pajamas, an unnatural flush blooming on his cheeks. She watched television before going to bed, though there was no bed for her to sleep in. She sold the queen-sized monstrosity and filled the space with toys. Her bedroom was now the nursery, and she slept on the couch. She planned to move to the suburbs soon anyway. When she turned off the television, she heard Ollie's hiccupped cries.

She walked into his room without turning on the light. At the window, she pulled back the curtain and saw the tallow waxiness of a glowing gibbous moon. Its light fell on her child. He was standing for the first time. She saw his pale face, the familiar signs of long crying, and his little fists holding on to the railings of his crib. His sobbing abated at the sight of his mother. He held out a hand to her. In that instant, time was both eternal and all-too-short, and she imploded with a love so fierce, she knew she could never love anyone else like this again.

Sylvie picked up her child and rocked him. "I'm sorry, Ollie, I'm sorry." She cried with her boy and looked at the reflection they made in the window by the light of the moon. Gone was the ghost of the bone woman. She was whole and she loved her baby and always would. She kissed the spot on his head where the whorl of his hair formed an all-seeing eye. The certainty of this love held her afloat now that her baby was nearly a man. When she submerged herself in the pain of watching her child grow, Grace buoyed her spirits. Without her friend, she would drift among the flotsam of her memories.

The record was near its end when her cellphone rang. She got up from the carpet and held on to an armchair. She was drunk. She considered not answering the phone at all, but she saw Oliver's name on the screen. She looked at the clock. It was past eleven.

"Ollie?"

"Yeah," Oliver said. His voice was little.

"Tell me you're okay."

"Yeah," he repeated. "I'm okay."

Sylvie waited. She was not a yeller. She waited for her son to speak and she waited for fear to strangle her. She put her head against the wall. Her temples pulsed and her knees buckled.

"I had an accident," Oliver said. She heard his loud sniffling. "I'm about twenty minutes from home."

"Is everyone okay?"

"I killed an animal," he told her.

She was relieved he was speaking of an animal and not a driver or a passenger or a suburban filled door-to-door with too many kids. Her stomach clenched and the acidity of the Shiraz burned her throat. She hobbled to the kitchen sink and stared into it. "Oliver, are you there?" Her mouth salivated. She was about to explode.

"Please come find me," he said in a tone so pure and full of fright that Sylvie would have run to him if she could. "I'm outside Chester Gap," he told her.

"I'll be right there."

Sylvie rested her forehead against the cold rim of her

kitchen sink. She worried about her son. His crystalline words rung in her ears. He needed her, and she could barely walk.

She called Grace.

"Syl, what's up?"

Even at this hour, she heard a child's pummeling footsteps and a kitchen stool scraping the floor. "I messed up hard, Grace. I'm so drunk, and Ollie needs me." Sylvie started to cry. "He hit an animal near Chester Gap."

"Is he at the hospital?"

"He's fine. I just—I just need to go be with him. Help him drive home."

"I'll pick you up in five minutes. Get your ass ready. You are not puking in my car. Are we clear?"

Grace was such a soldier. Sylvie placed her cellphone in the pocket of her jeans. She put on her running shoes and tied them as best she could. She looked at the sad loops and remembered teaching Ollie to tie his shoes when he was in preschool. She hummed the little rhyme to herself.

Bunny ears, bunny ears, flapping by a tree.
Crisscrossed the tree, trying to catch me.
Bunny ears, bunny ears, jumped into the hole,
Popped out the other side, beautiful and bold.

Sylvie walked out of her house and leaned on the storm door. It seemed her veins crackled with static as she waited for Grace, though she knew that was impossible. Her body itched and burned, and she scratched her wrist at the pulse. Her thoughts circled from Oliver to Grace to the dead animal. A deer, most likely. They bounded in Virginia woods on spindly legs, bodies emaciated by the coming winter. She'd seen a herd of fawns the week before, crossing the street behind their mother. That's what doe did nowadays: they crossed streets and walked their children. Had one pushed a shopping cart willy-nilly in a parking lot, she would have watched with polite curiosity. She pitied the deer, bloated postmortem on roadsides, hooves held up to question passersby. It was a common sight. Now, coincidence or bad luck had turned Oliver into a culprit.

Grace picked up Sylvie in her minivan. "You smell," she said.

Sylvie fastened her seatbelt. "I'm such a fool."

"That you are."

Grace was wearing loose pants, one of many pairs made by Bangladeshi women who'd escaped the rotted caves of sex trafficking. The fabric was green and violet and her hoodie turquoise blue.

"You don't match," Sylvie said.

Grace was not amused. She was driving just five miles over the speed limit, which irritated Sylvie.

"Step on it, will you?"

Grace snorted. "Would you like to walk?"

Sylvie touched Grace's arm. "Look—I'm a mess. I'm

sorry." She meant it, cloaking herself in the rankest guilt for being drunk and incapable of reaching her son alone.

"What the hell were you doing anyway?"

"I was having a Joan Baez moment."

Grace said, "You and a stupid record player, and too much alcohol. You're pretty dramatic when you want to be." She pushed on the accelerator. "It's the downfall of civilization, if you ask me."

Sylvie's heart beat in her temples. "No," she said, "this is how new democracies are made."

Grace turned onto the highway and said, "What a bunch of bull. That little bout of drunken revelry landed you in hot water, Miss."

To appease Grace, Sylvie said, "I might regret this, but I think I need to give your taxes a try." She made a face and turned down the corners of her mouth.

"Oh, praise be, Grumpy Cat. What changed your mind?"

"Something Ollie said this morning. I need to get my shit together. I need the money to fix his bathroom, pay his tuition, and live my own life."

"Your own life. Gee whiz. Imagine. I'm holding you to this."

Grace turned on the satellite radio to her favorite station, a mashup of obscure international singer-song-writers wailing about the state of humanity. The current song was South African and featured the synthetic arrangement of an instrument buzzing like a vuvuzela. Sylvie found the sound irritating. Though her mood had improved, her head still throbbed. The drive totaled fifteen minutes of two string-happy rancheros howling *ya-ya-ya* like coyotes and one Trinidadian steelpan drummer. She was hammered in every way.

They found Oliver's pickup on a narrow stretch of Zach Taylor Highway, the only road through Chester Gap. He had parked on a shoulder of soft dirt, his truck blinking in distress. Grace stopped her van behind it. A collection of new bumper stickers shone in the beam of her lights.

"The truck looks just fine. I can hear it running," Grace said.

"Good God, what am I going to do?" Sylvie asked.

"You can start by getting out of my van." She ousted her. "I need to get back."

Sylvie opened the door and hopped out, holding on to the handle. She saw her friend giving her the sharp nod of women of courage. Grace the Riveter. She nodded, too, and closed the door.

Grace drove away. Sylvie breathed in the cool air and saw a constellation of stars. No dim signs of heaven could slow the drumming of her heart. Here was her boy and she—his strong-willed and able-bodied mother—was grasping for the right words to make him whole again.

She knocked on Oliver's passenger window and waited for him to open the door. He was sitting in the driver's seat. He didn't move. She opened the door with its terrifying creak and she sat next to him. She shivered. Oliver removed his jacket and placed it around his mother's shoulders.

She rolled down the window and listened to the night. The highway was no more than a one-lane lazy stretch of country road, some miles outside their town. The national park was close by. She knew trees and mountains beyond teemed with life. She heard an owl hoot in the distance.

"Where's the deer?" she asked. She hated to break the silence. These weren't the right words. Even with her son's jacket, the cold seeped into her skin and she wanted to go home.

Oliver put his forehead on the steering wheel and turned to her. The truck's headlights were off. At this angle, a slice of moonlight bathed half his face. She could see the blue of his right eye, the line of his eyebrow, and part of his cheekbone. *He's a handsome man*, she thought.

After some time, he answered her. "It was a bear."

"I checked around your truck. There's no way you hit something as big as a bear." She squeezed his shoulder and rubbed the back of his neck, afraid he might swipe her hand away.

"It was worse than a bear. It was a cub. Soft paws and little black eyes. I saw it too late."

Oliver leaned on his mother, trying to put his head in her lap. His torso was too long. She lowered his head on her shoulder. His cheek prickled with faint stubble.

"It wasn't your fault. Accidents like this happen."

"I couldn't leave it in the middle of the road. He was hurting. I can see those paws of his. He looked asleep. I could hear his breathing. I thought I heard his heart. He was lying on his side with his back leg bent a little. You know, like when kids fall asleep."

Sylvie thought of the Syrian child on the beach. His little legs had been bent, too. She didn't mention him to Oliver. "Did you call authorities?"

"Mom, I called *you.*"

He hadn't said mom in so long. When he spoke to her, he no longer addressed her. It made her feel invisible.

He said, "I waited for the cub to die. I wanted to pet his fur, to let him know it was almost over, but I was too scared. It didn't take long. When his pee rushed out, I knew he was dead. I carried him away from the road so cars wouldn't run over him. He slumped against me like a baby. He probably weighed less than fifty pounds." Oliver lifted his head and pointed. "I put him down on a patch of pine needles over there. I hope his mother can find him, to see him one last time." He started to cry. "I'm sorry I made you come out here. I was just so spooked. I've never killed anything but bugs before."

She confessed, "Grace picked me up because I drank too much wine and couldn't drive."

He wiped his face. "You're shitting me?"

"I wish I were. I was drunk as a skunk when you called."

He laughed, sheepishly, and then so deeply Sylvie was unable to control her own outburst. She now knew her son was both oblivious to and aware of the world in the same ways she had been when she was his age. He had to get through these uncomfortable years. And she realized she had to do the same.

She said, "I'll call the forestry service in the morning. It will be all right. I promise."

"No, I'll call," he said, "plus you'll be nursing that hangover." He half-smiled at his mother. "Thanks for coming out and helping me."

"Always."

They drove home in silence. Sylvie was afraid the thread holding them together, fragile as spider's silk, would break under the weight of her words if she dared speak. She pictured the smallest of letters hanging from the web, forming sounds that sliced a space between them. She wanted to remain with her son in the cab of his truck, in this iron lung that sustained both their breaths as one.

At home, she undressed in the darkness of her bedroom. When she removed her phone from her jeans, she read a text from Grace, who sent it before driving off. "You got this," she'd written. Sylvie texted back: "Get ready, girlfriend, those teenage years ahead are a real bitch." She could have written more, explained the trials of separation, the bizarre years of longing for and dreading a child's departure into adulthood, yet she chose to bestow Grace the gift of ignorance.

She looked at the apps on her phone. The little white ghost hovered in the yellow square of her Snapchat account. When she tapped the icon, she imagined her phone was a living, breathing thing. She typed a message. At the other end, on the screen of Oliver's phone, the letters would appear, sink, and disappear. Gone in three seconds. She wrote the same message again, and to make sure he would see it, once more. Her words frittered away into the void of the abyss that divided what life afforded and what it didn't.

I love you

I love

I

A Baby of the Ganges

The flight to Kolkata had been long, interspersed with the kind of turbulence that made Anne feel as though the heavens dropped from under her into a void she couldn't name. In the dark, slow ride in the taxicab from the airport to their hotel, Reed had said, more to himself than to her, "So many goddamn air pockets." She ignored him, looking out the car window at the enormity of the city and its colorful buildings, and thought only of the infant she'd seen hours before, a tiny thing swaddled against his mother's breast in the seat across the aisle. When the turbulence subsided and the mother fell asleep in turn, Anne reached over and covered them both with her thin airline blanket. She reveled in these moments of private beauty when she could accept her own insignificance and forget, for a flash, the loss consuming her.

They arrived at the hotel tired and hungry. It was early in the morning, at that hour when the stillness of night slipped into sound: in the lobby an employee swept the marble floor, in the courtyard two gray langurs wrestled under a banyan tree, and in three bedrooms upstairs, tourists' alarm clocks announced daybreak. Four and a half million people rose like a single breath from the city's congested lungs, and the five a.m. haze slowly burned on the horizon.

Reed rang the bell on the lobby desk. A girl wearing a cobalt sari answered him. Anne hoped he wouldn't banter, yet before the girl could greet them, he pointed to the painted sign behind her and said, "The kerning's off."

"Kerning?" Anne asked him. She put her elbow on the desk and held her head. "Not now." If he started laughing, she'd leave the lobby. He'd learned to laugh again, and she begrudged him this ability.

The girl said, "It means the spacing between the letters. Dr. Thompson taught us this the first time he came to this hotel. We still haven't fixed it, you see. He made us laugh so much. It was Dr. Thompson who helped me get this job—"

He cleared his throat. "I'm sorry, Pooja, this is my wife, Anne." He turned to Anne. She was looking at the girl. To Pooja, he said, "It's so good to see you again." He leaned across the wide desk to kiss her cheek.

Anne noticed the girl's delicate skin, the clarity in her deep-set eyes, and the richness of her hair, braided down her back. Bangles of various widths adorned her left arm.

Pooja tapped his hand. "What was the joke about the monkeys?"

He thought for a moment. "Why did the monkey like the banana?"

Anne wished to cut them off and tell her the room was for Thompson and Bezuidenhout. At least he hadn't presented her as Dr. Thompson. She hated when he called her his wife. They were unmarried, which was her choice.

Pooja must have sensed Anne's discomfort. She forgot the monkeys and gave them two keys.

Reed asked her, "How's your little sister?"

"Priya is very well. My mother prays for you every day."

Reed explained: "Priya is Pooja's youngest sister. I closed her palate five years ago."

"She could not drink milk or eat properly and we thought she would die."

"That's a beautiful bracelet," Anne said, to distract them from their memories. She and Reed did not share the intimacy of a small miracle as he and Pooja did.

Pooja unclasped the bracelet and held it up for Anne to see. "This one belonged to my grandmother."

"You must think of her when you wear it." Anne touched at her neck a delicate chain from which hung a solid gold pendant in the shape of a bean. She remembered when Reed presented it to her *to celebrate our little bean.* How similar the first sonogram photo of the baby had been. "This necklace reminds me of a loved one, too."

Reed took her arm. "Thank you, Pooja. Point us to our room and we'll be off." He pulled Anne away from the desk.

"I am so happy you are staying with us. Please let us know if there is anything we can do to make your stay a most pleasant one."

Following Reed, Anne turned to look at Pooja, who shouted to them, "I remember the joke's ending: because it had appeal!" And the girl lifted her arm and waved, her bangles sliding down to her elbow.

*   *   *

Reed had surgically repaired cleft lips and palates in many countries, and he was returning to India. He begged Anne to accompany him. *You need fresh air, a change of scenery,* he told Anne. *And I need it, too.*

She agreed to go because her body had grown gaunt and she paced from room to room in their big farmhouse without knowing what to do. The door to the nursery remained closed. She forbade those who rallied around her before and after the funeral to enter the room. They volunteered to pack it up for her, so when the time came to welcome another child, she could rearrange the treasures she bought and made. She even asked Reed to stay away from the nursery for good after he stopped falling asleep in the rocking chair, holding in the crook of his arm a stuffed lamb she'd sewn out of a pale wool sweater.

She was stuck in the months between her completed doctoral research in botany and a job she deferred when she was put on bedrest during the third trimester of her pregnancy. The baby had been gone for months. Everyone said the passage of time would mend her heart. Some ventured, in a particular, unfeeling religious tone, that everything happened for a reason. When they said this, she wanted to torture them with the most gruesome of medieval devices.

*   *   *

Anne awoke alone every morning under the leaf-dark canopy of a Victorian poster bed, and she could see in the distance the brown serpentine body of the Hooghly River through the window. She avoided looking at the blue belly of Vishnu painted on the wall with his four hands presenting sacred objects, among which she recognized a lotus flower. "*Nelumbo nucifera*, eudicot angiosperm, order of the proteales," she recited. She thought of covering Vishnu with a towel.

Reed had already gone to the clinic. He performed a dozen operations every day and when he returned to the gloominess of their bedroom, he collapsed on the bed next to her without undressing. He no longer tried to hold her close. Anne settled into her own routine. She showered and went down to breakfast just before noon, toured a monument or a museum, and later strolled the market streets of Kolkata among fishmongers and fabric dealers and sellers of spices. Strong smells, a mixture of coriander and a certain sourness, nauseated her. Everywhere she went she was looked upon as a curiosity, her blond hair a beacon of her own strangeness, an emblem of someone who simply didn't belong.

Crowds overwhelmed her, especially when she saw signs of destitution. A woman wrapped in rags beckoned her closer like she had something important to say, yet Anne crossed the street instead, knowing she would not understand her words. She felt powerless. She counted the remaining days until they flew home. She'd had enough of Reed's change of scenery, and she considered his experiment of bringing her back to life, as she once was, a failure.

*   *   *

One afternoon, Anne slept for nearly two hours. The phone rang and woke her, but she didn't pick up. The soft drowsiness of too much sleep fogged her mind, so she stepped into the bathroom to take a long shower. She thought she heard the phone again, but the ringing seemed distant and hollow, coming from a room above or below her. She dried herself and sat on the rim of the bathtub while wrapped in the hotel's monogrammed bathrobe. She sat in the silence of her own breathing and the occasional clanging of a pipe resounding through the tiled walls when she heard a key in the lock and imagined Reed walking in the bedroom. When she opened the bathroom door, she was surprised to find Pooja rooting through his papers.

"What are you doing here?" Anne asked.

"Madam? Dr. Thompson needs a file. It's an emergency."

"He would've asked me for it, not you."

Pooja stilled. "You did not answer the phone. He called many times. I am sorry to bother you. Please call him back."

Anne looked about the room, annoyed at the interruption. Her annoyance morphed into suspicion. She went over to her nightstand and opened the drawer. She turned down the bed covers. Then she faced Pooja and said, "Give it back," holding out her hand. She towered over the girl and her wet hair dripped on her sari. "You took my necklace, didn't you?" She sounded both angry and full of sleep.

The accusation appeared to insult Pooja. She looked at Anne and said, "I am not a thief."

Reed appeared at the door, a flush to his face, his hair disheveled. He had run from the clinic to the hotel. "Did you find it?" he asked them both.

"Your wife will help you," Pooja said without looking at either of them. She left the room and closed the door.

"Why is she upset?" Reed searched for his file among scattered papers.

Anne folded her arms. "I think she stole my necklace."

Reed raised his voice. "What's wrong with you? Good grief, Anne. She's poor, yes. But you—"

"You're always defending these people."

He left the papers on the dresser and turned to her, his face impassive. "You're so difficult sometimes. I don't even know you anymore." He walked to her side of the bed, bent down on his knees, and fished the bean pendant from the floor. "You couldn't even look before accusing her. You see nothing but yourself. You don't know Pooja." He faltered and shook his head. "You're not the only one suffering." He threw the necklace at her.

To hide her shame, she said mockingly, "Oh, *suffering*."

"Do you even hear yourself?"

She regretted the sting of her cruelty immediately, yet she could not form an apology. "Reed."

He faced away from her now, neck craned toward the door. "It's always going to be a game of casting me out and reeling me in."

She studied his back and the familiar curves of his body: his long arms and legs, the hair at his nape needing to be cut, the protruding bone of his C7 vertebra. He taught her about the human spine in the first month they dated, naming and caressing every protrusion and concavity of her body while she lay very still, and she showed him the sexual organs of plants, demonstrating the wide variety of moist vulvar carpels and colorful powdery anthers, and the similarities between the folds of her labia and those of the butterfly pea. *Clitoria ternatea*, eudicot rosid, order of the fabales.

"I'm sorry," she said after a long moment. "Please."

"I'm done, Anne." He went to the dresser, picked up all his files, and left the room.

She watched him go, paralyzed by his sudden absence from this space, both foreign and familiar, yet she didn't move from the bed. She wanted to cry but couldn't. It had been such a long time since she let herself go. Sitting there, she remembered the early days of their coupling. They were graduate students at university when they met, she in her second year of doctoral research and he in his final year of his medical residency. She came up to him at a party, a little too drunk, and said, *What's your poison, cowboy?*

She missed his texts, or his sexts as he called them, the riddles, and the photographs. She had once laughed so well.

What starts with a C and ends with a T, and has a U and an N in the middle?

Give me a hint, babe.

It's fleshy and wet on the inside and hairy on the outside.

A coconut.

*   *   *

Hours later, Anne walked down to the courtyard and welcomed a slight breeze. She would apologize to Pooja, who was absent from her post, when she saw her next. She left the hotel and went to the nearby shore of the Hooghly River. The river calmed her. She heard of the powers of the Ganges, flowing down to her through these waters somewhere north in the plains, but she failed to believe in its holiness. The Hooghly was a poor substitute, she thought.

Next to her, a man sold effigies of Shiva, Vishnu, and the elephant-headed Brahma. He held up the blue god and she interpreted this gesture as a sign. The river and its molecules, and the plants growing near it, were what she believed in. The gods of science were either leading her forward or mocking her, she hardly knew which, yet she gave in to the feeling of being steered. "So help me, gods of this forsaken river," she said aloud. She looked out to the water, to kitchen boats floating fragrant bowls of peas and rice and meat in golden sauces; to birds flying low over the river; and to the halo of the sun, a red film flickering in the dying embers of the earth.

At the river's edge, she approached a two-passenger boat with a canvas awning strung with marigolds. She told the boatman she wanted to see the Hooghly and paid her fare. He held out his hand to her, but she refused his help while stepping into his boat. He pointed to himself and said, "Bilva." He lifted two long oars and began to push them away from the riverbank.

They faced each other in the little wooden boat, their knees separated by a few inches. Anne shifted to widen the gap. The sun on her back warmed her and the sounds of sellers and passersby lulled her with each stroke of the oars.

"You are tired."

She considered his voice, so unlike Pooja's. She shuddered, remembering what she said to the girl.

Bilva wore a loose linen shirt with the sleeves rolled up.

He put the oars down, pointed to the horizon, and said, "*Suryast*," while mimicking, with a broad curve of his arm, the overarching progress of the sun.

Anne noticed an array of objects bobbing along the boat, among them a forlorn sandal and a doll floating face down. She reached for the doll to turn it over. With a deft counterstroke, Bilva plunged the doll underwater while he waved to a man in a nearby dinghy and she, too, looked in that direction. When she turned back, the little doll was gone. She watched Bilva and he looked away. She imagined having seen the corpse of a baby girl, discarded shortly after birth. The image lingered, yet she reasoned that grief colored her thoughts, as it always did.

On the crowded river, pilgrims made their way north to Farakka and onward to Varanasi, the holiest city of the Gangetic plains, Bilva explained. Anne wondered what it would feel like to believe, to be enlightened by the candor of prayer. The length of the shores, so eerily hazy, sharpened her loneliness.

Bilva docked the boat on the shore opposite the bustle of Kolkata. The bank was silty, with a foamy edge. They sat in the shade of a peepal tree on the riverbank. He showed her the leaves and pointed to himself.

Anne said, "*Ficus religiosa*, eudicot angiosperm, order of the rosales. The sacred fig."

"Bilva is sacred leaf," he said, and she heard the word *life*.

When she came back to the hotel in the evening, Reed had moved his things to another room.

*　　*　　*

For two days, Anne slept on and off to accelerate time, although she felt indifferent about going home. There was nothing awaiting her there, her future with Reed uncertain, just as she had nothing to wait for in India, except offering the apology she delayed. She didn't go out into the streets of Kolkata. Instead, she ordered room service and ate alone under Vishnu's gaze. She tried watching television, but she tired of Bollywood music and the incessant happiness on actors' faces as they went about their business of singing and dancing.

Every time she called the front desk, someone other than Pooja answered the phone, and she imagined the girl watching her room number appear on a screen and refusing to pick up.

She had been so afraid of not saying the right words to her, yet now she needed to atone for her actions. She was running out of time. Even if she hadn't seen Reed in days, they would leave together soon, the seats of their flight booked long ago.

Anne went down to the lobby. She approached the clerk at the desk. "Where's Pooja?" she asked.

"Pooja is no longer employed with us," he informed her.

"Because of me?" Anne asked.

He looked at her, perplexed. "A good opportunity has come to her to go to university in Mumbai."

"So suddenly? What happened?"

"I cannot tell you because I do not know."

Anne walked to Reed's clinic, which she had visited only once, when he called the day after their arrival to ask her to bring him his laptop. He wanted to show the staff photos of previous surgeries, of the many success stories he liked to share. She hadn't taken the time to meet his new colleagues. She'd been extraordinarily selfish, she realized.

This time, she said to Fathiya, the woman behind the registration counter, "I'm here to see my husband, Dr. Thompson." Fathiya tried to hold Anne's hand, but Anne withdrew it from her, feeling unworthy of such affection. Fathiya took her by the arm instead and led her to the waiting room. There, she addressed in Hindi the two-dozen people seated and standing in the room. A woman holding a toddler lifted him to show Anne his post-operative recovery. He gazed at her with dark eyes fringed by a multitude of long lashes. She saw the sutures of the child's upper lip and the finesse employed in closing the opening. The mother spoke a litany of incomprehensible words as she rocked on her feet, explaining in Bengali evident gratitude. They were all standing now, observing Anne like she'd procured for them Reed and the small miracles of his practice.

Fathiya scurried out of the room, calling to Dr. Thompson. Anne, left with these visitors, quivered at the sight of what Reed had accomplished for this group of fathers and mothers who could now reimagine their children's futures. She didn't know what to say or where to turn. She fraudulently claimed she had come to see her *husband*. For the first time, she wondered if he felt the same—despoiled of the simple intimacy the ritual of marriage afforded, when he wanted to say, *This is my wife, Annie* or *My wife Anne and I or We've been married for X years.* She was sickened by a sense of utter failure and, disoriented, she leaned against a wall.

Reed, who appeared with Fathiya, took Anne's elbow and steadied her. "What are you doing here?" he asked.

"I feel ill." She tried to embrace him but stopped when he made no effort to close the gap between them.

He pulled her down the hall. "There's an office I use at the back. It's quiet." The room was no bigger than a janitor's closet with a desk and two chairs. Several anatomical posters hung on the walls, sagittal views of the human spine and skull, coronal planes of cleft palates and their descriptions.

"You moved out. And Pooja's gone."

He sat at the desk and opened a drawer. He took out Pooja's grandmother's bracelet. "She wanted you to have this, to go with your necklace," he said.

"What the hell is going on?"

Reed said, "I told her—of you and me—and," he hesitated, not knowing how to talk of their loss. "Pooja was pregnant. I took her to a good clinic nearby and I paid for her abortion."

"How could you—"

"What, you're conservative now?" He folded his arms.

She whispered, "Why would you?"

"You wouldn't understand what her life is like. I've known her since she was a teenager. Her boyfriend pressured her. When he got what he wanted, he broke it off. Her mother is a good woman, but she would have sent her away or she would have taken her to someone's kitchen. Here, the days of coat hangers aren't over, Anne. There are too many mouths to feed. Can you imagine?" He picked up a pen, turning it over his knuckles, a sleight of hand he learned in Korea years ago. "It had nothing to do with us." He gave her the bracelet. "She insisted on paying me back. It's the only valuable thing she owned."

Anne was crippled by an internecine morality she detested. She thought of Pooja as an adult woman, a woman whose life was complicated by loss and disappointment. With new conviction, she saw who she herself was becoming, wizened and unfeeling, and who Reed had been all these years. She'd forgotten his goodness, and she was sorry for it. "I've been thinking—"

He cut her off. "I can't. Not now."

She bent down and put her forehead against his. "Okay," she said.

*　　*　　*

Anne left the clinic and, not wanting to return to the hotel, followed a throng heading northward along the river. She understood, from what Bilva had said, that this was a pilgrimage, which she interpreted as a poor man's version of sacredness in the absence of the Ganges. In the streets of Kolkata, believers walked to the Dakshineswar Temple, unable to journey to Varanasi. They made do with the Hooghly, and the steps of the temple, in places so old, seemed swallowed by the river. The gray-green haze of nightfall descended upon hundreds of faithful, whose epicene bodies shimmered in the river, the last rays of the sun bathing them in light.

Anne shielded her eyes as she stood on a side terrace, watching the gathering. They lifted handfuls of water above their heads. She watched and saw strangers helping one another. An old man herded a young woman's frenzied brood separating in the throng. She saw colorful clothing on the strikingly rich, teenagers on mopeds whizzing by, musicians clapping ahead. And everywhere she looked, there were signs of grace and devotion. She wished Reed were here with her. He would have loved this congregation, when she had judged an entire culture so unfairly, so narrowly.

The sun disappeared. Pilgrims filled shallow vessels with flowers and tallowed wicks, which they lit and let sail. Anne understood she would never see Pooja again.

Next to Anne, an old woman asked in English for assistance down the steps. Anne took her hand and led her. With their feet inches from the waters, the woman turned to her and said, "This is for you. It's an *arti*." She gave her one of her vessels. A fire lily bloomed in the depression at the center. "Say your prayers and let go."

"Thank you." Anne held the little dish. She, the unbeliever, was willing to try—to test an unknowable faith—and to receive absolution from any deity. "*Gloriosa superba,* monocot angiosperm, order of the liliales," she prayed. She raised her head to find the woman had left her to stand alone.

In the beauty of the evening and the sound of chanted prayers, Anne finally wept. Her sadness came in waves, rising out of her and into the darkness. She was sobbing openly now, and she made no attempt to stop it. She welcomed the relief from these arduous months of anguish. She wept for her baby, for Reed, and for Pooja, who had also lost her baby, even if differently. She reached in her pocket and put on Pooja's grandmother's bracelet. Then, she unclasped her bean necklace, kissed it, and lowered it in the center of the lily. A stranger lit the wick. She placed the *arti* on the river, and launched it away from her.

She watched the little vessel glide, watched until its flame dimmed in the distance, watched until she thought she could no longer see it. Her throat constricted as it had before in that moment of weakness and crying released. She couldn't feel her fingers, her toes. If she stayed in place, she would become petrified on those ancient, moldering steps. What had she done? She hurled herself in the water, pushing past bathing bodies as she went, wading until she found space enough to swim. She was careful to keep her head from a baptism she never wanted and would never want. From the wake trailing behind her, she sent artis sailing fast, some of which tipped over and sank. She didn't care for the lost prayers she extinguished. Anne swam in the current of her own rage. She would reach her fire lily's dying flame and retrieve her little bean, blemished with the pearly wax of a benign ritual and, when she did, she would never again let it go.

The Kindness of Terrible People

Eve waited for Riley, her niece and surrogate daughter, to arrive at the cottage to spend a long weekend with her. The wind invigorated her when she remembered she would have to sell either her car or this beloved cottage, on the shores of Lake Gaston in North Carolina, which she purchased in her early forties. A few years ago, she renovated the kitchen and the bathroom, putting more money in the projects than she ought to, and she shivered in an Adirondack chair, thinking of what she might lose—more money and property because she decided to retire at sixty-three. She was unwilling to admit the folly of this choice.

Now that she'd vacated her office and packed her things—the rows of hefty books and stacks of papers, the misaligned brass frames and their faded photographs, and the large spider plant that had birthed countless potted gifts for colleagues and neighbors—she felt both free and discarded. Her young successor had slipped through the ranks of tenure like a yolk blown through the needled end of an egg. She could have stayed at the university a few years longer.

While her energy for publication waned and her numerous accolades seemed years old, she signaled to colleagues that administrative politics plagued her decision to retire, yet they couldn't fathom why she'd been in such a hurry to leave. The mystery of her departure remained between herself and Aidan Pitcairn, the university chancellor. No one had caught the pair in their claustrophobic trysts—wedged between her filing cabinets, hunched over her desk, hanging, yes, hanging from the ceiling chain that leveraged her bountiful plant—and, while moving the last of her boxes to the hallway, she thought of screwing black lightbulbs in the two wall sconces to show the department just how often she and Pitcairn had been together. She imagined the soft young professor flipping the switch.

Pitcairn had humiliated her by threatening to have her arrested for assault and battery because she slapped and kicked him after discovering his involvement with a Norwegian graduate student. Pitcairn said he might marry the girl. She was thirty-six years his junior. Eve had laughed at him: "She only wants money and a green card, you old coot." She secreted a few things from his office, and she revered these objects as talismans to ward off his evil: the daguerreotype of his great-grandmother, his only portrait of her; the Roman coin with the effigy of Caligula; and the silver ashtray she'd so often admired.

Sometimes she wished the Norwegian would fly home with a suitcase full of her own Pitcairn souvenirs.

Riley was now hours late. Eve would forgive her. She loved her strong features and olive skin. Both tall and wide-shouldered, their dark, thick hair grazed their elbows, though Eve's was maintained by boxes of dye. Eve had one brother, Roger, and Riley was his only daughter. Eve hoped Riley would mend the hurt of having been so swiftly discarded.

Riley arrived late in the evening in her mother's car and she parked next to Eve's old Mustang, her prized possession. Eve walked from the water's edge at the back of the property to greet her niece. She yelped when she saw Riley, whose hair was now cropped down to a few inches. Riley's torn jeans, the piercing in her nasal septum, and her plum-painted mouth reminded Eve of all the coeds who had streamed through her classes in the late eighties and early nineties, first with their oversized Doc Martens and then with their velvet chokers and butterfly hairclips.

"Evie," said Riley, opening her arms to hold her. "I'm late."

"Riley. Oh, my Riley."

Riley steered Eve to the passenger side of her mother's car. "I've got one hell of a surprise for you." The girl's words sounded like those of a stranger. "Meet Braverman," said Riley, waving to the passenger door. "I call him Brave."

A man in his late twenties stepped out of the car and held out his hand to Eve. She shook it. She had not expected him, and he irritated her simply by being there, so stupidly standing like a tree in need of pruning. *What did kids say nowadays? Basic.* Yes, Braverman was a basic boy with three-day-old stubble and a faded haircut. His arms were covered in tribal tattoos, snaking into the sleeves of his black t-shirt.

He pointed to them. "I'm working through my privilege. You know, the beauty of embracing all cultures," he said while kicking the driveway gravel.

"He's such an eloquent ass. You're going to love him. I know you will." Riley put her elbow on Braverman's shoulder in a territorial gesture. *This gorilla is mine to keep and to comb of nits.* "He's smart, too. Dropped out of Harvard."

"Rye likes to brag," said Braverman.

"You two look hungry."

Knocking on the hood of her car, he said, "That's one hell of a Shelby you got here."

It is, she thought. She led them to the house.

Braverman asked to use the bathroom, and, once he disappeared down the hall, Eve sat her niece on a kitchen chair and whispered, "Why?"

"What do you mean?"

"Why'd you bring a boyfriend into our girl plans? This was our weekend together."

"Mom and Dad hate him already. I thought you'd be different and we'd have a grand time, the three of us." Riley unlaced her boots and tossed them under the table. "He's really great, you know."

"How long have you known him? How long have you been with him?" Eve was grappling with the image of Riley the previous fall, as a college freshman, her pretty hair down her back.

"Two months. I met him at a party. My hallmate Inez knew him. They were together when he was at Duke."

"You said Harvard."

"Harvard then Duke."

"So he graduated?"

"He didn't."

Eve opened the pantry and took out a box of orzo. "I'll make you a bowl of your favorite *pastina*." She worried about Riley and the man she had brought into her home. "I'm sorry, Babe," she said into the hollow of the pantry, staring at boxes of dry goods and stacked cans of vegetables. They had called each other babe for years.

"Babe." Riley said, amused.

"What'd I miss?" asked Braverman to no one in particular.

Eve thought him a long-lost scientist, caught in the throes of discovery and disenchantment. He picked up a box of oolong tea from the counter, read the ingredient list with myopic interest, and put it down. He repeated his inspection with a pencil, a souvenir spoon, and the box of orzo. "Sit," said Eve.

Braverman obeyed and sat next to Riley. "Need help?"

"No. Pastina's a five-minute affair."

"That's what *she* said." Braverman held a little milk glass saltshaker to the light.

Riley whacked him on the shoulder. "Oh, Brave." She was blushing.

Eve had a vision of the two of them in the guest bedroom, under the worn pinwheel quilt, twisting their bodies to hold each other deeper. How she loved the sound of paper when Pitcairn toppled back on her desk. She wondered what spell the graduate student had conjured, what Norse rites she performed to secure him, whether she burned evergreens in prayer or shook a fine dusting of reindeer antler powder in his drinks. These thoughts plagued her often.

After dinner, Riley and Braverman retired to bed. Eve, fragrant with soap from her shower, a blue scent of ocean, sat on the reclining chair of her living room reading nineteenth-century poetry. She couldn't sleep. In bed, she listened for sounds in the room next to hers. None came. She moved to the living room with its bay window and distant sights. A sliver of moon trembled ever so slightly on the water's skin. She fantasized about talking with Riley all night to the violet hours of morning. She saw the image of that little girl, wet hair patted down and braided—a fishtail, a waterfall—the mermaid's hair now gone. How could she have thrown away the darkly beauty they shared?

Eve heard footsteps behind her. She knew it was Braverman before she turned her head.

"Can't sleep." He picked up Pitcairn's silver ashtray from an old tea table. "You smoke?"

"I did. Occasionally. Before," she said, putting down her

volume and the lines about the Sea of Faith and its melancholy. "Be careful."

"Let me guess. Lucky Strike?" He turned over the ashtray. "Wow," he said. "William Bateman silver." He looked closely. "Impressive. Look at the details in the gadrooning."

She said in a barbed voice, "Oh, you studied English antiques at Harvard?" To correct her sarcasm, she added, "You have the habit of inspection. That's a good thing."

He put down the ashtray with unnecessary care and sat down on the couch opposite the bay window. "I like the idea of smoking more than the smoking itself."

"Your generation can't even do that right," said Eve. "Oh, your vaping craze and those little pens and vials. I'd like to see you hipsters bring back snuff boxes. That'd be something."

Braverman laughed. "What can I say? I'm a sucker for good silver."

"Let me guess," she said, "you spent your youth rummaging friends' drawers for plated utensils and candlesticks?"

He winced. "Why, yes. Instead of playing Nintendo, I plundered household treasures. Grandmothers' leather Bibles, embroidered napkins, Georgian ashtrays. Every fifth grader's dream."

"The Bateman ashtray belonged to the man who broke my heart," said Eve, "and I stole it from him."

He smiled at her with what she thought was youthful excitement, yet his eyes were prematurely lined with crow's feet. "The price of a heart for a few pieces of silver."

Eve saw the moon through the window. "I can't tell if I'm Jesus or Judas in this story."

"Mary," he said. "Your long, dark hair."

"How did Riley find you?"

He sighed tenderly. "She followed the path of constellations. I am one lucky bastard. I don't deserve her."

Riley walked into the living room. "What are you two doing?"

"We couldn't sleep. Your boyfriend here is quite the purloiner of hearts," said Eve.

Riley stood between them. "The what?"

Braverman patted her on the hip. "Your aunt thinks I stole your heart. Why else would you be with me?"

"And he's quite the existentialist. Kierkegaard?" asked Eve.

Braverman rolled his eyes at Eve and ignored Riley's legs, partially blocking his view.

"Goodness, no. Really, Evie? If you pick a German, go for Kant. I'm an idealist."

Eve said, "Kierkegaard was Danish."

Riley tried to interrupt: "I have no idea—"

"Indeed," said Eve. She looked at Riley. "You should go back to bed."

"Why? Because I don't know who Kant is? What was he, some playwright or poet? You'd both be into old whites." She let out a false little laugh.

"Indubitably," replied Braverman. "I love Goethe and

Rilke. And Mann. Even though *The Magic Mountain* really isn't his best work."

"Be still my heart," said Eve. "You've fetched a wonderful literary critic, Riley." She lay against the armrest so Riley no longer stood between them. "Tell me now, what do you think is his best work?"

"*Death in Venice.*"

"Just like that? Do you stand by this verdict?"

"I do."

"My, my. I couldn't agree more, though his short stories demand serious attention."

Riley sat on the other end of the couch and glared at them both.

Braverman leaned forward and whispered, "But what of the Americans? That's the true test, if you ask me, Evie."

Riley flinched at his pronouncement. "It's Aunt Eve."

"Let's blow up the old canon. Give me their best: Fitzgerald, Steinbeck, Hemingway," said Braverman.

"A reader of men, I see," said Eve with the air of a coquette. "Oh, please. *Tender Is the Night*. Easily. It's messy and imperfect, but exceptional in ways *Gatsby* can't beat."

"Agreed."

She raised an eyebrow. "You have me cornered with Steinbeck. I'll go with *Tortilla Flat* for its compact length, yet profound descriptions of social constructs."

"Well, I'll surprise you here. Not his best, but my favorite: *The Moon Is Down.*"

"I haven't read it," said Eve.

Riley exclaimed with a flourish, "*You* haven't read it? Goodness, Aunt Eve, everyone knows this book is a masterpiece!"

Eve sighed. "Oh, yes?"

"Pages upon pages of *profound descriptions* of the lunar cycle! It debunks our understanding of human physiology, with particular concern for women preyed upon by wolfish men in sheep's clothing." She winked at her boyfriend. She pretended to smoke an imaginary cigar, tipping her head back to blow air to the ceiling. She said, enunciating every syllable, "Little do you know, the characters are metaphors for werewolves."

Braverman frowned. "The novel's actually a great allegory for the Norwegian Resistance Movement during the Second World War, but Steinbeck did indeed write about werewolves. An early novel, never published I think."

Eve said, "Rings a bell. I can't remember the title."

"The *Murderous Full Moon*? I can't remember either," he said.

"Aw, look at you guys. So cute with your encyclopedic knowledge of the humanities. What would I know? I'm studying political science."

Eve believed Riley studied art history. "You've—"

Riley shushed her. "Tut, tut! Let's not begin preaching." She laughed, "Hey, it's like Braverman could be your long-lost son. Maybe you didn't have that abortion after all."

Eve blanched. "Enough," she hissed. "You two should go to bed. Take your little theatrics with you."

Riley didn't argue. She left the room with long-legged strides. Braverman followed her, pausing to curtsy in front of Eve, mouthing the words, *I'm sorry*, before walking away.

The next morning, Braverman came to Eve, eager to speak to her. They were both early risers. Eve thought Braverman needed something to do to occupy his hours while Riley slept. He apologized for Riley's tantrum and her violation of Eve's privacy. "I'd be the last person to pass judgment on anyone," he said.

She hazarded, "I shouldn't have told Riley. I wanted to prepare her for certain situations. There's so much for her to learn still in the realm of bright awakenings and dulled disillusionments."

There was a restlessness about him, an energy both contagious and consuming Eve could only attribute to his experience of moving often. She accepted his offer to help her with the house. After sealing windows with plastic sheeting, they winterized the small garden at the back of the cottage. Around noon, Riley watched them from the bedroom window, and, when Eve motioned for her to come out, she turned away. Braverman said, "It's all right. Just let her be."

They wrapped burlap at the base of a few sapling bushes to shield them from frost. He assisted her with the tomato plants and suggested methods to counter the heaviness of clay in her soil. "Tomatoes will survive just about anything. Except for clay. That's what you get for being so close to the lake."

Eve wiped her brow with the back of her glove. "What can I do? The yield's been poor here year after year."

"A little sawdust goes a long way."

"Really?"

He rested his hand on her shoulder, his heat warming her neck. "Trust me." He looked into her face in earnest. "I come from good farming stock."

"I don't even know where you *are* from," she said.

"Oh, here and there. I am a citizen of the world." He curtsied. "My lady, let's go to the hardware store. We'll get sawdust. Got a tiller?"

"No."

"Add a tiller to our list. Next year, you'll be up to your ears in tomatoes."

"I don't know what to say." She touched his arm. "You've been great. Wonderful, even." There was mist in the air, a damp coolness on her cheeks. She breathed in and exhaled dramatically. "I wanted to be alone with Riley when you showed up."

"I know."

"She should come along. She's been avoiding me since last night."

"Nah. She's going through a rough patch. Things aren't going so well for her at school. She's doing worse this semester than last year."

"She didn't tell me."

"She doesn't want her parents to know. I really do encourage her to study, you know, but she's always looking for the next party. She's a bit lost. I guess I'm not the best example of scholarly success."

"I'll talk to her," said Eve, feeling the sudden pull of her kinship with her niece.

Braverman rubbed his hands together. "Well, you and me, Evie, we've got things to do. This house needs better tending."

The cottage was like an animal with special needs, like the dog Eve saw on television who could only eat while sitting in a contraption, beloved by its owners who slid a feeding tube down its throat. So the house needed work to stand: rotting fascia boards to be replaced, windows to be insulated, gutters to be cleaned of leaves. The list was never-ending and ever-growing. How nice it was to share the burden with someone like Braverman, someone who could appreciate that all these little nuisances were worth the investment of time and money, that to love a house or a dog or a partner was all happiness required of life.

Braverman told her not to bother with the Mustang. The sawdust would spread through every crevice. They borrowed Riley's mother's car without asking Riley.

At the store, he chose a box of long screws for the deck to fasten curling boards. He tested the push tiller, lifted sawdust bags for the tomato plants, and added masking putty to their cart, for the back edges of the kitchen counters, which he claimed hadn't been installed properly. She picked two new coppery carriage lights for the front and back porches to offset the wood of the cottage.

She longed for dark plantation shutters, but she couldn't afford them. He said he could build them for her. He sounded like he meant to stay when he and Riley would be gone the next day.

"Is there anything you can't do?" asked Eve as they made their way to the registers.

"Too much to name. I can't knit worth a damn."

Eve laughed. "Well, I could teach you."

"Wait for me here?" He nodded toward the end of the aisle. "Bathroom. Be right back." Leaving her, he pulled out his cellphone from his back pocket and his wallet fell to the floor. Eve picked it up and called out to him. He was at the bathroom door already and passing through the jamb. The wallet was thin and made of soft brown leather. She opened it. There were credit cards, his driver's license. He was born in June. *A Gemini.* Twenty-seven years old. Alistair J. Braverman. *No wonder he goes by his last name.* She pulled out two credit cards. These were in the name of a David Johnson, as was a 2001-2002 library card from Amherst College. She panicked, pushed the cards back in their slits, and closed the wallet.

When he returned, she gave it back to him. "You dropped this."

"Thanks," he said.

When Eve and Braverman unloaded the car, Riley scowled at them from the porch. "Hey," she shouted. "That's my mom's car. Where the hell have you two been?"

Braverman walked to the back of the house heaving sawdust bags on his shoulder. He didn't answer her.

"You could have texted us," said Eve. She carried the screws, the putty, and the carriage lights toward Riley, who blocked the front door.

"Oh." She crossed her arms. "*Us*. I see."

"Don't be a brat."

They walked in the house and Eve placed her purchases on the kitchen table.

"Seriously."

Eve turned to her. "What?"

"You!"

Eve stared at her. "You've been sleeping all day. You foisted your boyfriend on me. He had nothing better to do." She opened the boxes of the carriage lights. "And I'm grateful for his help," she said.

Riley poked Eve above her left breast. "Bet you like that foisting."

"Excuse me?" yelled Eve.

Putting on airs, Riley said, "I have doctoral degrees in literature and philosophy and all the subjects of the humanities. And I'm just so, so sexy."

"What the hell has happened to you? Who the fuck do you think you are?"

Riley stood there, in front of Eve, and her eyes reddened. She stormed off, retreating to the guest bedroom with a slam of the door.

Braverman entered the kitchen a few minutes later.

Eve was sitting at the table, holding her forehead as if her whole head needed to be buttressed. "You all right?" he asked.

Eve thought of confessing her spat with Riley but reconsidered. She wouldn't alienate Braverman. She enjoyed his company and his conversation. She wanted him with her. It was he who was salvaging her wounds, he who was making the space of all her losses brighter and airier.

He smiled at her. "Cheer up, Babe."

"Babe is our word."

"After all this work, no initiation for me, eh?" There was a small pile of books on the table and he began leafing through the pages of a poetry collection. "Susanna Moodie. Would I like her?"

"She's a little matronly, dowdy even, but easy to like."

"Mature women are easy to like," he said in a tone that insinuated mischief. "So, why that word, *babe*. What kind of anecdote sprouted its use?" He sat down next to Eve and scooted the chair closer to her.

"Once, when I was visiting Roger's family for the holidays, I went shopping with Riley at the big mall in town, the one with the fountains and glass box elevators and overly jazzy jingles. Have you been there?"

"No. Rye knows me better than that."

"You've been to Roger's, seen the big McMansion?"

"No. She knows *them* better than that."

"She told me they don't like you."

"Cat's out of the bag, Evie." His smile was wan. "I kind of knew it, so don't worry."

"It's not my place to say, but she's so much younger than you are. Her new look's not great. You should have seen her before. And you haven't graduated—" She stopped herself.

"Woolen bullshit. I want her to succeed in ways I haven't."

"I'm sorry."

He played with the pages of the book. "And the mall?"

Eve lowered her voice. "Out of nowhere comes a boy from Riley's science class, and he yells at me for all to hear, 'Whoa, Sexy Mama!' He was small for a middle-schooler and he was mentally slow. I shouldn't say it this way. I didn't think too much of the incident until the boy's father caressed my hip to feel me up. That's when he whispered, 'I'm sorry, Babe.' Before I could put him in his place, he vanished in the thick of the crowd, holding the boy by his elbow."

"That's unfortunate."

"I remember the father's breath on my neck and the warmth of his hand through the fabric of my skirt. I nearly lost my footing. You know, something about his casualty, his compliment—the whole goddamn Christmas scene and the crowd, something there was both comfortable and uncomfortable and I hated my unacknowledged anger—the righteousness of it—and the arousal I didn't want to feel."

"Girls my age never use words like *arousal.*"

"I'm not a girl anymore," said Eve. The blouse she was wearing opened at the neck. She leaned forward. "We made it into a joke between the two of us. It removed the sting of that man thinking that he could, and that I would. Riley was too young to understand." She told him, brazenly, "I was a true child of the Sixties. I read Anais Nin for the first time when I was fifteen." She added: "I pity your generation and your sad, sanitized porn with its parade of slick vulvas shaven to baldness. Bleached anuses. Those inflated breasts."

"Nin?"

"Ah, someone you don't know? She is a woman, you reader of men. She wrote great erotic fiction. An iconoclast of her time." Eve got up and pulled from the living room shelf a paperback. "Here. Give it a go. Can you handle a woman writer? There's nothing dowdy about this one." She extended it to him and brushed her leg against his as she sat back down into her chair. His nearness gave her a frisson of pleasure and she patted his knee.

He neither shifted away from her nor further invited her attention. "Thanks." He looked at the cover, the black-and-white photograph of a young girl, a fringe on her forehead. "I'll go rest a little now. We've been working hard." He took Eve's hand in his. He kissed it with childlike tenderness. "I can feel Rye stirring under the covers. I know how she sleeps. Her napping skills are legendary, the stuff of Sedentary Olympics." He wouldn't turn his face to her.

"Well, you know where to find me," said Eve more to

herself than to him. She watched him go to the bedroom with her book. She wondered if Riley was indeed sleeping or if she was waiting for him.

Braverman and Riley went out to dinner that evening and Eve was disappointed. While she was upset Riley had been so unfeeling, she craved Braverman's company. He had ignited the pilot light of her body, and she pictured a cougar seeking the advances of a younger man. *What does Riley know of true love?* She ate dinner on her own and poured herself a glass of brandy, which she brought with her to her favorite chair by the lake. The sun was down, emitting its orangey hues. Braverman approached her and said, "Rye's showering." He offered Eve a pack of cigarettes wrapped in cellophane. "Here. I bought you these." She took the gift, a woman dancing in a curl of blue smoke. They were *Gitanes*.

"How did you know?" she asked. "Where in the world did you find these?"

"Magic." He opened his hands like a bygone Cabaret performer. "Ta-da."

"In the book you gave me I found a cutout of the pack logo. A bookmark long ago? I like the smell of them." He raised his head to watch a bird flitter on the shore. *Always observing*, she thought. "I liked the book, too. Some of it at least. It's a bit out there. I stopped at the story of the guy balancing on the chair with his dick hanging out. And those boarding school boys? Christ, that's sick, don't you think?"

"She was commissioned to write those stories. For a lot of money. You can't blame a woman for her survival. Those were different days."

"We all try to survive one way or another, even with our vices and our secrets." He asked, uneasily, "How could you have read this book as a teenager when it was published posthumously in '77?"

She answered, "And you went to Harvard and Duke? Really?" She gave him a pointed look, and she smiled with the immediacy of her affection for him. "Thank you for the Gitanes." She turned the pack over and admired it. "It's been a long time since anyone gave me something meaningful." She was flattered by his gift. She'd been so good at seducing men. She considered Riley's feelings and the complications of the guilt that would accompany the overmorrow of whatever she did with him. *How easy he would be to love.*

After a long moment, Braverman sat down in the browning grass next to her chair, his forearms resting on his knees. "It's nice here. Peaceful."

"Yes," she said. The air was full of pungent fall scents: the burning of leaves, a hint of coming rain, and something else Eve couldn't place, which was both mineral and vegetal. She considered the vastness of the lake. The sun dimmed further. She looked at his face. "I think I might lose this place."

He waited for her to continue.

"I speculated. What a word." Her tears welled. "I resigned

and retired and took a second mortgage and made some unwise investments. I'll have to sell the cottage or the car." She drew in her knees. "The car's worth quite a bit. It's a 1968 King of the Road."

"How much is a bit?"

She hesitated. "Oh, one hundred thousand, maybe more at auction."

"Holy Mother of God."

"It will come down to choosing between the two. I'm thinking of moving here. For a little while, until I can decide what to do and where to go next. At home, I live in a rented Craftsman house right by the university. It's too large for me and the owners want to sell."

He patted her arm. "You know, you were right. I didn't go to Harvard. Or Duke. But I did go to Amherst. I hung around so many colleges."

"The library card."

"We all have our little mementos." He sighed. "Some people believe anything for the sake of appearances. This much I've learned."

"Anything." Eve understood his meaning from her relationship with men: they wanted anything and everything, and she gave them what they wanted. She was the victim of her own appearance, of a self she so desperately wanted to project. She desired their admiration and now she craved Braverman's.

"The truth is, I was somewhat of a grifter. Riley caught me off guard. She saw me, you know, really saw me." He turned to Eve with the wide-eyed look of a man in love. "She changed me. I know it sounds ridiculous. We've been together two months, but it's true. I'm a new person with her."

"She's far too young and inexperienced to be with someone like you." For the first time, Eve no longer wished for her relationship with Riley to be restored to what it had once been. Here was an opportunity to start fresh and, inhaling the sharp air, she was awash with relief. Yes, she could begin a life with a man like Braverman.

"Here's one more secret for you: I'm thirty-two," he said. He dug the heels of his boots in the soft earth.

"Holy Mother of God," she said, imitating him. "She's not even twenty."

"I'm sorry, Babe."

"Who's David Johnson?" she asked.

He looked at her, quite sadly, and said, "I am."

Overhead, a flock of wild geese flew in a V. She wanted to recite lines of poetry and tell him, *you do not have to be good*, yet she wouldn't. The evening remained unmarred by an abundance of words. She knew his romance with Riley would peter out, and, when it did, she would be at the cottage, waiting for him. They understood each other, and there was beauty in the silence of clarity. The lake, overcast by a fine mizzle, reflected nothing on its surface. Then, breaking the spell of their shared communion, he said, "This weekend has regenerated me. I didn't know I needed this escape, but I did, and you offered me shelter.

I was afraid you'd be—like Moodie, matronly—wanting to turn me out, but Riley said you wouldn't. And you know, she was right: You really are a cool old lady."

He would have hurt her less if he'd hit her, just as she'd hit Pitcairn. She was blindsided. There it was, the truth of what she was to him served cold. She lifted her glass of brandy, rose from the chair, and walked to the back door of the cottage while counting each of her steps. And when she entered her bedroom, shame and humiliation burned brightly within her breast. Like a schoolgirl, she cried herself to sleep.

Eve was anxious in waking, knowing Braverman and Riley were leaving. She had dreamed terrifying images she could not remember, and what remained was a foreboding sense of vengeance in her body, her spine tethered to the evil of nightmare. She recalled her conversation with Braverman and his confessions. Her stomach soured. *Old lady.* She thought of the library card from Amherst she saw in his wallet. If he was David Johnson, why had he been a college student in 2001? *He must be lying about this name.* He was Braverman, and he had stolen credit cards and identification from a David Johnson, someone he conned in the past. The library card was a memento of his misdeeds. She imagined a body—even her own body—rolled in a rug, slowly dropping to the bottom of the lake. And she was filled with apprehension at the thought of being a victim. Pitcairn had done this to her. He had made her fearful of men's intentions. Braverman had led her on, she was sure of it.

The phone rang. At the cottage, she still had a telephone on the wall, its long coiled bungee cord woefully hanging. She didn't answer. She didn't care to know who was calling her. The ringing ceased. On the counter, her cellphone pinged. She stood to look at the screen. It was her brother Roger. *Call me. Please.*

Riley walked out of the bedroom, her hair matted on one side of her head. "Jesus, you've got to cut your landline," she said. "No one has telephones anymore."

"Is he in bed?"

Riley kept her distance. "Brave went out to run errands. I thought he'd be back here with you already." Her eyes were half-open.

"Your boyfriend's not what he seems."

"Was that Dad on the phone? He called me already to tell me to get you up and leave the cottage. What did he tell *you*? That Brave is really a thirty-seven-year-old former convict? That he sells drugs? Don't believe him. You know Brave by now." Riley sat at the kitchen table.

Eve took her hand. "I had a feeling there was something off about him. He probably *is* thirty-seven and after your father's money. His real name is David Johnson."

"I know."

Eve waited. "You don't seem disturbed by this."

"Evie—I know him. You know him, too. He's been helping you with the house and you're buying into this?" Riley began to whimper. "I'm the one who's fucking everything up. I'm failing my classes so early in the semester. I was put on academic probation last spring. My hair looks like shit and this damn piercing keeps getting infected and crusted with blood boogers."

"Oh, Riley, my Riley," said Eve. "I thought he was real, too." What a fool she was for thinking of wasting herself on yet another gasbag of a man. It was Riley she should have shielded from the hurt of the world.

"I think he overheard Dad on the phone. He left, but I know he's coming back for me."

She seemed to look through the window. It framed a small curve of driveway.

"You don't need him, Riley," said Eve. "You have me."

"Don't turn him in. Please. They'll lock him up for things he's done before. He's told me his story."

Eve searched the spot on the wall by the telephone. Her car keys were missing. *Of course they're missing.* Was this the feeling that engulfed her all morning? Not the lingering effect of his insult and the cost of her fantasy, but a need for revenge against a wrong she now understood? Braverman had taken her car, one of the many impulses of her life. How Pitcairn had admired its body, its faultless construction. A ride in her car was the one thing she refused him. He hadn't earned it. Braverman hadn't earned it either.

Eve pulled Riley into the guest bedroom and told her to pack her belongings. She would text Roger and tell him to be there soon, for his girl, to brace her for what was to come. She kissed her niece's forehead and closed the door gently behind her. She looked down at her phone. Instead of replying to Roger's text, she found in her contact list the phone number for the local police station. She promised Riley not to turn in Brave, but what promises were truly worth keeping? Not the half-truths of life, the wild dares, and the precarious choices. There was no kindness to be gained in obeying the wishes of others, only folly.

She rummaged in a kitchen drawer and found a disposable red lighter. From the cupboard, she grabbed the pack of *Gitanes*, lifted the corners of the cellophane, and drew a cigarette, which she put between her lips. She walked out to the yard, her Georgian silver ashtray in hand. She flicked the little gas flame and took a drag. The lake was flat and unmoving. Behind her, in the distance, she heard the familiar rumbling of her car's engine. He was coming back, as Riley said he would. Eve thought of the song of sirens, mere minutes away, and of the men in blue who would take him from her home. She savored her choice. When Braverman slowly drove on the gravel toward her, she turned to smile at him through a ring of smoke.

Last of the Viking Seals

Look at that little cretin sitting on the train with his mother. She's wearing an absurd chenille cardigan that wouldn't cover her low-slung breasts if she tried to button it. Her hair is dyed burgundy, the only color Northern Italian women choose once they turn forty. How they love that color instead of the one they inherited from their parents. And how they love to bear children later in life. I am assuredly seated diagonally from one such woman. She tries to read a heavy book with bold lettering, a thriller in translation. With so many empty seats in this carriage, I expected her to choose a different row of seats for her tornado of a child. I should have sat elsewhere once they boarded the train.

"Micetto," she says. She tries to soothe the holy terror, whom she calls *kitty cat* and Amoruccio, a boy who is five or six years old, with brown hair, brown eyes, and chocolate sauce down the front of his polo shirt. He wears the collar flipped up like all the football stars he probably watches on television with his father, if he still has a father. By the look of his mother, I'd venture to say the father ran off with a cubista, one of those girls who

147

dances on a raised platform at the discoteca when the place bounces *unz, unz, unz.* It must be hard to raise a little tyrant while hiding the shameful loss of a husband who ran off with a cubista.

She tries to get my attention: "Signora, mi scusi," she says, but I have years of practice pretending to be asleep on public transportation. If I were a man, she would leave me in peace. Men have the luxury of sowing fear throughout the furrows of their years, and the requests for my help never cease because a woman of a certain age traveling alone inspires confidence. That's what the abandoned or destitute or helpless say, not to mention the hopeless, and I believe them. I spy through one half-open eye 'Amoruccio' and his burgundy-haired mother. Her eyes are green, glowing above two semicircles of purple veining that announce how tired she must be of being saddled with such a burdensome child.

She overpronounces her syllables in a singsong, "A-mo-ruc-cio." She calls him *sweetheart*, but she's neither thrilled with nor particularly attentive to him. He's mewling—mewling!—like a drowning kitten because his Kinder Sorpresa didn't contain the figurine he wanted. He's already opened three Kinder eggs since boarding. Each chocolate egg holds an orange plastic capsule shaped like a robust suppository with one of two types of surprises: a collectable figurine or a dumb assembly-style miniature toy that would test the most stubborn IKEA enthusiast. A glossy square of paper lists either the full figurine series—this season it's a set of Viking bearded seals—or the instructions to the horrid consolation toy, which is exactly what the boy found in those last three eggs. His mother puts together a cardstock bird with a plastic beak that's supposed to bob inside a water glass when its feet are clipped to the rim. The boy's juice box has no proper rim, the bird won't perch, and he wails.

"Mi scusi," the mother calls out again. Her skin is pale and waxy like she's sick with syphilis or gonorrhea or one of the many diseases spread at the discoteca. She turns to the child and says, "Matteo, zitto." *Be quiet.*

I want to support her need for quiet by saying, "Si, zitto, gattaccio," but I'd disclose my availability to help her with the hellion that is Matteo. Voglia sottozero. No desire whatsoever, *a subzero level of interest.* I'm waiting for her to blow up, but she tells him to be good and to suck on the straw of his juice box. "Porco cane, Matteo," she says. *Pigdog,* a fitting compliment for his smug, piggish nose.

"Voglio una Coca-Cola!" he screams.

She ignores his request and chants Amo-ruc-cio, interspersed with the word basta, as though she's a disabused and underpaid tutor from a Venetian school of witchcraft, and if she says the spell correctly—*enough, enough, enough!*—the little bastard will turn into an obedient piglet-pup. "Basta, Amoruccio, basta." She pulls out a discman from her bag and tries to shove padded earphones on his head, but he slaps her hand and the earphones fall in her lap.

He tells her she is ugly. "Brutta cattiva!" *Mean and ugly.* It never ceases to amaze me what children get away with these days.

But they have their own spitefulness, those mothers. They call their children bruttino and bruttina, *little uglies,* as they coddle them in infancy. They're stocking up on insults, in preparation for growing children throwing fits and calling them both mean and ugly or, as teenagers, porca putana della Madonna. At the thought of besmirching the Virgin's name with an assortment of insults reserved for servile whores, I mentally sign myself of the cross.

"Signora," says the mother, blocking the aisle by holding opposite headrests, "per piacere." I wait for a strident appeal to action. "Mi sente?" *Do you hear me?*

I feign awaking and look about me at all those empty seats, searching for someone, anyone, who could do her bidding. "What can I do?" I ask in resignation.

"It's an emergency. The bathroom. Can you please sit with him? Solo un attimino?" *Just for a little moment?* She speaks in diminutives.

I gather my things, cross the aisle, and sit in front of her dastardly son, who scowls. I want to wish her una buona pisciatina, *a good little pee,* but she's already disappeared from our carriage into the next one.

"Sei vecchia, tu," he says. *You're old.* He doesn't pronounce it *vet-shia,* so I know he's not from Venice or Treviso.

"Where are you going?" I ask him as he tugs the window latch and looks for his mother.

"A casa."

"E dov'è la tua casa?"

"Close to the kiosk of the edicola where we buy magazines and my Ovetti Kinder." He is suddenly quiet and restrained.

"I'm going to Udine," I tell him. "But I'm from Campania, in the south."

He tucks his feet under him and says, "Me too."

He clearly has no idea in what city or on which street he lives. The mother should have him memorize these things. She must think all the strangers in the world are here to help her—in her neighborhood, on the train, in doctors' waiting rooms—the lot of us hoping for a chance to spend time with the little brute. He is the product of an odious generation of ingrates. "Didn't your mother tell you not to talk to strangers?" He scoots back in the seat, folding his legs against his chest. He might start to cry and there will be no end to his wailing, so I say, "Never you mind. I'm not a stranger. My name is Edna."

"Edna," he says with a sniffle.

"You can call me Eddi."

"I don't like Edna, but Eddi is okay."

I ask him his name even though I know the answer. One can never seem too preoccupied with the affairs of others.

"Mattia!"

"Mattia? Are you sure?" A lying child. He's ignored too frequently at home and he'll become the next Volpe or Guerrieri, joining a band of Satanists. It's all over the news. That kind of degeneracy proliferates, but I prefer to be an optimist: the child is ignored at home because his mother is exhausted from working long hours and taking care of him alone. I consider asking about his father and the cubista.

He screams, "Mattia! Mattia! Mattia!"

What a nuisance. "How old are you, Mattia?"

He cackles like a budding maniac, doubled over. "I'm not Mattia. I'm Matteo!"

I pray he's not a Volpe or Guerrieri in the making. "How old are you?"

"Fifty," he says. He shows all fingers of his left hand and forms a circle with his right fist. He must think me a fool.

"Zero-five, I see. You're five." He's bound to explode with resentment. Instead, he nods yes and bursts out laughing again.

"I'm a hundred and twenty years old," I say.

He grows serious. "You'll probably die tomorrow."

"Magari," I say. *Maybe so. If I'm lucky.*

He raises the moveable tabletop from underneath the window and fiddles with the mechanism to keep it upright. He'll pinch his fingers. And then the mother will come back from her little pee and accuse me of abuse. "Let go," I say, swatting his hand away. I fix the bar and he plants his elbows on the tabletop.

Between the wall and his legs sits a brown corduroy drawstring bag with the name Matteo embroidered in blue. "Show me what's in your bag," I say.

"La Nonna made it, but she lives far away." He pulls on the strings of his bag and extracts two small picture books, a squashed merendina in the form of a round carrot cake sealed in cellophane—though carrot must surely be one of the last ingredients on the list given its neon yellow-orange color—CDs for the discman, and one last wrapped Kinder egg. He cradles the egg like treasure and shows me the catalog of the Viking bearded seal figurines. Before this series, Kinder launched the Russian bears, the Canadian caribou, the French poodles—I remember a mime, a pastry chef, and a can-can dancer with a jaunty red beret—the Majorcan hedgehogs, and the Egyptian camels, painted to resemble the gods of hieroglyphs. Ridiculous trinkets forming an international circus of moronic animals.

He points to one of the seals, a female wearing an iron corset and a horned helmet. Two thick blond braids frame her face. She sings opera. "I'm missing this one. I have all the other ones." He taps on the letters of her name. Griselda. "I have multiples of Viggo with the ax."

"Bella collezione," I say, "and nine out of ten isn't bad."

I lean in and he holds the wrapped egg to my face before yanking it back. He slides his index finger across his lips and says, "Shh."

"Do you think—"

"Shh."

I whisper, "Is it Griselda inside?"

He nods yes. "She's sleeping," he says, wiggling his bottom jaw horizontally while raising his eyebrows to an unknown beat. *Unz, unz, unz.* Does he know about the cubista?

"I hate asparagus," he says. He takes a deep breath and exhales with the air of a tragicomic actor. "Sempre, sempre, gli asparagi." *She always makes asparagus.* He sighs again. "My neighbor Nadia hit her head at the playground and now she's home from the hospital and they shaved her head and cut it open to fix her brain." I await his next non sequitur. He lifts his shoulders, once, saying, "Allora?" *So?*

"You must be sad," I say, "for Nadia."

"Mi rompe le scatole." *She bugs me.* "My mamma makes me go to Nadia's apartment after school. I hate it." He looks out the window at rolling hills. "I hate broccoli."

His mother better return soon. We are approaching Conegliano, which means I have an hour and a half or so on this train until my destination. I ask about the father's whereabouts before I'm released from this infernal duty. "E il papà, lui, cosa fa?" *What does your father do?*

"Mio babbo è morto."

"Are you lying?"

He answers, "No," and he neither smiles nor cackles.

I didn't mean to sadden him, and he'll surely start to cry. "Non piangere," I say. *Don't cry.*

"Non piango mai." *Never.* He must have learned to suppress his emotions.

"Me neither," I say. "I stopped crying a long time ago."

He asks, "One hundred years ago?"

"Maybe more."

"Me too." He lets out a long, petering toot and laughs without apology. "Old people have a lot of farts stuck in their butts."

Oh, Santo Cielo, he's bound to ask about sex. I might tell him babies come out of women's behinds, too, to befuddle him out of his grief, but then he'll tell his mother the shiny new thing he's learned and there will be no stopping her indignation.

He says, "Mio babbo è morto in un incidente di rally."

A rally accident. I should have known. The father is a semi-famous renegade and he has his choice of cubiste. Such a waste of a human life to drive at breakneck speeds for entertainment. Every year, someone is pronounced dead: the driver, the navigator, bystanders lining village streets and outfields in the middle of nowhere. Those damn rally cars sputter mud everywhere. A disgrace.

"Pilota?"

"Si." Matteo comes closer to open my purse, and he begins to extract each item as if the contents belong to him. "What's this?" he says.

"Milk of magnesia tablets."

"My nonna gave me some." He chews one and spits on the floor. "I hate chalk." One by one he asks, "What's this?"

I answer, "My glasses, an address book, an old lipstick, a wallet, an identity card, a train ticket, a crossword booklet—*La Settimana Enigmistica*—paracetamols and heart medicine, mint chewing gum, and a blue pen."

Without asking, he breaks free a square of gum from its blister packet and puts it in his mouth. He pushes a second piece between my lips. Oh, the thought of his fingernails harboring the dried-up dust of dirt and poo. I mumble, "Grazie mille," and he answers enthusiastically, "Prego cinquecento," like a professional gum distributor. Boys that age never wash their hands. I doubt his burgundy-haired mother taught him hygiene, and Nadia's mother is too busy with her poor Frankenstein of a daughter to clean dirty fingers. How did I forget to bring tissues?

I ask, "What will you be when you grow up?"

"Pilota di rally."

Goodness, there's no saving the child from a treacherous future. I turn to subterfuge. "I'll tell you a trick. About the Kinder eggs." His face glows with attention. "You can find the figurines without opening the eggs—"

"How?" he whelps as he squirms on his knees.

"You weigh them with your hands. The next time your mother takes you shopping, place one egg in each of your palms. Put back the lightest of the two. Pick another, and weigh those two. Do this until you find the heaviest." He flashes a smile that demonstrates the possibility of vestigial intelligence. "The seals weigh more," he says.

"Yes." The little imp must indeed be brighter than he appears.

He rises on the seat and wraps his arms around my neck. I pat his elbow, which digs into my collarbone. *There, there.*

"You smell like a closet," he says.

"You smell like a wet dog," I say.

He howls with delight. "Bau, bau, bau," he barks.

I push him off me and force him into his seat. "Settle down," I tell him.

"Uffa. You're no fun, Eddi."

At the end of our carriage, a conductor opens the sliding door and lets it close with a loud smack. The mother isn't back and she's taken her purse with her. She's been gone more than thirty minutes. Good God, is she constipated? That must be why she cooks vats of asparagus. For the fiber. With her husband dead, she no longer cares about the stench of her urine, and constipation taints her breath with the rancidity of her congested intestines. "Matteo," I say, "where's your ticket?"

"Boh," he answers, raising his shoulders.

The conductor could be in his sixties. I can't divine younger men's ages. And look at the shamelessness of his balding pate and stubby salt-and-pepper mustache. He's not even wearing his conductor's cap. I might report him for dereliction of duty.

"Tickets, Signora, tickets." With great flourish, he holds his ticket-punch forward like a gun. "Ecco, uno!" He turns to Matteo and says, "Il secondo? Signorino?"

Matteo snubs him and crawls over my lap to the table-top. He covers his head with his corduroy bag.

I explain, "He's not mine—"

"Ah! I'm not an idiot," says the conductor.

"His mother went to the bathroom."

"The boy needs a ticket." The conductor observes Matteo with a sharp eye. "Is the mother a gypsy?"

To my great bewilderment, Matteo turns his head and yells, "Si! Siamo zingari!" *We are gypsies!*

The conductor says, "There, see? The good old trick. The mother goes to the bathroom while I'm doing my rounds, leaves the boy with an old woman, and when she comes back, I've passed her in the bathroom, and later she can get off the train without paying."

I testify, without proof, that "he's not Romani—"

"He doesn't have a ticket. The boy and his mother must get off at the next station."

Matteo creeps along the facing seats and tugs the con-ductor's sleeve. He whispers, "I am a gypsy."

I yank the boy by the waist. "Porca miseria, Matteo!" *Pig-misery!* The heavens are testing me for whatever sins of impatience I committed in my youth.

The conductor grins and says, "That's all right, Signora. I'll come back."

Taunting old women and children must be the only pleasure of his life. Look at his benighted face with that awful mustache. I want to tell him to reserve what little power he wields in this world for grander occasions, but

I restrain myself. I might hit him with my empty purse. "Bene," I say. I replace my belongings in my bag to give it some heft. Sono pronta, I think. *I am ready.*

The conductor moseys along the aisle before turning back to us. "Without tickets, they either get off in Conegliano or I'll have the carabinieri at the ready."

"Stronzo," I say. *Shit turd.* He doesn't hear me.

Matteo chants, "Stronzo, stronzo, stronzo," like a disco beat. *Unz, unz, unz.*

I raise my arms above my head and implore the heavens, and to Matteo I say, "You'd test even the benevolence of Santa Scolastica di Norcia."

Thinking of the sanctity of Scolastica, patron saint of students and convulsive children, a horrifying truth occurs to me: the mother is unwed. She never married the rally driver. The pilota left her the gift of a precocious child. She's gone to the bathroom to refresh her makeup and spray perfume to mask her sewer odors. That's why she looks so tired. She works at all hours to bring in money. And once she gets off the train, she'll have to rush home, drop off the boy at Nadia's house, and head straight to work. Poor Nadia's mother. I don't know how she'll manage to watch over a vegetable and a potential delinquent.

"Ho fame," says Matteo. *I'm hungry.*

"Eat your merendina."

He pounds the tabletop. "I want a panino and a Coca-Cola."

"If it were up to me, I'd give you a swift spanking instead."

He wiggles his lower jaw and raises his eyebrows again. "I'm too quick." *Unz, unz, unz.* He pulls out my lipstick from behind his back. "See?" He takes off the cap and swivels the tube so it's fully raised to attention. He makes lightsaber noises. *Più, più, più.*

"Put it on," I say. "Go ahead. An angel with red lips. Don't you want to look like your mother?"

He turns the tube counterclockwise, slowly, and puts the cap back on. "Here," he says, "I don't want it." He squirms on the seat and grabs his crotch. His face paints a plaintive picture of pain and impending doom. "Mi scappa la pipi!"

"And you couldn't have gone to the bathroom with your mother?"

He's gripping his privates with both hands now. "I didn't need to," he says. There's logic in his statement. Maybe he should study law instead of fantasizing about driving rally cars designed by speed demons.

"Are you a gypsy?" I ask. One can never be too sure.

He says, "No."

I pack up our belongings. If he's not a gypsy, then someone else here will be. Only a halfwit would leave anything behind on a train, and I won't beg a stranger to look after the boy's things when that task was foisted onto me by his burgundy-haired mother. "Mannaggia," I say, already out of breath at the prospect of walking through moving carriages. "Come on," I tell him, "your pipi won't suck itself back into your bladder."

"Can it?" he asks with round eyes. He looks altogether too happy.

I push him along the aisle while holding his corduroy bag, my purse, and his mother's book in my arms. The things I do for charity, a veritable plague these past two decades of my life.

In the third carriage ahead of ours, we find at last an unoccupied men's bathroom. "You have to go in with me," he says, with his puny arms crossed defiantly. "It's the rule."

"Then with the little girls you go," I tell him. We enter the women's bathroom, and I manage to close the door behind us in this minuscule space that reeks of month-old urine. Why isn't the mother in here clogging rattling pipes with her compacted poo? She must be further up the train. Matteo pulls down his pants and releases his tiny penis over the elastic band of his underwear. He braces himself by leaning his thighs against the toilet bowl. He wiggles his pisellino before tucking it back out of sight and pulling up his pants. Of course, he reaches for the doorlatch without washing his hands.

I force his arms into the sink bowl and soap him up to his elbows. The paper towel dispenser is empty, as I expected—good public transportation staff who do their job and replenish towels do not exist—so he shakes his wrists like they're two fighting puppets and splatters water on my blouse. A real hooligan, that one. While I steer him back to our carriage, I discern the beige edges of two train tickets inserted in the mother's book. I am a miracle worker sometimes. Matteo prattles about opening his last Kinder egg. "Griselda!" he sings in an operatic voice. "Mia, mia!"

When we return to our seats, we find his mother and the conductor gesticulating like two braying donkeys undergoing the neutering of their testicles. "Matteo!" she shrieks, and the boy runs to her like he, too, has been maimed. To me she points, saying, without thanks, "How could you leave?" Her syllables echo along train-track turbulence. *Unz, unz, unz.* Only an acerbic cuckquean would assign the blame of her terrible parenting to an innocent old woman.

"It was Eddi!" Matteo accuses me of I don't know what.

She soothes him with her velvet tongue. "Amoruccio," she says. She tries to embrace him, but he wriggles himself free.

"He would have urinated on the seat," I explain.

Meanwhile, the conductor lectures me on recent sensational kidnappings. "Families need to be vigilant!" he declares. "There's evil lurking. And when it's not the forces of the adversary, then it's gypsies and Albanians entering homes and taking all they can while incapacitating owners with sleeping gas. The gas gangs are strong this spring. Heed my advice and keep all windows closed and locked into place."

I drop the corduroy bag and book on the tabletop and, in doing so, I slip the two tickets up my sleeve. Let the cuckquean and her little Judas get off in Conegliano. Good riddance. I've done her a favor and now she has no use for me.

"Our tickets." She reaches for her thriller in translation and shakes it while holding its spine. "They were bookmarks." She searches the pockets of her cardigan before rummaging through her purse. "I swear." Matteo takes a swig from a juice box he's found among the contents of her bag. She yells at him, "Where are the tickets?"

"I don't know," he says.

"Matteo! Non scherzare!" *Don't joke around!* "He does this," she groans, sweeping the air in mid-distance.

"The tickets are your responsibility, not his," I say, but she continues her beratement.

She says in a low voice, "I will count to three, Matteo. I swear to God I will count to three."

The conductor taps the side of his nose knowingly and asks the mother, "Is your husband with you?"

"What does it matter?" She appears frantic and deranged. "He left us, the imbecile." She fingers the tight space between seats and fishes nothing but soft emptiness. "Matteo! Where are they?"

He guffaws and says, "In my butt-crack!" as he toots three gusts that sound like deflated trumpet notes. "My butt counted to three!"

She screams, "Basta!" and slaps him across the face.

He is stunned into silence, a red handprint appearing on his cheek. He holds his bag against his chest, the blue letters of his name facing outward like an announcement of his claim to life. Matteo, poor child. Those big brown eyes lost in the smarting of his skin.

"Was that necessary?" asks the conductor.

"You're the one harassing us!"

For Matteo's sake, I confess, "There!" and pretend to retrieve the tickets under her seat. I hand them to the conductor, who punches each one with great fanfare. He's like a circus clown laughing and biding his time while we queue to see the bearded lady and the strongman.

The mother begins to weep. "Micetto," she says, but Matteo turns away from her.

He wraps his arms around my legs. "Eddi," he whimpers.

The conductor returns the tickets to the mother and leaves, whistling "O Mio Babbino Caro," a fool lost in his own megalomaniacal thoughts. The mother huddles against the window. I tell her to rest and try to sleep until her stop. She says they are going to Udine, and I tell her I've lived in that sunless city since I took a secretarial position there in 1961. I don't tell her I wanted to leave when I retired, but I had nowhere to go. I say, "Matteo is safe with me."

Then to Matteo, I say, "Vieni con me," leading him by the hand. He clutches his Kinder egg and I help him sit on my lap. He wipes his nose on the shoulder of his polo shirt and I fold down his collar. "There, a proper little gentleman." He doesn't flip the collar back up. He asks for my help with his egg. We peel back thin, silver-lined foil to expose two halves of a chocolate shell, one of which he devours like a lion. He tries to give me the second half, but I tell him the chocolate is for him. "Kinder means for children." He's trembling in anticipation, perhaps trying to will the appearance of his beloved Griselda.

I won't bear his disappointment if he doesn't find the last of his Viking seals. I say, "You can visit me in my apartment in Udine. We'll go to the market down the street and weigh their Kinder eggs, one by one. You'll test my method and we'll buy all the heavy ones." I put my arms around him and he leans back into me. "We'll buy eggs every time you visit me." I kiss the top of his head. His hair smells surprisingly fresh, like newly-mown hay and the coming of spring.

"I won't tell her I'm coming to live with you," he says, pointing to his mother. "Shh."

"Is that so?" I say, "and where will I put you to sleep? In the bathtub?"

"Si!" he exclaims, "like a secret! If the thieves come for you, I'll crawl out of the bathtub with a sword and— swish!—they'll be gone. I am a ninja. No one can see me."

"I see you, Matteo." I poke his little round belly and he releases his giggles. "No flatulence on my legs," I say.

Before popping open the orange bullet by squeezing its middle, Matteo commands, "Eddi, close your eyes." I cover my face with my hands. I hear the rolling wheels of the train, the exhausted snoring of his burgundy-haired mother across the way, and the squirrely chittering of his fingers, prying loose a plastic shape from a rolled paper catalogue. Matteo taps my raised elbow, in happiness or distress, I cannot guess. He whispers, "Eddi, look!" and, like the god Odin of his Viking bearded seals, I open one eye. I see what he cradles in his hand, a blue and green globe hanging on a keychain.

"Don't be disappointed, agnellino mio." *My little lamb.*

He holds up the world for my inspection and says, "It's not so bad, this one."

"No," I tell him, "this one isn't so bad after all."

Over the Mountain Steep

(based on a true story)

Martha Moats Baker stirs and burrows deeper under the pines. Her wool coat holds what little heat her body pulses on this January morning. After a long night of fluted shrills, the Whippoorwills have gone silent. *They don't sing in winter*, she thinks, as she hears the wind and sees snow blow down from above in great whirling gusts: it was the whistling of trees, swaying and cracking, she mistook for distant song. *There aren't any birds.*

She's been in the snow too long now. Her body is numb and sleep comes for her. To shake it off, she pictures what her mother must be doing at this carly hour, rocking by the pot-bellied stove, a floury apron protecting her dress, the good book in her lap. At her mother's home on the other side of the mountain, eleven miles from where she is lost, bony branches rattle against the windows and, on such cold mornings, nails sometimes thump in the walls. Her mother always interprets this sound, loud as the whack of a gavel, as an omen to pray.

Martha remembers the postscript of her mother's letter—"Come, great news!"—scratched in her familiar childlike hand. When she received the letter, she thought of her sister Dorcas, melon-big with her eighth pregnancy, and of her brother Silas, who was soon to return from months of logging in the south. She thought of Dorcas's middle son, whose leg was mending from a bad fall, and of Silas's oldest girl, who had a beau all the way in Franklin. Might he not propose sooner or later? She thought of her brother Lazarus, who died of Spanish flu some six years earlier. Lazarus's pain, though deep, had come to an end swiftly. Since the burial, hasty and small, all remaining siblings and their children put their pennies, nickels, and dimes in a Mason jar to replace the wooden cross of his grave with a proper stone. At her last visit, the jar had been nearly full. Tragedy had blessedly kept its distance in recent years, and possible good news came aplenty in the Moats family. She was eager to discover which particular happiness spurred her mother's invitation.

A cold blade of wind pushes its way beneath the collar of her coat and stings her neck, but she can't summon the strength to huddle harder against it. She thinks about the roles of time and chance in her predicament. Had the mail been delayed by a day, she would be home at breakfast now with her husband John and their only child, Roy. He's the joy of their life, this boy, and a smart one, too, recently accepted at the Virginia Military Institute in Lexington. He would be the first in a long line of Moatses to get a proper degree. She had studied to become a schoolteacher but didn't consider herself a true scholar. "He's a Baker, that one, all right," she guessed her mother would say. How she longed to see her face during their exchange of news. The desire to best her had been fresh on her mind when she decided to visit her family.

"There's news in Fletcher," Martha told John when they were settling for bed two nights before. "I'll be gone four or five days to get back in time for the start of school."

"Storm coming, Martha. I don't like you going one bit."

"Is that so?" She led him to their bed. Even after twenty years of marriage, she could make him see her way with what he called a little night magic.

The next morning, she packed in wax paper a few whipped lard and sugar sandwiches and slung an aluminum flask on her shoulder. She kissed John and made her way to the bottom of the mountain.

By mid-afternoon, it was clear her husband had been right. The path became so difficult she had to make several stops and lost, somewhere after the first blanketed peak, the markings of the trail. She berated herself. *My foolishness never ends.* Time after time, her stubbornness gets her in trouble, her biggest flaw in a varied lot. She's intelligent but close-minded, decent yet full of pluck, and strong though naïve. To whomever will lend an ear, her mother sings a similar backhanded litany of her daughter's faults with an air of desolation masking deeper pride.

Her body is being claimed now, the price of her foolhardy willfulness. Her mouth is dry, even after she put lumps of snow in her mouth to drink along the way when the flask was empty. In this spot, to which she's been rooted for hours, she breathes in resin and bark, though her moist lungs expand and contract by imperceptible degrees. She thinks she understands where she is and she recalls that in summer bellworts and bluets cover the ground, releasing a heavy scent of moss. She can't feel the snow banked against her legs and she repeats in whispers the arithmetic lesson she taught her students right before Christmas in the one-room Mount Solon schoolhouse where she's taught since she was twenty-six. Numbers soothe her, just as a cup of chamomile tea and a bedtime story comforted Roy when he was a boy, and this multiplication table of prime numbers is her favorite.

She is halfway between her home in Stokesville and her mother's place near Fletcher's Run. This she knows. She's made the twenty-mile trek across Brushy Mountain countless times on foot, but she tries in vain to calculate where she went wrong while numbers tumble in her head. She enumerates the trees and crags and views she knows so well. She's crested Little Bald Knob, eight miles up, in the shoes she bought last fall, but on the trail to Reddish the snow fell in blinding sheets and the sky took on the hazy yellow hue of an unseasonal thunderstorm.

She brings the tips of her numb fingers to her mouth. They taste bitter yet sweet. She took off her mitten hours before to scratch pine bark and cull its gum. There is no pain, simply a dull feeling in her hand. She takes a long breath, and another, slower, much slower. In each bronchiole of her lungs, tiny ice particles crystallize. Snow falls on her face. Her fingers rest on her cheek, this part of skin she can no longer feel. She is both herself and not herself, a stranger in the snow, cool to the touch, with a face smooth as a skipping stone.

There's only the smell of resin to remind her of her own body, lost in the Alleghenies. Against a great darkness, this lingering odor evokes the small block of rosin that in the early days of their marriage John rubbed on the strings of his fiddle bow. Light filters through in thin blue lines and there he is in the distance, with the fiddle, playing the melody she likes best. He's never played on such a finely tuned instrument. How young he looks. And Roy at five years old is dancing with a little fox as snow twirls about them. She sees her life as a picture reel, all the years she and John have built and lived together, the joys and sorrows and the sicknesses and health. Her vows are ringing with the beauty of the violin and its music, and she is filled with love and grace.

There's a cloud of crossbills and waxwings, of buntings and wrens in the sky. They fly to the music, which grows loud and pure. It's as much part of her as the marrow of her bones and the frozen lashes of her eyelids. A single mountain bluebird descends on her shoulder. It hops across her breast, leaving the tiniest of prints, a repeated letter M, to signal where she rests. At the bluebird's whistle, the birds swarm down in patterns and peck at her coat, her shoes, her bonnet, and her mitten. Carefully, they lift up her body, in a slow ascent above the trees, high above the peaks of mountains, and she sees beyond the storm, so clearly now, a luminous promise of early spring. This, she knows, is the best news of all.

Godfrey Green

I thought I bombed my job interview with Tamsin Godfrey, the woman I referenced in my master's thesis. Tamsin Godfrey's fingers had deftly repaired the fibers of the great hanging canvases Picasso created for Massine's ballet *Parade*. She oxidized her own pigments in paint pots numbered in the hundreds, replicating the exact shade of blue of the Virgin Mary's veil in more than a dozen frescoes, in small flashes of light and shadow in the depths of ancient chiaroscuro. During the interview, she presented me with two challenges, which consisted of identifying a paint chip containing albumen and discussing the transparency and layering techniques of lead hydroxycarbonate. I thought these tests were too simple, and I believed she'd already dismissed my candidacy. Before I left, she said, "Now, we drink." She offered me a glass of red wine. "I brought this back from Veneto. The grapes are *corvina* and *rondinella*. Taste it." I put my lips to the glass's rim. She watched me. I knew little about wines, but I could taste notes of sour cherry, and I said so.

Afterward she told me she hired me because I held the glass by the stem and not the bowl. She believed all wines needed the filter of light, to develop and to breathe. I was honored by her selection, yet disappointed neither my portfolio nor my recognition of the correct paint chip had won her over. She said I had elegance and a quiet air, and it was all she required of an assistant.

*   *   *

Some months after I became Tamsin's assistant, I painted her portrait. I'd earned a dual master's degree in historical conservation and fine arts, with a concentration in painting, hoping to establish my own career as an artist while working as a restorer. I carried the canvas from my Brooklyn apartment to the station platform, setting it against the bench where I sat, waiting to board the train. I lumbered with this canvas all the way to our studio. When I entered the building, the security guard asked me to unwrap it.

I made a face at Sebastian, puffing my cheeks to show the task was insurmountable. "It's for Tamsin," I said. "I painted it. It's her birthday."

He crossed his arms and pursed his lips at the canvas. Sebastian was Ecuadorian and pointed with his mouth. "Rules are rules."

I peeled back the tape with great care to preserve the wrapping and asked, "Is Monica's mother still with you?"

He told me weeks before, with a long, plaintive sigh, that his mother-in-law would be staying with them for a month. It was the low point of his year whenever she visited.

He rolled his eyes. "Good painting. Looks like her, but fuzzy."

"I like to make abstractions of portraits. Small strokes of paint layering larger ones. Her eyes, there. They survey everything and reveal nothing. She's an enigma, even in the painting." I tried to close the wrapping, but the tape had lost its stickiness.

"It's no Mona Lisa, if you ask me, but it's pretty good."

I took the elevator and inserted my key in the lock that opened the doors to our studio. Tamsin sat in front of a large easel, working on a self-portrait of Mme Gabiou. She had in mind to illuminate Gabiou's career and revive interest in her art. She liked to work by the large window facing north to keep even sunlight throughout the hours. Sometimes I could forget iron bars reinforced our windows and downstairs Sebastian monitored the building and every person who entered it. The first time Tamsin said, "Leonardo taught me to paint by a northerly window and in late afternoon, to diffuse harsh shadows," I imagined her in conversation with the master. I envied Da Vinci his convivial friendship with Tamsin. She sensed the presence of the painters she restored and she often spoke to them in whispers. She said they guided her through every stroke of her paintbrush.

"I have something for you," I said. I loosened the wrapping and showed Tamsin the canvas.

"What's this?" She placed her glasses, which had been perched atop her head, on the bridge of her nose. She held the canvas away from her and inspected it. "Well, my dear, you are a restorer. Unless you want to go down the annals of history as a mimic of Graham Sutherland, you'd better stick to the practice of reviving women's work."

"I thought—"

"I'm not saying you can't paint, but there are thousands upon thousands of artists like you now, women who paint whatever they like." She eyed me with woeful patience. "What we do, you and I, is give voice to women who rose against impossible social mores to produce art in an age when they couldn't. They defied the limitations and constraints of their sex."

Tamsin pushed the canvas against my body so I would hold it. "They seated themselves at the artists' banquet when the place settings had already been assigned. And yet they managed this arduous feat. From whatever dusty corners in those rooms, they found chairs and pulled them up to the table, elbowing their male neighbors for a chance to fill their plates." She patted my shoulder, not without affection. "It's a question of legacy. Who else will do this work but us? The men who rarely include them in retrospectives? The visitors who take a quick glance at small placards and move on to those paintings selected to correspond with an odious audio track, which *explains* to them why they are there, staring at beauty like befuddled children? We live among the intellectually bereft who can't decipher anything without self-guided tours. Will anyone ever write anything worth a damn about Mme Gabiou? About her sisters, her cousin, that entire ingenious family of Lemoines, pupils of Adélaïde Labille-Guiard? About you? You, one in a million women with dreams and the luck of a little talent? I think not, my dear, I think not." Adélaïde Labille-Guiard she most respected. "The Royal Academy took her in. Imagine. She'd been offered a seat in the center of Parisian culture. She was a true champion of women. She and the Lemoines are the ones you need to study." Tamsin often wished I adopted a permanent predilection for the artists she loved most.

*   *   *

Tamsin's reputation for her artistic talent rose with her creation of Godfrey Grey in the 1970s. She mixed resins, her own lamp black and lead white, until she achieved the tone of Marie-Antoinette's dress folds in a portrait by Madame Vigée Le Brun. She said to me while discussing this work, which, until then, was considered her most important, "Marie-Antoinette was misunderstood. She wore a dress the color of stone because she could and no one else would, until *she* did. That gray was all the rage at Versailles. A real triumph. How else was she to show her influence and her permanence, she the Austrian child-queen?"

And of Vigée Le Brun, she said her ambition was earned. "There's a woman no man ever crossed. She looks soft in her portraits, but she was anything but romantic. Nerves of steel, believe me."

Sometimes I wondered if Tamsin's success in restoring Marie-Antoinette's portrait was due to her affinity for the painter, and, after my failed attempt to give her a portrait of herself, she discouraged me altogether from pursuing my own work between our projects. I interpreted her rejection as a portent of things to come, as a sign that she couldn't love me as a woman, a colleague, a painter. She told me, "Your art is too modern, too vague, and you'll ruin your hand." I hoped to keep my ambitions in check and not resent her criticism. After this defeat, I substituted artistic gifts for Tamsin with generic ones—choosing to give her a scarf or a coffee table book instead—and I relayed my good wishes for her birthday with a kiss on her cheek.

*　　*　　*

Our lot in the art community considered Tamsin's work restoring female painters her strongest gift. She brought vitality and calculated gentleness to those pieces, qualities that were absent in her Italian religious work. When she repaired a series of Carpaccio altarpieces, her brushstroke was imposing, crass even. She inhabited the painter's personality and channeled his spirit. Carpaccio, she said, was self-indulgent and a great whiner.

In the years we worked together, I failed to become fully acquainted with Tamsin, maybe because her preference for restoration over the origination of new art offended me. She intimidated me.

Tamsin was in her seventies. I was twenty-seven when I first took the job. She kept her white hair trimmed short, above the ear like a boy, and her cheeks powdered to a flush. She drew her eyebrows in two fine lines, which were too dark, though those arches above her blue eyes framed them with certainty. She wore long, loose tops and pants that reminded me of jodhpurs. Her air was regal and timid, and there were times when she seemed almost fragile.

My admiration for her excellence and my disillusionment with my mediocrity corroded what could have been a beautiful friendship. I knew little of her personal life, yet I was as familiar with her work as my own.

Once when I visited the Getty during a traveling exhibit on eighteenth-century portraitists, I leaned in as closely as the cordon would permit to a Marie-Gabrielle Capet. I saw the delicate weaving of a torn canvas, the slightest application of gesso layered with paint covering the mend, the deep mystification of Tamsin's repairs. Her work was meant to be undone, so precise that every retouched surface could be easily dissolved for future restorations. She understood the effects of time.

*   *   *

During one of her winter absences from the studio, when she traveled to Italy, I worked in the bakery below my apartment in Bed-Stuy and returned to painting. My work was uneven and uninspired. I considered moving closer to Tamsin's studio to avoid the C train. Traveling to and from work swallowed hours of my day, yet I enjoyed the smell of yeast and sugar in the air of my building, my cup of coffee in the morning, the long train rides with strangers, the lengths of bread I brought Tamsin, which had to be scanned by Sebastian, his beeping wand traveling the length of my body to catch me concealing files for our iron bars upstairs.

I hesitated to leave my neighborhood for Manhattan. And like a hipster cliché, I'd begun dating a tattoo artist who specialized in do-overs and cover-ups. He lived nearby. He, too, was a restorer of sorts, a miracle worker in the province of regret. His name was Nathaniel. He named his shop *La Longue Carabine*—the frontier name, he told me, of Natty Bumppo in *The Last of the Mohicans*. No one understood this reference or the name of one of his tattoo guns, Killdeer. I loved to hear him speak of his favorite things: his grandfather's collection of black bowler hats, his knowledge of the old card game whist, his love of gin tonics. He gave the impression of being a man from a different era. Sometimes we spent hours in bed talking about food from places we'd visited: *cuor di bue* tomatoes from Liguria (him) and *kouign-amann* pastry from Brittany (me); *tom kha gai* from Phuket (him) and *quiaude* from Gaspesia (me). We dreamed of Indian street food—*chole bhature* and *jalebi* from Punjab—holding hands in the dark. In the hours of morning or evening, Nathaniel listened to me talk about the art I wanted to make and the visions I had for our future.

*   *   *

On a Monday in March, Tamsin began to speak to me differently. She had just returned from Venice and I hadn't seen her in months.

She said things aloud to herself, little fragments of sentences like tattered pieces of paintings: "Keep the beads of your rotting rosary," or "A simple apology would have sufficed," or "This deterioration is of your making, you evil witch of God," and when I called to her, "Tamsin?" she looked up from her work with an air of not knowing she had even spoken. She often ignored me. We worked in silence, complacent in this comfort.

Tamsin seemed altered and loosely dreaming, her eyebrows drawn higher, which gave her the look of a Modigliani, a painter she despised. Her eyes appeared lost underneath those arches and opened to a vacancy of feeling.

"Tamsin?" I asked. I approached her with her name like a solution to a great problem.

She sat motionless, her wrist supporting her elbow, an exclamation mark too heavy for its sentence. "It means twin." She turned from the light of the window and looked to a spot past my shoulder. "I am a twin." She returned to her canvas, and I saw little movement of her instruments in the following hour.

Days later, she told me during our lunch break, "Thomasina also means twin. Little twin. She was smaller. Always frail." Tamsin ate baguette and brie with fig compote. There were crumbs on her blouse, a saffron-colored silk buttoned to her neck. She didn't brush off the crumbs.

"She passed away?" I gave her a napkin.

Tamsin dismissed it. "Oh, leave it, dear. What I can't see doesn't exist. Tidbits and morsels will always find their way to the floor." She picked up her plate and returned to her work.

I asked Ruth, who came to sweep the floors and dust the studio every week, if anything had happened to Tamsin while she was in Venice. Ruth opened her mouth, to speak, yet she lifted her shoulders and turned from me. Ruth had worked for Tamsin for fifteen years and I imagined them conspirators.

Tamsin always brought back delicate things for Ruth: a lace handkerchief from the tiny island of Burano, a glass paperweight from Murano, a bound journal with the effigy of Colombina etched in yellow leather. I'd catch them looking at each other sometimes in ways friendly or familial. Without malice, I told Nathaniel that, perhaps in a secret world, those two were intimate.

"Wouldn't that be something," he said. "The grand dame of restoration and the housekeeper. It's so Ladies of Llangollen."

Nathaniel was a great reader of many different genres and I was not. He listened to LibriVox while he tattooed to dull the sound of his drill. The Ladies of Llangollen, he said, were too fabulous to discuss in passing. "Look them up," he told me. "You'll understand what I mean." When I searched their biographies, I couldn't imagine the connection. The ladies lived and worked together in Wales. Theirs was a life of open communion.

That spring, Tamsin worked quite slowly, and I felt I should help her by becoming something more than a background specialist. I hoped for peculiarities, small pinpointed challenges like the restoration of a sea of miniature faces in great Flemish vistas or the reflected portrait of the artist, so easily missed, in the cup of a Clara Peeters still life. I had newfound energy. I was buoyed by love.

I held on to this feeling of rightness even as pile drivers in the street woke Nathaniel and me too early in the morning, even as the weather warmed my apartment and leeched the walls of their deeply-buried naphthalene smells, even as I let him tattoo the skin over my hipbone. He urged me to paint my own canvases. I prayed for the return of the muses. I prayed for inspiration.

*   *   *

"Vespers at dawn or dusk?" Tamsin asked me one late

afternoon.

I explained things to her like she was a child. "Evening vespers, Tamsin," I said. And, because I wanted her to speak to me, I asked, "Praying?"

Did she sense I wanted something from her she was unwilling to share? She answered, "No."

I approached her at her seat. We were commissioned to restore a few of the lesser-known works of Mme Gabiou. We received portraits in which Gabiou painted herself in ivory silks with blue velvet ribbons, fresh roses in her hair, gathered not in high Rococo style, but with the aesthetic efficiency of a young woman needing to paint, to keep strands from her eyes. She was a lovely girl, perhaps not as striking as Marie-Gabrielle Capet, whose self-portraits mirrored the beauty of Labille-Guiard's renditions, yet Gabiou's gaze seemed to follow us throughout the room. She was roundly enchanting.

Before Tamsin was a portrait of the artist as a pupil of the arts. I looked closely at the area she was repairing where small paint particles had fallen like molting scales. We'd scanned the canvas using infrared, X-ray, and ultraviolet imaging to note any discrepancies in past restorations, misused pentimenti and palimpsests of color in the painting that, like wallpaper in an old brownstone, peeled back decades of history.

She'd analyzed and mixed the colored resins by hand. Yet in front of me were lines too stiff, abrupt layerings, and a shriveled application of green shadow surrounding the young woman that gave her an unnatural halo. Tamsin's muddied green imbued a darkness to the painting that had not been there before.

I did not recognize Tamsin's work.

She held her paintbrush close to the canvas, and it quavered. "It's no use," she said.

"Tamsin." I rested my hand on her shoulder.

She looked at me. "You finish it." Her voice was firm.

I felt two things at once: the stabbing ambition of opportunity and the force of my betrayal. How could I sit in Tamsin's chair and take her place? I had waited so long for the chance to take charge of my own restorations and I hardly knew what to do with it.

"You've been patient," she said. "You've done tedious work." She laid her brush on the little table next to her where she kept all her instruments and jars of solvents. "These paintings are houses. I treated you like the plumber and the electrician. You did all the maintenance, the backgrounds. You took care of the pipes and wires behind the walls of these canvases. Now it's your turn. You can decorate. Set the furniture as you wish. Replace the wood-burning stove with a stone fireplace if it's what needs to be done. What we see as a good restoration today might be mocked in one hundred years. There are fads, ways of doing things. Nothing lasts." She stood up and hugged me with an awkward thwap on my back.

"I don't know what to say." I could neither find the words to apologize nor to show gratitude.

*   *   *

I saw perhaps in our last moments together that Tamsin had sacrificed thankless years, cooped up in the folds of our profession, which required so much of our time and dedication. She'd been a devoted disciple. She succeeded in channeling every artist's virtue and vice. She was the crucible for the resurrection of their art. She effaced herself, invisible to the ordinary eye, recognized only by her ability to recognize others. Yet she provided generations of museumgoers, art collectors, and promising artists the means to gaze through the corridors of centuries and to vanish beyond the perspective of history, of her story.

I failed to know her, not the doyenne in a world of salvaged art, but this old woman in the cerulean blouse and dark-lined brows. I saw her eyes, and I saw through them. And that's when I knew I would take her seat and finish her work. I would become Tamsin Godfrey becoming Marie-Élisabeth Lemoine—Madame Gabiou—who had imitated her teacher Adélaïde Labille-Guiard, whose paintings had been restored on so many occasions by the great Tamsin Godfrey. I would become part of this circle of women who breathed studio air infused with the fumes of men's varnishes and liniments. *Nothing lasts.* I would take my place as a new layer in the sediments of art history, in the ancient house of beauty.

*   *   *

Tamsin died of heart failure shortly after I completed the work on Mme Gabiou's portrait. I repaired those swatches of flat green, which she mixed incorrectly. My restoration launched renewed interest in Tamsin's work after her death, and my green resin, which resists oxidation to yellow, is named after her. I didn't confess to anyone this green was of my creation. I owed it to her, but now I understand my misguided devotion. I'd been afraid of becoming Tamsin Godfrey.

I'd been afraid of a life of loneliness dictated by the whims of collectors. She showed me something with her words: Nothing lasts. Not even a girl's ambition to become a great woman in her field. Not even the pulse of the artist's life, which clarifies the light of a troubled chiaroscuro. And I understood, finally, why Marie-Antoinette wore those gray silk dresses and why she hired a woman portraitist. Tamsin had known, decades ago, that the desires of a young queen were more incisive than mere flights of fancy. She found a way, however elusive, of opening her gilded cage. Grays, like tarnish, remain. They flicker between the white of dove feathers and the darkness of a raven's wing.

Women of past eras understood life often was, for them, mere shadow. In not knowing Tamsin because I was afraid of her, I had become a grayed version of myself, moving toward the permanence of lost artistic sensibilities.

*   *   *

Nathaniel and I moved out of Bed-Stuy when I became pregnant with our daughter, who is now eight years old and a stubborn artist. In our neighborhood, she's known for her sidewalk chalk portraits of her classmates: here a girl with Titian hair, there another holding a basketball to her chest. My daughter captures their likenesses in bold strokes of temperamental blues, glazed oranges, and charred browns. Her art is made of fire. She is better than I ever was, having inherited her father's fearlessness.

I take Tamara to the Metropolitan Museum of Art as often as I can. There, she declines the headset whenever she is offered one by the elderly volunteer at the ticketing counter. I follow her, allowing her the joy of choosing her own rooms to visit. She heads straight to the eighteenth-century French gallery where she sits on a bench and admires the work her mother once restored. I say nothing to her about it, but, given her interest, I suspect Nathaniel may have informed her. Her face angles to one side: the painting is next to the large doorway through which visitors come and go.

She sees a man passing by this self-portrait of a young woman. He does not glance at the canvas or at my daughter. He's an older gentleman burdened with a slight limp. I don't recognize him, but he has the very look of a curator: the crisp shirt collar tucked under a wool suit jacket, the vintage watch with its original leather strap, the hat Nathaniel would rather like, though not in the style of Magritte. Removed of his accoutrements, the visitor is one of Rembrandt's men.

Tamara leaps from her seat and stops his progress. "You forgot this one," she says. She hesitates to take his hand.

I want to say something droll or appropriate, but I cannot. Instead, when the man looks at me, I purse my lips like Sebastian, the guard of our old studio, to indicate the canvas. He turns and imitates Tamara's side steps to the painting, the pair scuttling like crabs. She is holding him by the cuff of his jacket. When she is satisfied by their position, at center frame, she releases him.

He leans into her. "And what can you tell me about this painting, young lady?"

Then she begins to explain.

*   *   *

Over the course of almost a decade, I began to find my place in my family. I quit the work of restoration when Tamsin died. In that world, everyone expected me to be the new Tamsin Godfrey when I simply had someone else to be: a partner, a mother, a woman producing her own art, however unsuccessful with the public her vision might be.

On the walls of our home now hang my paintings, even the portrait of Tamsin. She surveys our dining room where we sometimes eat compote and brie and forgo the use of napkins. I attached a small placard next to the frame, which reads, "Tamsin Godfrey: Principal Restorer and Savior of Women" (2010), by Julienne Doyon, oil on canvas." Nathaniel nicknamed the painting "The Resurrectionist."

Tamara, who understands the importance of such things, added underneath this canvas a square of white cardboard bearing the black horseshoe shape of head-phones, at the center of which she drew, with the pedestal of a serif, the number one. She will tell anyone who wishes to listen the importance of the woman portrayed in the painting and the intent of the woman who painted her.

*   *   *

I thought I would carry endlessly the memory of Tamsin Godfrey with feelings of guilt I tried so hard to repress, until I ran into Ruth at a Midtown department store. I recognized her immediately, though she aged since we were last in the studio together. She held a pair of oxblood-colored gloves, contemplating their quality and their price. I could imagine Tamsin wearing them.

Ruth and I talked about those years when we really didn't know each other.

"You see, Tamsin worked on all those altarpieces and frescoes in Venice to be near her sister Thomasina," Ruth said. She was still holding the gloves in her hands. Her skin was chapped, perhaps from the chemicals of cleaning. "She joined an Italian convent in the 1950s, you know."

"Tamsin?"

"No, of course not. Thomasina." Ruth looked at me as though I were a bit slow. She spoke to me as I had so often spoken to Tamsin, in a childish explanation of the obvious. "Thomasina liked to torture Tamsin by telling her she'd wasted her time and talent on those French tartlets—that's what she called those women Tamsin worked on—instead of pious men who painted the birth of Christ. She told Tamsin God would take her sight. Like a punishment. And you know what? He did. Your Christian God is a brutal one. When Tamsin returned from Venice that last spring, she was going blind. You asked me about it, about Tamsin being different. I remember. I just couldn't tell you. It wasn't my secret to share."

"Her work *was* different. Even the curators knew something was wrong, but they were discreet and didn't complain."

Ruth put down the gloves on the counter. I touched their leather. "These are lovely," I said. "I think Tamsin would have liked them."

"Yes, probably. I miss her very much."

"Were you good friends?"

"She gave me a job when no one else would. I had arthritis and I couldn't keep up with the young chickadees who worked for the big cleaning companies." Ruth patted me on the arm and said, "Good to see you, dear." She smiled, turned, and walked to the exit.

When she was some distance away, I hollered, "Do you

want the gloves?" She must not have heard me well because I still hear her answer: "She told me all would be well with the art, even with her failing eyes. Because you were there. Because you would finish the painting in her place."

✳   ✳   ✳

I thought of the green I created for Tamsin. It came to me like a revelation of light, the gift of restoration in exchange for Tamsin's faith and my renunciation of our profession. I watched Ruth leave. Then I turned to the girl at the counter. Her hair was piled on her head in a knot, tied away from her eyes in a sensible, yet elegant style. "You look like a wonderful French painter," I said. She smiled.

I didn't tell her Mme Gabiou and her sisters, the entire Lemoine clan, fell into obscurity during their lifetime, rediscovered through the dexterity of an old restorer two centuries later. Tamsin may not have created the green that saved Gabiou's canvas, but she'd been the one to give her importance, to rescue her best work from the shadows of anonymity. I told the girl at the counter, "I'll take the gloves." She wrapped them in tissue paper and placed them in a box, and I discarded both as soon as I left the store. I slipped on the gloves. I felt airy, the weight of my betrayal lifted.

On the street, cars hurtled toward their destinations in a symphony of sound. Trees lined the pavement in a powerful show of survival: here they stood in this urban landscape, long-limbed and capable. And green, so green, sunlight pierced through their leaves and marked the concrete with dappled grays. I made my way home to my family, one among a million travelers crossing the city's great canvas in quick strokes. Everywhere there were colors by the thousands—tint upon tint, shade after shade—of everything the spectrum of beauty satisfied. Everywhere, there were signs of the renewal and restoration of life.

*   *   *

When Tamara will come of age as a young woman studying fiber arts or jurisprudence or dental hygiene, whatever path guides her artistic sensibilities or sense of practicality, I will give her these red gloves among other objects. Until then, I will wear them to celebrate my work with Tamsin and to remind myself, with fondness and joy, of her irascible genius.

The future of this pair of gloves, much like Nathaniel's collection of old bowler hats, will depend entirely on Tamara. She will either wear them or drop them off in a donation bin after years of neglect, my gloves found buried in the back of an old dresser, her father's hats boxed in an attic or displayed as a gallery grouping on her living room wall. My paintings, our photo albums, the toys of her childhood—the legacy of her family life—will be hers and only hers to love or abandon, as will be the path of her career, her romantic relationships, and her secret ambitions. All these choices will be hers to make.

What Came After
the Harvest

Ben Salvato was seventeen the summer he picked fruit on a farm in eastern Quebec. For five months, he boarded with and worked for the Sheltons, a family consisting of Matthew and Fredda, parents to three teen-aged children: Charlotte, pretty and round; Timmy, shy and sandwiched between gregarious girls; and Gertrude, bony and decided. He arrived on the farm in early May, in snows of apple-blossom petals.

Ben learned to prepare soil for rotation crops using homemade fertilizer (cow dung, horse droppings, food scraps, autumn leaves, rotting pinecones, and copper powder from the abandoned Capelton and Albert Mines, an excellent natural bug repellent). Matthew Shelton, a believer in biodynamics, had lately taken to reading books on anthroposophic thinking by pioneer scientist Rudolf Steiner. He rotated crops differently that year and he concocted horticultural solutions and theories on natural composting versus chemical treatments.

In June, they picked early strawberries, a proud yield

for the Sheltons who were first in fruit. Then late July rains fell in patterns. The weather seemed calculating. It rained when the workers weren't out in the fields, while the sun scorched at lunchtime. By September, the season of 1962 had broken multiple harvest records.

One of Ben's tasks was to drive the old pickup truck, bumping along dirt roads, and to carry loads and bushels to Dunham and Cowansville at four o'clock when he completed his regular chores. He lied to the family and told them he was eighteen to get the job. He quit school the year before and his parents approved the work. The farm was a family business, yet the older girl, Charlotte, was sure her future lay elsewhere, and she dreamt not of crops but of war and soldiers. She spent her youth harvesting, and she learned her skills at triage with apples and cabbages. She was ready to attend nursing school at Notre-Dame Hospital in Montreal. Her decision to leave the farm allowed Ben to board with the family and to take the space of her bedroom. Her brother wasn't old enough to drive, her father said, when in small communities boys were allowed to drive not by provincial law but by rural concession. In some families, even twelve-year-olds were seen plowing fields. Timmy, now fifteen, had once ruined an acre of newly overturned soil by driving the truck straight through it. So the Sheltons had chosen to hire Ben.

The pay was low but Ben's work earned him a few friends and invitations to supper from neighboring mothers displaying eager daughters. Although he enjoyed the dinners, he never asked out any of the daughters. He was too preoccupied with his work to bother with younger farm girls. Perhaps because he saw himself as wiser and more mature than he actually was, he was unprepared for the attentions of a woman more than twice his age, someone for whom the world held little mystery. He first met the Tahitian woman while unloading from the dusty pickup the strawberry baskets Alphonse Laporte had ordered. She came up from behind, and he put down his load. He smiled at her. Her name was Nanihi O'Shea. She was a rare sight in the town of Dunham and somewhat of a green-thumbed phenomenon. Townsfolk gossiped she could revive any sort of plant. A real Lady Lazarus, they said.

"You're more of an attraction than I am," she said to Ben. "How do you like it over there at the Sheltons' farm?"

They talked for a while on the sidewalk, in front of the co-op grocery store window. The women inside turned their heads, pretending to read can labels. They looked up at the pair and faced one another with inquisitive stares. He drove Mrs. O'Shea home, and she offered him some tea and a plate of fruit. She was lonely. She married an Irish-Canadian tourist who visited her home country when she was a young woman, still a girl, really. She planned the wonderful adventures she would have in America. She soon discovered the unending months of snow and darkness and she regretted her marriage.

When Ben said it was a good year for harvest, trees overflowing and cornfields growing high, she furrowed her brows.

"You know, in my country it isn't so good to have so much fruit. A plentiful year will bring many deaths." She bit into an apple and said, "Of course, a year of disastrous harvest also brings death, but I doubt the beliefs of my people. This year the fields are full."

She had an accent when she spoke. Her husband had settled in the English-speaking part of the province, which excluded her even more. She stayed because everywhere else was just as foreign to her anyway, and her French sounded different from Quebecois. She had nowhere to go. "Why do you speak English?" she asked. "I thought only people from these parts and the very rich were Anglophones."

"I kind of speak both," he said, "though I'm not awfully good with French. I was brought up Italian. My parents immigrated and got stuck on the north side of Montreal like the others. I was born there."

When the time came for Ben to go back to the Sheltons' farm, she gave him a plant of African violets for Fredda and some of her homemade rhubarb jam and raspberry butter for the girls.

"The youngest is just sickly thin, *trop maigre, c'est pas joli*," she said.

He drove away in the dirty pickup with the seldom-working brights, humming tunes to the beat of puffing exhaust. The stars were magnificent and numerous that night. Much like the trees of the bountiful season, they bloomed in the black sky.

When Ben walked up the stone path to the house later in the evening, Matthew motioned to sit with him on the front porch. "She's a nice woman, Nanihi, but she's lonely. Sometimes it's best to leave women to comfort each other. Fredda's there for her, you know," he said, and when Ben stared ahead blankly, the man of the house stood to go back inside. Ben didn't quite know what to say to Matthew, so he followed him into the house and gave Fredda the violets and jams. He believed Matthew meant to tell him he should befriend Mrs. O'Shea just as the family had. Ben knew Fredda remained kind to a woman who ten years earlier had been so aggrieved by gossipmongering regarding her character that she left the province to make a fresh start out in Newfoundland. He could learn from the Sheltons in the way of kindness. He resolved to talk to Mrs. O'Shea and keep her company.

*   *   *

Many months after he left the farm and returned to his family's apartment in Montreal, where he worked loading docks at the old port like many of the men in his neighborhood, Ben received a letter from Lottie Shelton when she was studying at Notre-Dame. She was full of news about the techniques she learned: how she found blood at the first prick on a woman whose veins were hardly visible, how this skill had gotten her praise, and how she could assist with just about everything without the slightest nausea. On the last page she wrote that her brother had broken his ankle trying to walk wooden planks over some marshlands. No one else would have broken a bone by falling in mud water, but Timmy Shelton could and did.

She added a postscript: *Madame Tahiti—what was her name? She died late November when the harvest was well over. They can't say what took her. They just found her in bed. The woman next door went over because she noticed her outdoor plants hadn't been winterized. You'd think it would have been a disgusting thing to find, a dead body like that, for who knows how long, but the miracle of it is, she didn't even smell. The ones who saw her said she dried up like a wildflower. No one ordered an autopsy and the husband didn't make it back in time for the funeral. It could have been anything, maybe an aneurysm, or the thrombosis of a vein, or viral pneumonia, or an ectopic pregnancy. There were rumors of men in her life. I assisted with surgery on a woman whose right Fallopian tube burst and she died from the infection. I wish I could have been there for Madame Tahiti.*

Ben took the letter and pressed it between his palms. His heart pumped loudly. He felt guilty for not seeing the obituary and for missing the funeral. He sat at the small desk in his parents' apartment and tried to answer Lottie's letter. He started to write several times, bunching up page after page, which he sent sailing into the tole-painted wastebin in the corner of the room. In the end, he didn't know what to write and he marveled Mrs. O'Shea could be dead. He regretted never saying goodbye, though at the time he couldn't face her. He was plagued by thinking she might have used him, yet he also wondered if it had been the other way around. And now this woman who marked a milestone in his life was gone.

*   *   *

He last saw Nanihi in early September. He'd been driving the old pickup on his usual route when further ahead construction workers laid the foundation for a thick coat of asphalt and blocked the road. He turned onto a small dirt lane and bore right. After crossing Ruisseau Selby, he saw a lake on the horizon and drove to it. The temperature was furiously high. He wanted a break. The truck bounced on its wobbly suspensions while long blades of flax and wild wheat whipped its sides and crackled under the tires. The ground near the water turned to marshland. He put the vehicle in reverse. A pit of mud spun out in flying bursts and bogged the pickup. Ben got out and bent over to shovel under the tires with his bare hands.

While putting together a makeshift lever from the slats of a fruit box, he looked up at the lake, blue as stone and flat as glass—trees mirrored on its surface. There were willows and firs, cypresses and pines. Small swallows busily swam the sky like minnows. Ben savored the accidental detour, and he picked out the best plum of the bushel.

If he were lucky, he could still deliver to Dunham and Cowansville and be back at the farm by sundown. Fate was on his side. Long trilliums and blades of flax swayed. He heard footsteps and turned toward the sound. She wore a white sundress held by two thin straps knotted at the shoulders. Her hair was tied at her nape.

"What are you doing in these parts?" asked Mrs. O'Shea.

"You scared me—"

"I'm sorry," she said, "I heard the truck. I thought I might help. I've never seen you coming this way." She pointed at the tires. "Too close to the water."

He thought she looked happier out in the middle of nowhere. Maybe she looked this way in her youth, on her island, where everyone was beautiful like her and where they spoke a language that communicated who and what she was, and not the things he and the other townsfolk thought she should be. She was not the coming winter, she was not the Atlantic, and she was not the Canada of maple syrup and lumberjacks. Her presence mystified him. Around her the willows became Ati trees and lake water turned salty. He'd read about Tahiti in Matthew Shelton's encyclopedia and studied the black-and-white photographs that accompanied the entry.

She said, "Well, don't just stand there, come down, there's not much you can do but keep me company," while holding out her hand. He noticed how much her palm was like the underside of a seashell. He thought of the things and the men she had touched.

Ben walked by her side. Her feet were bare. She held her canvas shoes in one hand and curled her wrist in the crook of his elbow. He'd taken off his shirt and left it hanging on the sideview mirror. With the rhythm of walking, she stroked his flank, much like a child would caress a sleeping dog. She took him to the best part of the lake, on the opposite side of where the truck sat. The bank was dry with a clearing of smooth dust on the ground. There were fewer grasses growing by the water. Her bicycle leaned on a tree. In its basket were flowers of all kinds, wrapped in silk paper, their roots covered with wet gauze. *My mother does the same*, he thought. Yet Mrs. O'Shea was so different from the woman who, at that hour, baked afternoon bread in a Montreal apartment. "You came all the way out here, on your bike?"

"I ride my bicycle every day when the weather's warm. I can't stand the cold. It's very hard for me to live here in the winter. I try to be out as much as I can. I go everywhere on this bicycle. I know all the lakes and the rivers, the hills, and hidden trails." She pulled from under the flowers a small container filled with fruit. "Have some cherries," she said. "They're imported from France. Look at their color. It's so much deeper than the kind they grow here. I'd like to think they come from Provence. It's nice to think something so good grew in a beautiful place, don't you think?"

"I guess," he said, ashamed by his own lack of cleverness, and he accepted her offering. They were the best cherries he'd ever eaten, and he told her so. "Why do you stay?"

"Because I can't go back. Now I am here, and I have to stay. I'm tired of moving. My husband is a sailor and I followed him from Tahiti to Hawaii to San Diego and, when he got ill, he wanted to go home, so we did, and I stayed. He's better now, and he's gone again, but women like me can't be sailors. I think he's in the Pacific right now. He could be anywhere. I receive a postcard once in a while. It's no matter. We've both drifted apart—sounds like a joke, doesn't it, drifted apart, when you're married to a sailor." At this she smiled, and she sat down in a sunny spot on the ground, spitting cherry pits in the water.

"Where are you from on the island?" he asked, not wanting to think of the man who somewhere on a far ocean might have the picture of his wife hanging by his bed. He sat next to her.

"Bora Bora. It's far from the main island. When I was three, my family moved to Papeete, the capital. My father was a fisherman and my brothers also. My mother stayed home to cook and clean and sew, and I sat by her and learned." She asked, "And you, what about you?"

"There's nothing much to me. I've always lived in Montreal," he said, planting his elbows in the grass, "but my dad's family is from Italy. Now there's an interesting story for you. He's Sicilian, from a port on the sea, close to Catania, on the south side of that big island. His father was a fisherman, too, though he was famous not for the fish, but the treasure he caught in his nets."

Mrs. O'Shea listened with her eyes closed, her face turned to the sun.

"You're not going to believe this but one day as he was off the coast to the east somewhere out on the Mediterranean, he fished up in his nets an original bronze from the Hellenic period, half eaten up by salt and covered up with green. It was worth a lot of money and when museum people got there, he became the town hero. The fishermen even called him old *Giuseppe degli Argonauti*. I guess they didn't know their Greek mythology too well. At least that's what my mother says."

"Well, this story's not about you, so tell me about you."

"There's nothing to say."

"I don't believe you," she said, always with a long, drawn-out ooh—I don't believe y-*ooh*—and she plucked a trillium blade from the back of his shoulder. "How old are you, Benjamin?"

"It's Benito. My parents left Sicily in the Forties, when Mussolini was big and people thought he would save them from poverty and hunger. They thought they would end up on the winning side of the war. So, I'm named after a dictator. I go by Ben, just Ben. I'll be eighteen in a few months, but I told the Sheltons I was already that age. You can't tell them." He implored her in mock pity with a thick Italian accent. "Please."

"If I could go back to being your age, I would have done so many things differently." She sighed. "My people do not believe in looking back. It's bad luck. You take what you have done for what it is, and you continue on your road."

He was glad to be young. The road ahead of him was long. "Would you," he hesitated, "have stayed home?"

"I don't know. I would change things, but I don't know what I would have done instead. I had many possibilities. I could have married the young man my parents preferred. I could have studied or learned a trade—perhaps my father would have let me—I'll never know since I never asked." She moved so she lay fully in the sun. "I only know there was so much more. Maybe this is the feeling of regret." She motioned for him to lie back with her.

"I should get the truck out of that mess. I still have to make my deliveries and get back to the Sheltons' farm, you know, before dark. I wouldn't want them to think—" he fumbled for words, "something happened to me. You know how they are."

"You can't leave yet," she said, "it's four-thirty or so, and we haven't gone swimming—don't you want to swim with me?" She undid the bows of her cotton dress.

He tried to stop her from undressing. "No, really, I should be going. I'm not a good swimmer anyway, and you know what they say about getting into cold water after eating. I wouldn't want you to get, you know, *malade*."

He lied. He was an excellent swimmer. Somehow, she seemed to know. She did not listen to his protests. She stood and her dress fell to the ground. She wore a swimsuit, a corset-like suit, held up by her breasts. She looked like Esther Williams in a movie he'd seen about a Pacific island girl whose American lover whisks her away in a helicopter. He remembered the ending and the scenes with all those swimming bodies curling and expanding like pieces of a kaleidoscope. "Twenty minutes. I don't want to be too late." He took off his jeans and stood there somewhat ashamed in his briefs.

"Come on," she said.

The water was cold. She took a few strokes. Her movements were graceful but not as strong as he imagined for a woman who grew up in Tahiti.

She swam *à la grenouille*, as she called it. "You should see the water of the ocean by our islands. It's nothing like this. You can see your whole body in the water, even very deep, and we have so many fish—all the colors." She trod water, saying, "And to impress the tourists young boys feed the sharks. It's always such an attraction, you would like it, I think, seeing the sharks." She tried to keep still in her spot.

"How do the boys do that? I wouldn't want to go near one. Those tourists could pay me a fortune and I wouldn't do it." He thought of a shark, circling him.

"Sharks only attack if they are hungry. Our sharks are fed, like circus lions—same thing, they put a long rope in the water, and the sharks know they have to stay on one side. The boys dive in and feed them. It's a show really. Think of the *dompteur*, what is he called, the man who puts his head in the lion's mouth at the circus, just like this." She held both her hands out like jaws and put her head in them.

"I mean, how do the sharks know not to cross the line?" he asked.

"They just know. How does the lion know not to bite his master's head off? They've learned food comes their way if they stay there. Sharks would make Dr. Pavlov very proud."

"Dr. Pavlov?"

"Yes, the Russian scientist. You know the one with the dogs and the little bells? He would ring a bell and his dog would come eat dinner as soon as it heard the sound. Then Pavlov would ring the bell without having a plate of food and the dog still came. So the sharks stay behind the rope because they want to be fed—no different from the dog or the lion."

"Well, still, I wouldn't trust a rope. It's not going to save any of those boys when one hungry traveling shark comes along, not knowing his new friends learned not to cross the line. Really, what would happen if another shark, maybe lost, or just one of another species, just dropped by? Oh, what's this? A boy wants to feed me a little fish?

I think I'll eat his arm instead!" He pretended a shark pulled him under and he disappeared with a scream.

After a minute, she yelled, "Ben, come out! I'm serious." She kept turning her body to look in every direction. "Ben, please, come out."

Just as she was about to dive under, he emerged and pretended to bite her. She splashed his face. He dunked her and she swallowed too much water. She coughed a great deal.

"Are you all right? I was just playing."

"Let's get out," she said, still coughing.

He helped her by holding her shoulders. He thumped her back, saying—*ça va*—as if she would get better somehow if he spoke French.

"I'm fine, thank you," she whispered.

"Thank you for drowning me. No problem, any time!" He ran his fingers through his hair.

"No, thank you, for the company. *Merci.*"

Her eyelashes clustered like the tips of stars and her hair fell to her elbows, almost blue in the sun. He looked at her, feeling older and important.

He held her arms. He'd kissed girls in his neighborhood. He even had a girlfriend for the whole of six months, though he failed to go all the way. A good Catholic girl, she told him they could do things to each other as long as he didn't penetrate her. She made such a fuss about the importance of virginity that he wished for the power to skip that middling interlude altogether. He wanted all the experiences that came *after* without going through that first time. At nearly eighteen, the combined weight of his own ineptitude and Nanihi O'Shea's experience crushed him.

She kissed him on the shore of Lake Selby. She drew him down. He knew what she would do to him, and he let her, though he couldn't quite concentrate on the act from sheer nervousness. He would never again come back to the person he was *before*. Weeds poked his back. So still in the silence of the afternoon, a hummingbird hovered above her head, green tail feathers gleaming in the light.

After it was over and their bodies came apart, they both got up. He was shaken and he avoided her gaze. He didn't want to know what this tryst meant to her, and if he had been good at it, lying there while she straddled him. And he didn't want to know if she picked up hired help every summer or if he was special, the first to break her wedding vows to a far-off sailor. He didn't want to think of her husband. He was afraid.

They half-dressed, their backs to each other. She took his arm and said, "You say that you have nothing to say about yourself, but I believe you can do anything you wish." She added, "*Vraiment, tu es un bon garçon...*"

You are a good boy.

He was offended by having being so deluded. "Well, I better go," he said.

He walked away from her in the brush of weeds, his

mind full of words he didn't want to say. She didn't follow him. He thought he heard her laugh. When he got to the truck, he noticed the crud around the wheels had dried off in the sun. He put on his shirt without buttoning it, and he worked the lever of staked box slats behind the tires. On the first hard push of the accelerator, the truck jerked back. He was going home. He wouldn't need her help and he was glad.

The way back confused him. He forgot about the bushels and, halfway to the farm, he remembered, cursed every saint of his religion, and turned around. At almost nine o'clock, he walked up to the Sheltons' door. Fredda came out of the house, telling him how worried she'd been. She even called the grocery store in Dunham, and they said Ben never showed up. "I was worried sick," she kept saying, "worried sick." For all her chiding, she rubbed his back the way his mother would have.

He did the best he could to reassure the Sheltons everything was fine. He gave his version of the story. He got lost after the detour, the truck deep in mud, and he fell asleep in the hot afternoon sun. He said when he woke, he wanted to deliver everything as fast as he could. He didn't think to ask to use the telephone. He excused himself and went upstairs.

Alone in his room, he kicked the metal bed. He tried not to cry. He pushed the quilt aside, smoothed the bedclothes. Fredda had changed the sheets. They must have been Timmy's, patterned with tiny looping cowboy lassos that looked like nooses. He was overcome with shame. He pushed the image of her body from his mind. He had succumbed to something he hadn't wanted or the opposite: he had yielded to pleasure, but thought it unnatural because of her age. Or maybe he had wanted to seduce her, using her loneliness to his advantage, and she hadn't known how to refuse him. He was a fool.

After much tossing, during which the objects in the room grew large and ominous in their half-lit shadows, he fell asleep in his clothes, his face buried deep in the pillow. That night, he dreamt he was a pilot—slick and wise and experienced—and of Esther Williams in her island-girl getup. She was lonely and unsure of herself in this wilderness of green. He heard her laughter trill, and she swam toward him in an elegant breaststroke. He pulled her out of blue waters and, with his arm around her shoulders, led her to board his helicopter. He would carry her to a distant, foreign land where the weather would cool her skin. He would be the man to keep her safe because, in the dream, he could.

Olympic Hopeful, 19, Dies After Winning U.S. Figure Skating Championships

My sister at nineteen died folded in a laundry hamper. Death came for her on many occasions before: while she bit the corners of a stale cracker after practice for gymnastics or skating or dance; with the words of a boyfriend who watched her stumble along the corridor of his house, drunk as a sailor on leave; through her surrender to every stolen pill—nibbles of a thieving mouse scurrying through our mother's purse and strangers' pockets. Quite early, Death marked my sister with his wizened hand, and neither her sustained starvation nor an overdose claimed her as we expected.

My sister died of thirst.

My sister died when no one was watching. No one, who was alive and near her, put a mirror to her nose or felt her wrist for the faint ticking of her pulse. No one called the emergency medics. I suspect no one even noticed her body until morning, when sunlight flooded that dingy hotel room, groggy with dust motes and stuffy with the odors of greasy jacquard curtains, bong water, and urine.

*   *   *

My sister's name at birth was Anna. After our parents released her from the cold cradle of her Soviet city and adopted her, they renamed her Svetlana. Our mother dreamed of a girl twirling like a gymnast through the grass of our backyard or like a figure skater gliding on the frozen ice of our New England pond. She settled on both images after watching too many reruns of the Olympics' Greatest Hits, a smorgasbord of girls, reed-thin yet full of ambition, bearing the satisfaction or disappointment of their nations on their shoulders. *Watch them stick the landing*, our mother told the two of us, though she was speaking to Svetlana.

My sister's joints plied and her muscles stretched, and she became our mother's angel, an underfed urchin with hair slicked back in austere buns, her eyelids powdered blue, a smile stretched upon her face, teeth bared for the judges.

Svetlana hated competing, but she loved to dance. In the parking lot of the studio, she tugged on my arm and said, "Look, look," showing me the mastery of a long pirouette, the polish on her nails circling her body with each flip of her head. Her toenails, painted sparkling red, cracked and bled in point shoes and skates.

In our bedroom, her foot atop the dresser, she pulled off toenails hanging loosely from their beds of spongy flesh and she preserved them in lidded baby-food jars. "Here you go, little guy," she whispered, dropping the latest sliver to nestle among the others. She had collected enough nails to make three whole feet. Eventually, the nails on her big toes stopped growing, coming in as nubs of yellow keratin.

Her favorite flavor of baby food was plum, which she ate with a teaspoon. Sometimes our room smelled of bananas or pureed pineapple. Mostly our room smelled like marijuana, a scent she tried to cover with a spray of Giorgio Beverly Hills, her favorite perfume, a gift from our father. By then, he was already living on the other side of the country, in Southern California, a place we'd never been. He gave me a bottle of Escape, because it smelled like the ocean, like water, for his little swimmer.

It was Patrick who first provided weed and filled her belly with clouded air. Even high, she looked invincible, a girl awaiting a video montage of her past and future: the old buildings of Novgorod a backdrop for the first home recordings of performances, the procurement of a state title, and a win at nationals. Svetlana Hanond-Jones, gymnast and figure skater. Olympic hopeful. Prodigy. A resurrection of Cold War dreams made manifest in a star-spangled leotard.

*   *   *

I was born in another communist country, which bordered Russia for hundreds or thousands of miles, yet the exact location never mattered to our parents. Sometimes they spoke to me of my birth in rice fields fertile in long terraces and sometimes I came from slums overshadowed by factories. Our mother kept my birth name because it was foreign enough for her. Our parents stripped away from me everything but my name and those features, which would never be theirs. My body, like Svetlana's, held promise. Our true identities did not. When *The Joy Luck Club* came out, our mother bought the book and read it *for her Asian daughter.* She made us huddle in the theater, the three of us, to watch Jing-Mei reunite with her sisters, the gift of a swan feather clasped between her hands.

Money was hard to come by, and we lived in a two-bedroom bungalow on the edge of a sad town filled with rusted minivans driven by harried mothers. They yelled at their children, strapped in seats sticky with the remnants of juice boxes and the moist middles of Oreo cookies. That's what Svetlana and I imagined when we drove past those vans, and girls pointed at us—*it's Svetlana and her sister!*—fingers slick with treats we weren't allowed to eat. Svetlana held up a baby carrot, an orange middle finger she bit off while watching those girls' faces change from delight to consternation.

Our training siphoned all the money our mother made. We knew where she hid a few bills for the emergency that in her interpretation of danger never came, dollars shoved in the sand of psyllium husks, hidden among jars and ointments and bottles of medicine. At the community center, our mother coached younger girls—who hoped to be nothing more than high school cheerleaders—to pay off the mounting expenses of our sports, yet it was never enough. We had our private lessons and coaching, Svetlana's costumes and leotards and soft tumbling shoes and hard skates, and my swimsuits and good goggles. I told my mother I would quit so she could keep the money, but she said to me, holding my chin, "Keep that sweet face held high, darling, because if I have my way, you and your sister will grace the boxes of cereals. You hear me? You'll be the next Wheaties girls. *The Wheaties Sisters*, the sickle and the hammer sisters. And you'll grow up to be judges on *Star Search* and *Miss America*. I just know it." Her jaw muscle would twitch sometimes in the middle of her daydreams.

For all our mother's wishes and desires of fame, Svetlana and I felt alone and unloved, transfixed in the present like the static noise our television made late into the night. It was our future, and only our future, which concerned our mother. To us, the future lay ahead like a long, empty tarmac with no plane in sight waiting for departure.

*　　*　　*

Our mostly unfurnished house echoed our whispers. Our mother assembled what little furniture we owned in an ascetic collage betraying the disease of her determination. We couldn't tell the difference between the polarities of mental health and illness: there were so few joys in that paneled house. We were each damaged in our own way, and no amount of practice could have corrected the form of our desires.

I only wished to be with my sister, and we traded roles to suit our needs: one of us played daughter and one of us played mother.

Together, Svetlana and I loved to watch cartoons and sitcoms with laughing tracks. The TV had been a gift from a neighbor who wanted to get rid of the hulking thing. Sitting on the floor in our pajamas years ago, Svetlana's blond hair appeared thin against my dark braids. We watched *Full House* on that old television set, jangling the antennas to clear the image before us, of sisters we could never ourselves be, and we sucked our thumbs, a fuzzy blanket draped over our heads and shoulders, which made us look like one nesting doll holding two girls or a womb sheltering twins.

*　　*　　*

When I stood on the diving board, high above the pool, the scent of chlorine burning the lining of my nose, I thought of my sister—my white-haired half—who bent her body backward and flipped acrobatically over a beam, with nothing beneath to catch her.

I had water.

It was there, like a safety net to buoy my fall, though at the time the quaver of deep blue refracting long, black lanes painted on the concrete below seemed an ominous path to my death. Our mother stood at the edge of the pool, her arms crossed, watching. She settled on diving for me because those little girls who looked like me, some-times not even five feet tall, excelled at it. *Oh, those girls, flying into the air,* our mother repeated the movements—*pike, turn, twist*—hoping I'd catch on to the sport, like some miserable germ passed on to a new host, when all I heard were her words slithering across a dinner plate. I was hungry. Svetlana and I were both so very hungry.

*   *   *

We were born a few months apart, sisters of two adjacent continents, girls saved by an American couple who soon divorced after we entered their lives with our nightly wails and shitty diapers. We were our mother's dream but not our father's. He soon defected the committee of our family, long before Svetlana's photograph appeared in an issue of *Sports Illustrated.* When he saw the picture, on a rare visit to our house, he stared at our mother and said, "They're doing too much." He said *they,* but he meant *she.* Svetlana practiced her gymnastics in the morning and her figure skating in the afternoon—each coach bemoaning the strain of her other sport—and I dived in the evenings. On Saturdays, Svetlana danced. We were homeschooled, though the learning was thin.

Along came Patrick, the tutor.

He loved her immediately. We thought nothing of his devotion. My mother said he was gay. He loved Svetlana the way my mother also loved her, yet differently. He loved her for her movements and her abilities, for her wandering ways, for her personality split in two, one part girl and one part fairy. She was that already to everyone, but not to me.

*   *   *

"Help!" a young Svetlana cried out to me. She hung upside down from the top bunk of our stacked beds and waved her arms, her hair spilling over like a veil. I put my own arms around her waist and slowly took her down while breaking her fall. "There, there."

Sometimes she did the same at the playground, hanging from monkey bars. Once she fell hard on her wrist and our mother blamed me. I waited two hours in the emergency room corridor while Svetlana was being X-rayed and prodded by nurses and doctors. When we returned home, our mother pushed me to the kitchen and pressed my forehead in the corner of two walls. "Stand here," she said. "That'll teach you to be a better sister." Svetlana cried while observing the scene, her arm bandaged in a white sling, little wing bent and held in place. Even without turning my face to her, I saw her lips forming the words, "I'm sorry." Our mother slapped the back of her head and told her to go lie on my bed, the bottom bunk, and she did so, only to crawl sometime later on her good arm and knees, like a soldier avoiding barbed wire, to bring me a note. *I'm sorry,* she'd written. *I'll be good for you.*

*   *   *

With Patrick she was anything but good. He was a college student, a former gymnast himself, one of those short, pretty boys who would look young in middle age. He wore Girbaud shorts and high socks with Birkenstocks. Sometimes he showed up in red Doc Martens, unlaced, with a British flag painted in Sharpie. He was preppy and angst-ridden like he lived inside the lyrics of every Smiths song he'd ever heard. When I discovered he was having sex with my sister, I started to hate him.

"Patrick," I said, fists on my hips, imitating our mother when she deplored our form, "no one wants you here." To Svetlana I jeered, "You're better than this."

Svetlana laughed, her head poking out from the blankets of her bunk. "Oh, Little Ding-a-Ling."

Patrick guffawed. "Ha!"

"I hate you both," I said. I left them in bed and went to rummage through the back of our kitchen cupboards. I found an old box of Triscuits hidden behind cans of corn. I would have devoured the whole thing, but Svetlana left teeth marks all around the crackers. She chewed off the edges like they were crusts. She felt alive eating little things that were not whole; she could claim not to have eaten them at all. I tossed the box in the trash and ate tablespoons of honey instead.

There were no boxes of Frosted Flakes in our house, no bottles of cola in our refrigerator, no packaged cakes crinkling in their cellophane. Our mother had even forsaken the microwave because *you could never be too sure*, and Russians banned the use of microwaves. She believed in a breakfast of yogurt and muesli. Our lunches and dinners consisted of salad, fish, and cruciferous vegetables. Sometimes we ate lentils. When she thought we earned it, she allowed us jars of baby food to replace desserts. "This is what we call wholesome. It's just better for you," she said. Yet, always, we were hungry.

*   *   *

I knew Svetlana would die when she quit gymnastics. I thought our mother would kill her. I was both relieved and surprised when she didn't.

Our father convinced our mother, from his office in Pasadena, one sport was better for her anyway. He had always believed in the value of a single pursuit. To us, he'd become nothing more than a monthly check, so his opinion hadn't mattered before. When Svetlana yelled at our mother, "See? He understands. He knows," it put an end to the discussion and to our mother's dreams of a Summer Olympic podium. I alone remained on the platform of her Atlanta dreams, so she doubled my time at the pool.

She thought it was great luck that after Albertville in '92, Lillehammer followed only two years later when the committee chose to alternate the summer and winter Olympiads, which rescued Svetlana's chances at earning her gold.

Svetlana came in fourth at the U.S. Championships before Albertville, missing her chance to compete by one spot. Our mother was enraged, throwing her participation medal against the glass case where she kept Svetlana's trophies, a real Cobra Kai sensei from *The Karate Kid.* That's what Patrick said. We'd never seen this movie, so we believed him. Patrick had been fired as our tutor long before, but he still picked up my sister whenever she snuck out our bedroom window.

*　　*　　*

At sixteen, Svetlana developed full-blown osteoporosis. Cavities riddled her teeth, and the doctor said she was malnourished. He told our mother she should rest. Our mother may have believed he was speaking directly to her, worn out as she was from the business of coaching one prodigy and one promising competitor. Svetlana weighed eighty-nine pounds. I was so big in comparison I could have bench-pressed her entire body. Svetlana tried to shake off the symptoms of malnutrition, yet I saw fear on her face when she plucked nests of hairs from her hairbrush. Underneath the bathroom sink, there were boxes of tampons she no longer needed—it had been months since she had her last period—that I used or threw away so our mother wouldn't be alarmed at the severity of Svetlana's deterioration, and, more than this, I wanted to soften the blow of truths my sister and I already knew: no alarm bells would ever sound loud enough in that house of ours for anyone to come to our rescue. Svetlana made me promise not to tell anyone her period had stopped.

Our mother found out, I'm not sure how. I stood in the doorframe of our bathroom. Our mother knelt by the cabinet. She said, "No worries, darling, this is what it means to be an athlete. This is what happens. It will happen to you, too," pointing at me, "when you decide to put in the effort. You could be a great athlete. Like your sister." Our mother bought Svetlana a case of prenatal multi-vitamins—*the best stuff on the market*—and said to us, "This should do the trick. Don't worry your pretty little heads, it's not about babies. The last thing we need here is babies. These vitamins are strong stuff. The very best stuff for this kind of thing. You'll wake up in a month and your nails will be thick as dimes."

Svetlana overdosed on iron for the first time some

months after beginning her regimen of supplements.

She eventually turned to drugs, which coursed through her veins like a mudslide we could not halt. She tried so hard to dull the pain of her body. Even Patrick stopped supplying her with prescription pills when she found a way to get crack or heroin from a guy who hung around the parking lot of the grocery store. She burned those crystallized pellets and pecked her syringes, a bird perched on the edge of a spoon.

She had dark circles under her eyes, and her makeup never looked fresh. Her physical pain worsened. She fell more and more on the ice.

I didn't know what to do.

*   *   *

Gradually, our mother stopped believing she could be the second American female to land the triple axel during competition. Svetlana tried so many times and failed, picking herself up and continuing her routine like the world wasn't watching her. "It's nothing but embarrassing," our mother said.

Then my sister skated for the last time. I wish I remembered more about that day, about all our days. It's nothing but fuzziness now: her eyes at the top of her tiny body, the smell of her Giorgio, the blown shapes of her smoking.

Near the end, Svetlana practiced a new routine. *I choreographed it for you,* she told me. *I saw the movements in my head. You'll see me and you'll know. You'll know it's for you, even if you were born in Kazakhstan.* We'd gone through our mother's things, her documents. It was her way of cheering me up, when she faced the most important competition of her life. She felt sorry for our mother's disappointment in my diving efforts. I achieved some notoriety in our area, but my scores weren't good enough to qualify for states, let alone nationals. I sat in the bleachers with the other spectators, white breath condensing in the cold of the coliseum. Our mother was elsewhere, watching from the sidelines in the coaches' box, eagle-eyed.

My sister skated to center rink in an ivory costume I'd never seen before. Her team had done her face so it would look bare, and for the first time in two years, she looked like herself. She arched her back and waited for the music, her arms forming a shape above her head that could be mistaken for a heart. The pause seemed too long, yet when the notes of a bamboo flute rang through the air, clear and bright, we all waited for her suspended release. She moved one arm, slowly, reaching into her costume to pull out a swan feather, which she held up to the light. I recognized the soundtrack of *The Joy Luck Club*.

She skated like she never had before, with the bravado of jumps and spins and extensions, perfectly executed, and the grace of a ballerina. She was the dying swan carried across oceans, awarding me her last feather.

I saw us as little girls, a flashlight underneath the blanket of her bed. I crawled in with her after wetting my mattress, and she hushed me with words we dreamed coming from our mother. "My darling," she said, "I'm here. It's going to be all right." She put my head in the crook of her bird-like arm, and I fell asleep in the hollow of her bones.

*　　*　　*

They found her body the morning after nationals.

She'd gone to a hotel with the brother of the girl who did her hair, and he brought along friends. They'd gotten high. She demonstrated for them her ability to fold herself in the smallest of spaces. They clapped and cheered, and fell asleep. She wedged herself in the laundry hamper inside the closet, next to the safe, under trailing plastic garment bags. Her leotard hung above her.

Death arrived at the hotel without the fanfare of sirens or a parade of paramedics. Death knocked on my sister's hotel room door, politely and patiently. *It's me, my darling girl. It's time.* My sister stretched out her hand and followed.

It wasn't the level of alcohol in her blood that killed her, though it contributed to her desiccation, but all those hours in the previous days she spent practicing and practicing without taking care of her body. The coroner likened her dehydration to that of dying patients in hospices and nursing homes: my sister, at nineteen, compared to a woman of ninety.

*　　*　　*

Our mother blamed everyone but herself. She sued the girl who did Svetlana's hair. She sued the brother. She sued U.S. Figure Skating, the organizational body of the championships. She went after our father, citing his negligence, bemoaning his abandonment of our family. She let herself go, and she began to drink. She fell asleep in front of the television, long after local stations went off the air and their programs ended. She rose from the living room in the dead of night, and, the last time I saw her, I awoke to find her face above mine in that gutted bedroom: "You," she said. And I heard the declaration she couldn't hiss: *Why couldn't it have been you?*

I packed my things and left at first light. I stole from our mother her emergency money, bills hidden in a tub of Metamucil, the old hiding spot a testament to her obstinate ways. In my bag, I tucked not only a photograph of Svetlana and me as children holding on to each other, but I also stole our mother's prized scrapbook, the one containing every newspaper clip and magazine article devoted to Svetlana. I took her favorite career medals, and I salvaged her jars of baby food.

I carried throughout my life my sister's nails like relics.

*　　*　　*

When I returned to the pool, years after the funeral, it wasn't to dive, but to immerse myself in dark water, body sinking to the tiled floor beneath. I opened my eyes and looked up, light wavering ghostly, and I came back to the surface.

I swam lap after lap until my legs cramped and my arms stiffened. I lay on the edge of the pool, breathing. I could see the diving board high above me, a tongue stuck out in the air, and I saw the fountain, bolted to the wall, next to the sign listing rules of conduct for pool patrons, with its admonitions not to dunk, splash, or run. Food was strictly forbidden. I pushed myself up and stumbled to the little silver bowl. I bent down to press the lever. A trickling of water fell away in an arc, and I put my lips to the stream.

For my sister, I drank until my stomach ached from being full.

The Beast Who Knew the Songs of Billie Holiday

The cat hadn't appeared on the porch in three days. It usually climbed up to the double bowl, which Barbara filled every morning, and weaved its body between and around her legs, leaving a coat of hair on her shins. She named the cat, a scrawny calico, Halloween, for its riot of orange and black fur. She stood looking down at the double bowl and then out to the edge of her property, willing the cat to appear, yet the horizon remained still. In the bowl at her feet, a skater bug flitted across the water. Since Halloween's disappearance, she hoped water and a heap of dry food would be enough to lure the cat back.

A yellow leaf fell from a birch tree and settled in the kibble. She bent down and plucked it from the pellets, pressing her fingers to feel its veins and serrated edges. After some whistling and repeated air kissing, she scooped up the bug with the leaf, flicked it over the porch railing, and went back inside her house.

There was breakfast to be made, the script of pouring a carton of milk into a ceramic bowl of bran cereal. The clock on the wall pinged eight in the morning. She calculated the number of breakfasts she'd eaten without her husband in this house, and there were thousands. She was neither happy nor fully unhappy in her life alone, but with the departure of this cat who had visited her for the past seven months, she sensed more keenly than she should have the pain of her absence. She realized, with a daughter in the next town to whom she spoke less and less frequently, perhaps solitude had turned to loneliness. While weighing her life on a scale of human interaction, she heard a rustling of the cat food outside, bits rattling in the bowl. She stood from the table and walked to the front door, thinking of the cat, but seeing instead through the screen an enormous raccoon.

They stared at each other, and the raccoon's dark bandit eyes shone silvery and unblinking. It hunched on its hind legs and held a handful of food in its right paw. She noticed its tiny human-like fingers, clutching kibble like a cluster of snacks, yet another animal surprised by a question while at a party Barbara was hosting, and she imagined him commenting on the elegance of the porch, the excellence of the music—Billie Holiday's "Gloomy Sunday" playing from an old Victrola perhaps—and now he answered, "*1941 I think it was...and she was only twenty-six*," because his fur shone with the patina of a long, careworn life filled with nocturnal home visits, jazz floating out of opened windows. He might be her age, seventy-eight, in raccoon years. She turned the knob of the screen door and the raccoon darted down the steps and into the shadows of the bushes beyond.

In her small office, which served as a storage space for all the things she hadn't organized in years, Barbara searched the word raccoon on her computer. She wondered what he gorged on to be so fat. She thought of feeding him a raccoon-friendly diet while continuing to search for Halloween. She thought of naming him Billy for his musical panache. Her good intentions vanished after she watched a few videos.

In one, a nighttime shot of an outdoor chicken coop: there among the clucking hens, wings aflutter in alarm, a raccoon. Its arms were slipping through the fence while he torturously pulled one of the chickens apart. The massacre completed, the animal yanked at poultry parts until, piece after piece, it ate its fill. It lumbered away, leaving the frenzied birds to circle a bloody patch of feathers. The video was gruesome, but not as disturbing as a news report of a raccoon, somewhere in a nearby state, that terrorized an entire neighborhood by killing its cats. A little girl cried, holding up for the reporter a handmade flyer—Missing: Mustache—written in block letters above the photograph of a kitten, a black stripe below its nose. The image switched to a hole by a barn where the bodies of a dozen cats were shown at various stages of decomposition. Among them, Mustache. The barn owner identified the perpetrator as a large raccoon, which he, town hero, cribbed with bullets, ending its cat-killing spree.

Barbara's morning visitor had seemed innocent with his serious gaze and intellectual disposition, but a horror film of dead cats filled her mind. She now dreaded his return, so she drove to the hardware store in town. She'd gone to school with the original owner: now his son Hank was in charge. She parked her car, never in the handicap spot, though her hip surgery a few years back qualified her for a special license plate. She walked straight to the counter, telling Hank about the cat and the raccoon.

"You need rat poison," he said.

She thought about this. "If the cat comes back," she said. "No, I can't have that. She'll gobble it up."

"Well, it's a trap or a gun, but what if this thing has rabies and you trap it and get bit? Imagine." He leaned forward. "They're vicious buggers."

A tremor ran down her spine. "I saw its face. I'm just not sure he'd kill the cat, that's all. How can I tell? Rabies won't show right away."

"You've got yourself a predicament." He wiped the counter as they spoke. "How's Kathleen? I haven't seen her in a while."

Barbara sighed. "We're not getting along. She wants me to move into a rest home. Shady Blossoms." Her voice went quiet. "Good name. Sounds shady to me."

"You know, Ma's been there a couple of years. She likes it. They do water aerobics and group trips to the big mall."

"This girl of mine, she thinks I'm a menace. When she's not trying to yank me out of my house, she's peddling essential oils with her wife. They have a distribution business. Some kind of pyramid scheme. She wants me to buy diffusers and arthritis blends and all sorts of pills. And on top of that, she's converted to some religion requiring she help the needy. I don't think it's Marjorie's fault. She just does what Kathleen wants." She waited for Hank to say something, and when he didn't, she said, "So now they have Jesus and I'm supposed to find my way in the shadow of the blossoms of the Lord." She patted his hand not unkindly. "Stay clear of her path—and Marjorie's. If they see you, they'll try to sell you salves. And salvation. Ha! They should package that as a value combo: two for the price of one. Talk about a better business plan." She winced from a muscle spasm in her shoulder. "They're probably smack in the middle of menopause, losing their minds from hot flashes and scratchy skin. Serves them right."

Hank straightened and said, "You have a gun at home?"

"Bill bought me a twenty gauge a long time ago. It's in the attic with his old hunting rifles, I think."

"You can't take your chances, Barb. Aren't there kids in the house next door?"

She drummed her fingers on her cheek and considered the question. "Oh, I haven't held that thing in years—but now, you got me thinking. Yes, little ones, too, running around with soggy diapers to their knees." She pictured the youngest baby with the pink hat playing in a pool of sand in the front yard. That toddler may have been the only one wearing a diaper still, but she couldn't keep up with those religious folk who just couldn't help themselves. It would be up to her to save that baby from the certainty of rabies if she couldn't save the parents by dropping condoms in their mailbox.

Hank left her and returned with a box of cartridges, which he put on the counter. "This is loaded with birdshot. I don't want it to knock you over when you shoot. You can always call Linda at animal control. She'll set you up with some traps if that's what you mean to do, but I think you'd better be safe."

Later in the evening, at home, Barbara fetched the shotgun from the attic. It took some time. First, there was the careful climbing of the pulldown ladder while holding a flashlight, then the rummaging through the dry, semi-dark space, and last, the business of climbing down with both the shotgun and the flashlight. She looked through the lit square of the room beneath her and dropped the flashlight to the rug, lowering the gun until its butt hung halfway down and settled on the rungs. *If Kathleen could see me*, she thought. She made her way down, sweat sticking to the back of her shirt. When she put a foot on the floor, finally, her ankle smarted. The flashlight at her feet had spilled its batteries, which rolled underneath a credenza. Barbara picked up the flashlight, but left the batteries to hide, and carried it with the gun to the kitchen table, where she'd put the box of birdshot.

She was tired. She could feel her heartbeat, a thumping not quite right in its rhythm. Sometimes palpitations woke her in the middle of the night. If she told her physician, he'd send her for testing, and then Kathleen, and maybe even Marjorie, would leverage these results against her. Best to wait it out.

The next morning, Barbara leaned the shotgun next to her on the house's exterior wall. She sat on the cushioned swing at the far end of the porch, opposite the cat's double bowl, and ate popcorn from a glass mixing bowl. She thought of Halloween and prayed in her own way the cat would be safe and come back. She missed the little creature, her regular appearance at her side, the way her fur hung in clumps she sometimes brushed—cat willing— to see her patchwork coat shine. Lately, Halloween had sat on her lap and let herself be petted while she licked her paws clean. Barbara hoped to take her inside, so she would sleep on her couch.

She herself fell asleep against the pillows, a breeze working wonders through the trees in a soft rustling of leaves. She awoke to the sound of metal scraping on wood.

There he was, enormous, dragging the double bowl to the porch stairs to purloin the goods without being seen. Barbara stood, slowly, and picked up the shotgun. The raccoon stopped. It eyed her, a paw curled against its breast, the other holding the edge of the bowl. She lifted the gun, braced it against her shoulder, cocked the thing cold. *There, there,* she thought, her cat on her mind. She sighted along the barrel the animal in front of her, yet she hesitated and blinked.

The raccoon let go of the bowl. It sat opposite her, not rabid at all, but supplicant and strangely feeble. Barbara saw a living being in need of ministry or succor or the balm of her friendship. She could save him. She saw the paws held against its heart, the wild beating of fear beneath its fur. This creature might or might not be a murderer. She no longer knew. She was the one holding a gun, birdshot ready to explode. What a mess would come of it, bits of fur, brain, and bloody gizzards spread on the railings. She might damage her porch. She wouldn't forgive herself, even if the murder could save a cat like Halloween. And why should he bear the burden of all his raccoon kin, the killers and the thieves, the ones who perpetrated these sins in their youth? He was just an old raccoon, its mask faded with gray. She'd accused him of the crime of survival. Let him take the food on her porch. She imagined he tipped his head and said, *"The kibble is lovely. Dry, but lovely, with just a hint of gamey smokiness. Might we have a little music you and I, 'Fine and Mellow' or 'A Fine Romance' on the old Victrola?"*

She put down the gun. She would place a new bowl for him alongside the cat's, wet food in cans that resembled chunky stew. He'd have no reason to prey if she fed him and, in due time, she would subdue her Billy. She had faith Halloween would return. Two creatures, suffering unjustly, needed her to survive. She would be the one to grant them mercy. Kathleen and Marjorie wouldn't be able to displace her now and Barbara would never set foot in the hellish, geriatric tenements of Shady Blossoms. Someday, her daughter and her wife, too, would know something of growing old and unwanted, like this fat raccoon, scared stiff some feet away from her. She extended her popcorn-filled hand and waited for him to come closer. She would tame and domesticate him with her own communion. Billy and Halloween would venture inside to live with her. She would attend to their needs for the remaining years of their lives. Barbara's home was safe harbor, and she had much to accomplish still.

The Words of All Our Fires

(for A. 1999-2020)

Paper

The pandemic raged on in blue and red states alike. Our youth watched mountains burn while the year reigned as a colossus risen from hell: it brought deaths and the cloister of quarantine, riots and protests to ignite bodily fires through sleeplessness and troubled starts. Breathing became a stolen privilege for those on ventilators and for those whose necks we pinned to the ground. Gunfire rang in Chicago. Gunfire rang in Louisville and Portland and Minneapolis. Wildfires glowed along the west coast. Newsreels filled our screens with the light of terrible things the youth of our country witnessed in silence, their words lost in the space between their lips and the cotton of masks.

Kindling

It had been nearly six months since Oliver had seen his closest friends, the ones who'd flown the coop of Front Royal for larger universities north and south of their small town two years before. They'd been sent home unexpectedly in March, but now they were surfacing from their quarters like cicadas after a long period of dormancy. His friends had been close by, yet they would leave again without so much as a going-away party.

Once, they parked in the high school lot, seven of them, sitting on the roofs of their cars and trying to talk, but they had to shout to hear one another, so they went home, frustrated. Oliver had never felt so alone.

When he FaceTimed his best friend, Trey said he couldn't hang out because his grandmother was now living with them to avoid proximity to strangers. He'd be back at JMU soon—pandemic or bust!—on a modified schedule of online and in-person classes, and he couldn't wait. "I'll catch you later, Ol," he said before hanging up. Trey's Snap stories highlighted his glorious return to campus and football practice, his living quarters on Greek Row, and his funny captions of professors' faces frozen on Zoom.

Months before, at the end of spring, Oliver decided to take a gap year after two semesters at the local community college. He'd been a star runner and swimmer in high school, yet he lost interest his senior year, dreading the departure of his friends and the void of the unknown. His mother, Sylvie, though disappointed, rallied. She loved having her son to herself for a little while longer. She'd raised him alone. They belonged to each other in ways both intrinsic and sometimes toxic. She watched him face the boredom of his college classes and his retreat into his bedroom, unable to sway him to activity. Long gone were Oliver's early-morning runs and twice-daily swim practices. She couldn't force him to compete anymore.

In the early days of the pandemic, when shops were closed and they couldn't eat out or catch a matinee at the theater, he lay on their couch, propping his feet on his mother's lap, and watched marathons of TV shows, entire series devoured in the space of days. His favorite: *Love Island*, the inspiration for the gap year, which was such a British thing to do. Her favorite: *Black Mirror*. They joked the producers had gone too far by putting their viewers inside the show. They were all living the episodes now.

Every time they went out, his mother whispered, "There's another sign." A line of customers, wrapped around the exterior of Home Depot, six feet apart, waited two hours to purchase bags of mulch or gallons of paint or hand sanitizer and bleach; doomsdayers who wore their masks on their chins ransacked big-box warehouses for toilet paper and gallons of milk; pizza delivery places promised a safe ordering experience; while everyone hailed grocery-store baggers as prototypes of a new kind of heroism. Everyone watched these details unfold. They were as powerless as the next person in line.

"There, see that guy?" she said.
"Yeah. Virologist in disguise," he replied.
"Russian?"
"Lithuanian."
"Yes."

Wood

The history of the world is rife with pleas to save human-kind. One believes himself to be the reincarnation of Er, Plato's hero, gone down to the five rivers, searching for meaning in the astral planes. The son of a carpenter proclaims himself the son of the living god and dies on a wooden cross, forsaken by his brethren, resurrecting as the Christian God. A young girl leads French armies, guided by her visions. Her countrymen burn her body to the ground, and the pyre of her ashes releases a dove, a symbol of her martyrdom. Five centuries later, she is canonized a saint.

And, yet, for all our scientific advancements—human ears growing on the backs of mice, cars running on electricity, or devices bringing hundreds of participants into virtual conference rooms—no one can say with certainty what awaits on the other side of life. No one can promise to return.

Match

Their neighbor Mr. Olson was dying of cancer. Oliver couldn't remember his childhood without a glimpse of this man, a decorated Vietnam War veteran and inveterate smoker, hosing his lawn with a Camel pinched between his lips.

Hullo, hullo, my boy.

The sound of his voice still clear in memory.

The invitations to come inside the house for ice cream.

The days spent playing backgammon and chess when his mother worked.

The hours pored over trigonometric equations Oliver couldn't solve.

All snapshots of the goodness of one man.

Mr. Olson was reduced to his bed and would soon be moved to hospice. Oliver sat by his side holding his hand. He wanted to hear his stories once more, but the rattling in Mr. Olson's chest was too deep. Oliver didn't want to cause him pain.

Mr. Olson removed the cannula from his nose and pulled on Oliver's sleeve. "Come closer," he said. Oliver bent his head to hear him. "It was a wonderful life." He squeezed Oliver's wrist. "As life"—a long breath—"should always be." He exhaled. "I'll be with my Hazel soon." He tried to wink. "It doesn't get better than that."

Oliver nodded. He held Mr. Olson's hand for what

seemed like an eternity. When it went slack, he held on until the warmth of his skin waned cold.

Spark

"Ollie?" She called him Ollie again now, the name of his childhood. He couldn't protest.

He'd hated the childishness of those two syllables, *Ol-lie*.

"Can you hear me?" She pushed the grass around the stone, dug up clumps of soil, the richness of loam filling her senses with longing. She remembered something different each time she planted his flowers: the sight of his little legs, running from advancing waves lapping the shoreline; the sound of his laughter as a child, tinkling, and later as a man, cavernous, yet golden and infectious; the smell of his infant head; and the softness of his downy toddler hair. He was always all of his ages at once, the conglomeration of layer upon layer of all the people he had been. His entire life compressed into this single moment of planting the ball roots of daylilies to decorate his name.

Ignition

"Oliver?"

There he was with a sandwich stuck in his mouth, thin slices of turkey hanging out like a wide tongue. He opened the catchall drawer in the kitchen and rifled through a bowl holding her bills. He removed the sandwich from his mouth and said, "Keys."

"Retrace your steps," she said. She always said this when he couldn't retrieve his belongings—his wallet, his sunglasses, the keys to his beloved pickup truck, which he purchased with his own money from lifeguarding at the community pool.

"Dunno." He took another bite. "I need to pick up Nilou and drop her off at work."

"Why does it always have to be you?"

"What can I say? She needs me."

Smoke

On television, they observed maps of the United States dotted in red, concentric circles growing large and wide over the city of New York, then up and down the east coast, a country bodily plagued with the pustules of chicken pox. Americans did not have the pox. They had been immunized years ago. This disease was more complicated, more virulent.

They subscribed to lists and refreshed their browsers, watching the number of cases on multiple dashboards rise through triage: active, deaths, recovered. The correct word should have been *dead*, but there was something aggressive in both the adjective and the noun: here are the bodies of your dead, lying in the morgues of your towns and your cities.

The word *deaths* assuaged our beliefs in our collective multiplicity while replacing the singularity of grief—because these deaths are not us, are not you. You are not yet a statistic on the map.

Bellow

Oliver stretched behind the starting block, flailing his arms and twisting his torso. He adjusted his goggles, pulled on the cord of his briefs, and slapped his thighs: this was his pre-race ritual when he heard the cheers of the crowd, clustered on bleachers and waving giant foam hands that bore his name. Sometimes he could distinguish the voice of his mother.

He stepped on the block and took his mark, waiting for the flash of the light and the blip of the horn. He lunged into a dive and a long pullout, his body a bullet underwater. His head surfaced farther than his competitors, boys trying to match his rhythm and the beauty of his breaststroke.

During his junior year of high school, he nearly won every race for which he registered.

Air

"Oliver?"

"Hello?"

"Did you send a message on Snap?"

"Do you even listen to voicemail?"

"Where are you coming back from?"

"I didn't get to read your message to the end. You know me and technology."

"Call me when you can."

Sylvie's messages to Oliver's voicemail sounded like snippets of a doleful, one-sided conversation. Oliver never called back.

Flame

Oliver drove through Thornton Gap and parked at the trailhead. He climbed his way to Marys Rock, passing boulders and brambles through switchbacks. Deciduous leaves turned yellow and orange, the color of lapping flames. When he reached the summit, no one was there. He dreaded having to wait for hikers to leave, yet now that he was alone, he both feared and welcomed the solitude.

He sat at the edge of the stone face, which fell away sharply below his feet. He could see the rolling green of the Shenandoah Valley—the peaks of Pass Mountain and the Marshalls—and opposite this yawning abyss, the range of the Blue Ridge mountains breaking the horizon to the west.

Up there, he could almost forget the world as it was now: the parade of masked faces, the constant nagging of shop associates who asked everyone to spread out or wait their turn or stand on a duct-taped X a few feet from the cash register and the credit card machine needing to be sprayed and wiped and disinfected after each transaction.

Up on Marys Rock, bushes, birds, and bears remained unchanged.

He'd seen videos of spaces cleared of their usual pollution: Venetian canals, blue-green as polished agate, suddenly filled with schools of fish swimming along old foundations residents had not seen, they said, in over a century. There was a strange rejoicing in the early days of the quarantine: Italians and Spaniards opening the shutters of their cobbled buildings and singing to one another across the way, some lingering on their balconies to glimpse at grandchildren standing below, waving.

Yet this rejoicing for animals and fish returning to the wilderness of far-off fields and to seas previously blocked by the waste of human consumption diminished with every passing month. By fall, in the Unites States, electoral ads and the great political divide eclipsed the pandemic, the wildfires, and the pronouncement of tornadoes looming near. A photograph of a black fly atop the vice-president's head heralded the nation's new intellectualism, a meme transformed into a thousand different jokes.

Oliver longed for his high school years, when he and his life had been important. He once found purpose in athletic competitions, in championing friends through difficulties, in being that kid on whom everyone could count.

What was left of those years? He had deleted his Facebook account. No one his age used Facebook anyway. His mother had insisted he join because she wanted to tag him in her photos and the small updates she sometimes posted. Nowadays, social media was a paltry stage for the hatred of strangers—friends of friends who attacked wayward posts landing on their timelines like bombs. He hated their memes most of all. He almost deleted his Snapchat account as well, but that was how he kept in touch with his old friends.

They seemed less perturbed than he was by the plagues washing over the country. Even Trey dismissed the words of sympathy sent to him after the murders of George Floyd and Breonna Taylor and the verdicts of grand juries. Trey sent a photo of himself taking the knee in his football uniform with the caption: *Blessed.* He received an onslaught of comments and deleted his story. And he asked everyone to stop sending their white-guilt shit his way.

"Wassup?" Oliver Snapped a week before his hike to Marys Rock.

Oliver's message lost traction among so many others.

Catch

In *Moral Letters to Lucilius* ("Letter 78: On the Healing Power of the Mind"), Lucius Annaeus Seneca, sometimes known as Seneca the Younger, wrote openly of his physical troubles and mental health.

Nearly two thousand years later, an excerpt from this letter, taken out of context, emblazons memes in a variety of fonts. A sentence transcribed onto t-shirts and bumper stickers and email signatures: "For sometimes it is an act of bravery even to live."

Yet Seneca did not survive with the force of his courage alone. Caligula, cruel emperor, suppressed a mandate to execute Seneca because his writings revealed he would soon die of his physical ailments. His words saved him, if only temporarily, until Nero—Seneca's former pupil—believing him an actor in the Pisonian conspiracy, ordered him to end his life. Seneca obeyed.

Roar

Oliver said, "Isn't it strange? Every year we pass the anniversary of our death and don't even know it."

"I've never thought about it, really," his mother said.

"Unless we choose or discover that date, at some point."

"Like the dating episode with the breakup countdown clock on *Black Mirror*?" she asked. "Were you thinking of a dystopian future?"

"When you just know it's time. Like a feeling. Like there's nothing left to do here."

"There's always something left. I can't imagine a day without a to-do list. I'd welcome it. No one ever feels like all their boxes have been checked."

Oliver asked, "What about Mr. Olson?"

"Maybe Mr. Olson."

"The bell tolls louder these days," Oliver said.

"Things will be back to normal soon."

"And if they don't? What if we're on the brink of the end-all? It's self-immolation to watch it all burn to hell like this."

"Oh, my," she said, "I'm raising quite the philosopher. Have you been reading Heidegger again? Let me guess: Kafka and Dostoyevsky?"

"Nietzsche."

"Well, that explains your mood. Make us some popcorn. When life gives you nihilism, turn on Netflix."

She would remember this conversation and the opportunity he'd given her to understand him, yet he hadn't confided the extent of his fears for the future. She wondered, with astonishing pain, if having a father could have made a difference. Mr. Olson had been a surrogate grandfather and his only paternal figure. In leaving this world, he'd unwittingly invited Oliver to follow his example.

Mothers soothed and cajoled. They combed hair and washed faces for school pictures. They prepared lunchboxes and afternoon snacks. Fathers, like Mr. Olson, went off to war. They were born to roar and combat, to inspire and to save.

Burn

This story is too long. It's not the word count, per se. There's a certain tedium and exhaustion rising from these pages—the point seems belabored. While the writing is, at times, quite compelling, the jarring shifts between—what?—journalistic flashes of this terrible year and the life of one young man seem incongruous. And notice the sections where the POV suddenly shifts to the mother—that's asking a lot from our readers. (Are you familiar with our magazine? We like stories that pop a bit more, that are urban, and that focus on the grittiness of the American experience. Where's Front Royal?) The mother's sections feel like separate vignettes: rushed and unformed and somewhat uninformed. We understand what you're trying to do here. We do. (We read with great interest your note concerning the life of the young man for whom you wrote this story.) We appreciate your effort to say something meaningful about our youth and their despair, and the culture at large. Please know your piece generated much discussion among the members of our editorial board and made it to the final round of consideration. Your story didn't quite resonate with us the way we hoped, so we must decline its inclusion in our pages. We wish you the best of luck with your writing and hope you'll think of us in the future when submitting your work.

Heat

Oliver tried to date Niloufar, who played the trombone in the marching band, but her parents were opposed because he wasn't Muslim. In turn, Oliver's friends expected him to date members of the cheer squad or the dance team, but he was attracted to girls who talked of climate change and immigration policies. He'd been raised by a strong woman with whom he discussed the state of the world since he was a child. His mother had once been a corporate lawyer in D.C.

Nilou also wanted to study law. She received top marks in their Principles of Government class. Oliver first noticed her sitting in the front row of their classroom.

During her presentation on the necessity for adequate

treatment for mentally-ill prisoners, she tucked a strand of her hair behind her ear and blushed from nervousness. She discussed the story of Jamycheal Mitchell, who died in a Virginia jail cell while awaiting trial for stealing a Snickers bar, a Mountain Dew, and a Zebra cake. She brought those items to class and placed them on the desk in front of her. The sheets of paper she held quivered while her words rang through the classroom in lilting syllables. A sophomore clucked his tongue and swayed his head from side to side because he believed her to be from India. Two girls rolled their eyes at him, yet they smiled at the entertainment. Together, the three of them snickered. Oliver pointed his pencil at the boy and made a face that shut him up. No one laughed at Niloufar in class again.

Conflagration

These are among the last photos he took: a flower growing in a crevice of rock. A little bird, curious, its head roving. Also, a sweeping view of the valley. Before that day: photos of his friends sitting atop the roofs of their cars, in the school parking lot, *a conference*; one meal, a burger from a drive-thru, yellow paper holding the bun, on his lap, while driving his truck, *a consecration*; Mr. Olson, waving from his bed, smiling even with the cannula fogging at his nostrils, *a commemoration*; self-portraits in various facial poses, eyebrow lifted, lips tucked, the bulging eye of disbelief, *a consternation*. Snapshots of people, animals, and things in their collectives.

Here are the objects of his room: on his bed a stuffed bear. No, not a bear, but a well-worn dog, ears curled with age. A gray-black dog he received when he was just a boy, from his mother's best friend Grace, an aspiring writer and artist, after the passing of Winston, her first Newfoundland. Identical stuffed dogs, mementos distributed to neighborhood children, in remembrance of the gentle giant she used to walk on their streets. How they loved to scratch his back and watch the fluff of his tail wag and wag. Grace and her husband Daniel soon surprised the neighborhood with a new puppy they named Abraham.

On his bed: nothing else. Bedclothes tucked in place.

On his desk: a mug from his childhood swim team filled with pencils. A laptop.

On his walls: medals and medals hooked on thumbtacks. More than one hundred orange *heat winner* and blue *first place* ribbons glued neatly in rows. Racing bibs from cross-country and track and field races. Photographs: his mother, his friends, himself. A dried boutonniere from a dance.

In his closet: rows of clothes, piles of shoes. The odor of a person, boy and man.

Smolder

They came to Sylvie weeping, six feet apart. Grace held her to standing. *To hell with the quarantine*, Grace said. Sylvie could not remember all their faces: acquaintances and near-strangers who had come to this outdoor gathering to support *her* and to remember *him*. His friends arrived, the boys from his teams: Jacob and Nick and Sung-ho, among so many others, their heads bowed, and the girls, some of whom were ex-girlfriends: Cassandra and Maddy and Jilly, red-faced and crying.

Trey dressed in a dark suit, wearing one of Oliver's ties. At the makeshift lectern by the picnic tables, he faltered and crouched to the ground. Trey's father read the last paragraph of his eulogy.

Niloufar and her parents brought platters of Iranian food Oliver had eaten, with them in their home, and loved.

His teachers and coaches, now docile and tender-voiced, wondered how and when they failed him. They spoke of his greatness, his compassion, his steadfastness. They spoke of his ability to encourage others to strive for their best.

They could not believe it was true. He was gone.

Sylvie was overwhelmed by everyone's attention and kindness, yet it would never be enough.

Embers

Next to him, a little bird pecked the rock landing for scraps. Oliver tossed a cracker, which the bird nipped before retreating to a crevice. He pulled his cellphone from his pocket and snapped a picture of the bird and the view before him. A breeze cooled the beads of sweat on his neck. He was filled with a temporary sense of reprieve. Perhaps he should live like a hermit in the woods for some years. He would become a trail legend, the bearded man-bear spotted by hikers and ultrarunners combing the area. Perhaps he should not live at all. He had come to this place for this, at last.

He looked at his cellphone. He understood the terrible pain he inflicted, yet he felt removed from it. It wasn't death he courted as much as disappearance. He wanted not to feel the world and its every heartbeat. Every day, he woke with a sense of dread that wouldn't fade. Every day, he heard fresh news of calamity and hatred. Fellow citizens lived separately in a divided country. Stores and schools and theaters shuttered. Faces half-hid. Bodies distanced. He never imagined the years of his young adulthood this way. Soon, he would wake up from this nightmare. Yes, he would awaken himself from the nightmare the only way he knew how. The episode would be over, and he and his mother would turn off their television for good.

He remembered a night he drove home in the dark. He hit a bear cub some miles from where he was now, and it died. He'd moved the body to the side of the road, out of cars' way, and his mother came for him to help him drive home. They returned to their house well past midnight. She hated technology, but she Snapped him, in those early days of that platform, when messages disappeared in the space of seconds. She wrote *I love you* in multiple installments, words appearing and disappearing with every contraction of her heart. He'd sensed her presence—the pulse of her being bounding them together—his body born of her body.

He pressed the icon of the little ghost wavering on a yellow background. He scrolled and scrolled to find his mother's avatar. Then he sent her his last message.

Ashes

Sylvie's friend Grace wrote a short story for Oliver, so he might live on the page, but no one wanted to publish it: all these words lit by the fire of their loss were left unread.

Sylvie sent messages into the void, words which disappeared before her.

Words consumed her now.

She opened her Snapchat, his last message long gone. She hadn't known how to capture it, and it vanished. She hadn't known its importance. She called him back immediately. He couldn't answer.

Those reading her Snap story wouldn't understand her

grief. They would only see letters separated into small signifiers, singular syllables trying to uphold the weight of her snuffed out world. It was impossible to move forward—to move *on*—as they said, when everything in her life was *off*, a blinking series of ones and zeroes that transformed into a coded language no one could translate for her. She tried to find the right words, the correct signals serialized through space and time to commemorate who Oliver had been—infant, boy, and man—and how much he would always mean to her. She typed her message and sent it out, again and again and again.

He was my son

He was my

He was

Boys and Girls Swimming Like Dolphins

He was sitting in the waiting room of the fertility clinic where his wife had scheduled an appointment. On the television above a row of empty seats, a nature program explored the rites of passage of Danish teenagers in the Faroe Islands, of which he'd never heard before. The teenagers spoke a strange language, subtitles shining their words in white. The camera showed these boys, just come from the sea, laughing and hollering on sandy beaches, their hair wet and disheveled. They exuded joy. They had just become men.

He watched the screen, unable to look away. On the half-moon beach, hundreds of pilot whales lay in tide pools of blood. They appeared more like dolphins than whales. Even the waves of the sea were tinted a magenta pink. Such was the scale of the massacre. In this country, the practice of whaling weaved itself with manhood: these boys had to lure the whales into the bay, wading first through shallow waters and then deeper into the sea, to sever the whales' spinal cords with lances, a custom centuries old. The boys pulled the carcasses onto the beach and danced and hooted in victory.

When he first looked up at the screen, at the boys and not the blood, he smiled, thinking of his wife at home. She watched documentaries lately and, just yesterday, one about Korean women diving into the ocean. Filmed from afar, their bodies looked like dolphins, encased in their charcoal-dark rubber suits. He wanted to call his wife, to tell her about what he just saw, but he was afraid she'd ask about the appointment. He would tell her later, when he got home.

He thought of his classroom of five- and six-year-old Kindergartners. He'd taught them for a decade now and before this as a substitute teacher, but that work was part-time, and with a few additional night classes at the local college, he earned the certification to become a full-time elementary schoolteacher. He loved the little imps, the unruly ones with their fingers exploring their noses, the prim and proper ones wearing their hair slicked back with a wet comb, the loud ones, the daydreamers. He liked teaching them to read, to count, to tie their shoes. Simple acts which would stay with them for the whole of their lives. He thought of them and of the killer boys across the Atlantic, and he didn't know how one could become the other, how in ten years' time some of his students might hurt each other or do drugs or have sex— the real kind, not this clinical thing he'd come here to accomplish—and he shuddered. He considered calling his wife again, but he hesitated and let the thought go.

He wondered if the nurses at the reception desk knew of the images projected on the television screen. He was grateful there were no children in the room, and he was relieved when a nurse opened one of the doors and called his name. She proffered a small plastic container with a lid on which his name had already been inscribed in black marker.

"In this little cup?" he asked her. He held it up for her inspection.

The nurse didn't answer him. "It's this way." She led him to a door and ushered him inside the room. "Take your time in here. There are magazines in the cupboards above the sink if you need them." She showed him a miniature fridge. "When you're done, put the cup in here."

"In the door or on the shelves?"

"Doesn't matter."

He was nervous. "Well, wish me luck."

She raised an eyebrow and didn't reply.

After she left, he sat down, only to get back up and open the fridge. It was empty. He welcomed the cold air on his face.

*　　*　　*

On the other side of town, in their kitchen, his wife rolled out balls of *pâte à choux* to make tiny profiteroles for dessert, just as he liked them. How he loved little pastries. She was frustrated by the composition of this meal, the preparation of a dinner of fish—choice Chilean sea bass—and mashed cauliflower purée. She'd make a beet salad right before he came home, so the meal would be perfectly cooked and warm while the beets marinated and cooled. She preferred steak and potatoes and biscuits, yet her husband liked to eat refined foods with names like distant provinces: amaranth, matcha, ceviche, rémoulade. She never cooked and she was afraid of not being able to follow instructions, she, a veteran soldier who had served in Afghanistan twice. She was a Marine. Now she was in her kitchen, cooking.

She knew how much he hated the thought of going to the fertility clinic. He fought hard against the appointment. His line of defense: "It's only been two and a half years. That's normal." Her reply: "I just don't want to wait, if there's something we can do." Since making the appointment for her husband, she'd been plagued with nightmares. They were all a variation of the same fear: their inability to conceive was her fault. She thought of herself as damaged since her body had been shaken by a minor explosion the last time she was out there, some miles from Kabul. In her dreams, he always told her, "I knew it." And then she cried, which in life she rarely did.

They both wanted a child, yet she sensed he suspected her body of being incapable of pregnancy. He never hinted at or said this. She simply believed he would look at her differently when they found out who was to blame.

What he actually told her was the opposite: "No one is to blame." To her dismay, he sang a Howard Jones song. She was four years old when this song became a hit; he was ten. He often belted out lyrics to punctuate their conversation, which sometimes irritated her, especially when she tried to say something she believed he needed to hear. She thought maybe his age had something to do with their circumstances. He was forty-two.

She wanted to pacify him. He told her just before leaving for the appointment he thought the performance embarrassing. She already had her appointment, which, she said, involved stirrups and speculums and the invasion of strangers' fingers into her body. Her doctor's consultation violated her privacy; his did not. To this he said, "Everyone will know what I'm doing in that room." She rolled her eyes at him.

She thought a fine meal and chilled pinot gris would bring them closer again. The exams now over, they would soon know results, and it would be a matter of making decisions and taking action. She was eager to move forward with their plans. To distract herself while she cooked, she turned on her tablet, which she set on the little easel he used to prop his cookbooks. She looked at the thumbnails of the available programs and clicked on an image of a partially toothless Korean woman wearing a diver's suit. The night before, she'd begun watching the documentary *Haenyeo* on the lives of the women divers of Jeju Island. She slowed her chopping of beets and mint, and in the process forgot the profiteroles in the oven, which, just ten minutes earlier, were rising golden. Now she smelled smoke and opened the oven door to find the little puffs blackened. "Shit," she said. She grabbed her mitts in haste and put them on halfway. While pulling out the cookie sheet, she burned her wrist on the oven rack. She slammed the sheet on the counter and placed her arm under cold water at the sink.

*   *   *

He could not rid from his mind the image of Danish boys lording over dead whales. He'd been in the room for more than thirty minutes. He even opened the cupboards to look at magazines, yet they didn't help. He grew anxious, pressured by time and his wife's expectations. He didn't want to be there. Maybe he couldn't fill the cup because he resented her for making him go through this testing. He wanted a child, but he was doing this for her.

He thought of their courtship when they were free to discover each other. He missed the simple selfishness of thinking only of their immediate needs—the long Sundays spent in bed, the walks through parks and the old part of town with the quaint shops and restaurants, the car rides to antique malls in the country. They'd laughed together and been happy. Lately, they were too enthralled by the idea of starting a family. Their early enthusiasm at the prospect of parenthood had been a bond between them. She invited him to contribute to a Pinterest board dedicated to nursery decor. To satisfy her, he pinned pictures of pretty painted walls, tall stuffed giraffes, cozy woolen blankets.

At one point she split the board in two: boy, girl. She wanted a boy; he wanted a girl. He remembered sending her YouTube videos of crocheted booties in the shape of baby ducks. "We need to learn to make animal booties," he said. They bought needles and yarn at the craft store. Their first trials resulted in shabby reproductions, yet he knitted a pair of black-and-white panda bears, with round ears atop their heads, which garnered him much attention on Instagram. "OMG. I can't believe you made those!" their friends commented.

They hadn't made crafts or shopped for their future baby in a while now. He wondered when they gave up or began to fear their efforts were in vain. He observed the fridge in the room, which seemed to whir with accusatory tones. He picked up the cup and stared into it. He just couldn't imagine what he could say to his wife when he got home. Maybe she would understand his predicament and feel a sense of vindication that he couldn't perform. He could present the problem as a means to flatter her: *This feels wrong without you.* Somehow, he didn't think she'd be impressed by this soft fidelity. He opened the door to leave.

He approached the nurse at the reception desk. "Hi." He held up the empty cup.

"It's all right," she said. She smiled, for the first time with sympathy. "It happens."

"It's the documentary you had on," he tried to explain. "There were hundreds of whales killed by these boys from the Faroe Islands. Some sort of rite of passage. I couldn't get the image out of my head."

"I get it," she said. "When I need to cry and I feel a lump in my throat, I think of puppies stuck in farming equipment or Sarah McLachlan singing to those cats with gimpy legs and milky eyes. Works every time. I just start to sob." She leaned in. "I guess you thought of the wrong thing at the wrong time."

He nodded. "Yes, I guess so. What can I do?"

"Take the cup home."

"Was that always an option?"

"No, because it's better here. We can't control your refrigeration or the possible contamination of your sample."

He put the lid back on the cup. "So, how do we do this?"

"You go home. When you're done, you put your cup in the freezer and you come back here within twenty-four hours." She handed him a sheet of instructions. "Take note of our hours. We're closed on Mondays."

At least he wasn't the only one who failed at the clinic. "Thank you," he said. And, to alleviate the mood, he told her in a German accent, "I'll be back."

*   *   *

The dinner was going to be ruined. Her plans to thank him for the ordeal of the clinic were unravelling. She held the edge of the counter and stretched her back, which had been aching all day. Months of physical therapy a decade earlier hadn't helped with her back pain. Sometimes her husband led her through a series of stretching exercises before bed, but lately this routine hadn't worked. He was limber and agile, a former gymnast turned high school cheerleader. Their team had gone to nationals. Sometimes it bothered her that he hadn't been a football star. He was the guy on the sidelines tossing girls into the air and tumbling in front of bleachers to mark every touchdown. She'd been a soccer star. After a serious knee injury, which put an end to her college scholarship, she joined the ROTC and then, after graduation, the military.

In front of her, the haenyeo were plunging to great depths without breathing equipment. She watched them gather sea cucumbers and abalone shells, loosening them from rocks with long knives, careful not to disturb a delicate ecology. Her wrist throbbed from her oven burn. She wrapped a wet paper towel around her reddening skin, which would blister. She would have a scar to remember this day by. To focus her energies and calm her growing anger, she prepared the vinaigrette for the beet salad. If she could cook the fish well, the meal might be salvaged.

She threw out the profiteroles, washed the cookie sheet, and put it away. They would do without dessert. She heard the whistles of the haenyeo calling to each other as they emerged from the water, signaling their location within the waves. She had never seen women of such ages swim like this, like the most graceful fish. Their bodies dressed in dark rubbery suits and their long fins reminded her of dolphins. Had her husband said this the night before? Some of the women were as old as eighty-five. She watched the praying rituals of these matriarchs, who, on dry land, formed an occupational society of women.

She wondered what it would be like to live on an island like this, to be the very best in her field, a chosen diver among many. She remembered feeling accomplished in her youth. When she was a little girl, she sold more Girl Scout cookies than anyone else in her council, which earned her a special patch. As a teenager, she studied abroad in Köln, Germany, for two years, and she learned the language well. She moved back to the States for her senior year of high school, and it took quite some time for her to lose the accent she acquired. Much later, when she was stationed in Stuttgart, the accent returned.

Even in the early days of their courtship, her husband made her feel like she could do anything. They learned to play guitar together, however poorly, and they sang a folksy duet at a party. She loved him for his playfulness, for the way he egged her on and dared her to go onstage when they went to see a comedian who performed magic and hypnosis. The comedian had her squawk like a chicken in front of hundreds of strangers. Afterward, when she saw the video, she laughed at herself until she hiccupped. Her husband was different from the other men she'd dated. He made her feel seen.

These days, she grew more serious and affected by small and large events alike. She didn't know if wanting a child somehow deprived her of her childlike curiosity. In trying to become a mother, maybe she'd also become matronly. When she was moody, he always said, while massaging her shoulders, "Oh, loosen up." Sometimes she followed his advice and sometimes she gave in to her mercurial feelings. If test results demonstrated her body was at fault, how would she survive hormone injections and accompanying mood swings? She'd be relieved if the culprit of their infertility was his lack of sperm motility. She knew her selfishness grew from her fears and nightmares. She apprehended his reaction when they'd sit, side by side, in the office of their doctor, who'd tell them what impeded the conception of their child. She would want to disappear if as she once read in a pamphlet—he described her uterus as inhospitable, like a no man's land in a war zone.

*　　*　　*

While driving home, he imagined cliffs and houses with the moss-thatched roofs of fairy tales, however marred by bloodshed. This was landscape to inspire the writing of Red Riding Hood raped by the wolf, the Little Mermaid killed by her own hand, and children cannibalized by the witch in Hansel and Gretel. Sometimes the monsters were young boys from small villages in remote island countries. Sometimes they were sons or fathers, brothers or uncles. Men so easily turned into monsters.

He remembered his father catching him with a book of tales about the rascally adventures of an orphan girl. He'd been reading in bed at the age of nine or ten, and his father laughed at him. "That's not good for you," he said. "Why don't you just pick up some Superman comics? I read those as a boy." His father hadn't been a monster, but he was unaffectionate and often distant, disappointed his son was better at individual sports instead of being a strong member of a team throwing or kicking balls. He was often busy, working long hours as a criminal defense attorney, a position that led him to drink too many whiskeys and contributed to his death in his early sixties.

He tried to make his father proud, but the effort of making his father love him crushed his hopes. He vowed to be different with his child.

He was preoccupied by his failure at the clinic, yet he found solace in the triviality of his situation. They would have a child, a boy, not only to make her happy, but also because she was right: a boy could protect future siblings, a boy could set the tone for their family. Their boy wouldn't grow up dreaming of killing whales that looked like dolphins. Their son's manhood would be tested the American way: by eating too many hamburgers and wrestling neighborhood boys and spitting on sidewalks and maybe even playing youth football. He wouldn't force his son to learn that sport or play the drums or raise a big dog, but he wouldn't steer him away from those things, either. Maybe he'd wanted a girl for fear of becoming like his father. He remembered him less and less since his marriage. His wife eclipsed the memories of his childhood with her love.

Through the windshield of his car, he saw the sun setting, a haze of pinkish orange turning to inky blue. The thought of going home to his wife comforted him. He would explain to her what happened. Together they would fill the plastic cup, for them now a sort of Holy Grail. He hoped she'd laugh with him at the absurdity of his predicament, that she'd realize there were bigger worries in the world than empty cups, like raising boys with enough love and faith to prevent them from becoming savage men.

*   *   *

She set the dinner on a pretty tablecloth. She pulled out the lacy napkins from the back of the linen closet and placed silver candlesticks in the center of the table. The beet salad turned out not as sweet as she wanted. The bass, which she tried to cook to a hint of flaky pink, was overdone and tough, and the cauliflower purée tasted too salty. She thought the meal a complete disaster. She wallowed in worry, yet she thought of the sea women of Jeju Island, who braved freezing temperatures, wind gales, and sharks. One of the women, eighty-two years old, spoke to the camera: her eyes, filmed with cataracts, glinted with mischief. She told the interviewer she would die by the sea. The subtitles explained she started diving as a child and been named a haenyeo at fifteen.

The wife sat at the table waiting for her husband to walk through the front door. She wished she could be an old woman on the other side of the world. How small her own life seemed, with her best accomplishments lodged firmly in the past. Now she worked in the publicity division of Veterans Affairs as an executive. She thought the work physically easy, there at the desk of her private office, but with this ease came other discomforts: the visiting lieutenant colonel who asked her for a cup of coffee as though she were his personal assistant; the nagging feeling she should be back out there, in the field, as a soldier, a rush of adrenaline coursing in her blood; the echoing clock above her desk that ticked and ticked and ticked, more slowly it seemed with each passing day.

Unlike the haenyeo, she had no strong currents to swim against, only terrible meals to cook and the luxury of fertility clinics to aid her body. Watching women swimming in circles, she knew she would weather the hormone therapy, culminating in the birth of their baby. She remembered running free on the soccer field, cleats lifting clumps of muddy grass with every foot strike, the smell in the air and the points of light like glowing embers against the shadows of dusk. She scored the winning goal of the last game that year and made the front page of the local newspaper. She was offered a full-ride scholarship to a good, midsize university.

She thought of her husband, driving across town. When he got home, tired and irritated by his appointment at the clinic, he would realize the hours she spent preparing this dinner and, when she'd say to him, *Nailed it!*, she hoped he'd laugh with her and pretend to love the meal. She sat there at the table thinking of a certain success in her failure when the doorbell rang. She stood to go open the door. A deliveryman pushed a crate on a dolly. She recognized the logo of her monthly Beers of the World Club shipment, which she subscribed to because she missed her European beers, especially the monastic centuries-old dark ales from Flanders.

"Looks like you'll have a happy man when he sees this," the deliveryman said nicely.

"They're *my* beers." She glared at him, this nondescript man who came to her door only to do his job. She wanted to say more, but she stopped herself from defending her choices. "My husband likes mojitos and Moscow mules," she said, moving aside so he could deposit the crate beyond the threshold. She signed her name on the pad.

"Well, you enjoy your beer," he said. And, halfway down the walkway to his delivery truck, he turned to her and waved. "Please thank your husband for his service. We need more men like him in this country."

She stood there, alone, and watched his vehicle disappear down the street. He must have read the personalized license plate on her truck: S3MPRFI embossed on a wavering American flag. She remembered a day when the pain of her lumbago was killing her, the old injury sprung loose through her nerves, and she parked in the veterans' spot nearest the grocery store entrance. A man in one of those matchbox electric cars, driver-side window rolled down, yelled as he passed her: "That spot is for vets only. Shame on you!"

She tried to run after him but couldn't, so she spat at his car and held up both middle fingers while shouting she was a decorated Marine. He drove off without glancing at her reflection, growing smaller and smaller, in his rearview mirror.

She'd wanted a boy so badly. How had she come to this, to desire one child over another because of the inherent simplicity of being male? When had she become so jaded by being a woman that she couldn't contemplate the joy of passing on everything she knew and was and had been to her daughter? A little girl running and riding her bicycle, screaming English and German words to strangers while shopping because she hated shopping and putting on nice clothes and playing with a doll while sitting nicely in the rolling cart pushed by her father. She would prefer to play with the toy hammer, like her mother, who gave her nails and wooden planks and a real screwdriver to make things. This girl of hers would build things, countries of new things. They would name her Aidan or Blake or Cameron. Or maybe Arabella. It didn't matter. She imagined her clearly: in the darkened suit worn by generations of older women, her daughter would swim against currents in long circles and icy lines.

She went back to the kitchen and assessed the meal on the pretty tablecloth. The beets leached blood-red over wilting leaves of young spinach. The mashed cauliflower formed a yellow crust, just as the fish hardened on the plate. She seized the bowls and the platter, scraped them clean over the trashcan. All that work for nothing. It didn't matter. She had other things to do, other plans to make, other sacrifices of her time and of her body to choose. There were bigger things in this world to consider than conciliatory meals, like raising a girl to hold her breath under the sea, a knife clamped between her teeth.

Notes on the Stories

All place names in the text are spelled correctly. Marys Rock in Shenandoah National Park does not need an apostrophe.

Although not entirely impossible, it is unlikely seventeen-year-old Liz Fraser read *Blood Meridian* in "The Ethics of Keeping Company with Strangers." While the story takes place in September 1986 and McCarthy published his novel a year earlier, few copies circulated at the time. The novel, much like McCarthy's career, gained widespread readership after the publication in 1992 of *All the Pretty Horses.*

I mention many historical and cultural figures in this manuscript. In most instances, the reference is brief, but I wish to note that all women painters in "Godfrey Green," such as Marie-Gabrielle Capet, Jeanne-Élisabeth Chaudet, Adélaïde Labille-Guiard, the Lemoine sisters—Marie-Victoire, Marie-Élisabeth (sometimes credited as Mme Gabiou), Marie-Geneviève, and Marie-Denise—Clara Peeters, and Élisabeth Vigée Le Brun were true iconoclasts of their time, showing their works, when socially allowed, alongside the artistry of more famous men. While paintings and drawings by Labille-Guiard and Peeters, and most extensively by Vigée Le Brun, are exhibited in some of the finest museums in the world, the oeuvre of the Lemoine sisters and their cousin Chaudet fell into semi-obscurity until recently. From June to October of 2023, a great selection of their works was gathered for the first time at the Musée Fragonard in Grasse, France in an exhibition titled "Je déclare vivre de mon art" (I declare that I live from my art). I was in Grasse with my husband and my sister a few months before the opening, and I am so sorry to have missed this inaugural and crucial exhibition. The cover of this book features a detail from the painting *Madame Grand (Noël Catherine Vorlée 1761-1835)*, 1783, by Élisabeth Louise Vigée Le Brun, courtesy of The Metropolitan Museum of Art's Open Access Initiative.

With the exception of Martha Moats Baker, all characters in the stories are fictitious. Not much is known about Martha and, where possible, I included details I knew to be true: She was married to one John Baker, she had a son named Roy, and she wore nice leather shoes on her fatal hike to the other side of Brushy Mountain. All other details in the story are pure speculation on my part. Today, on what is now known as the Wild Oak Trail, a plaque reads:

MARTHA MOATS BAKER
BORN 1880
FROZE TO DEATH NEAR THIS SPOT ON BRUSHY MT.
JANUARY 1925
FOUND ON AUG. 30, 1925

I became interested in Martha's story after running the Martha Moats Baker Memorial 50K in 2013. Denis Herr founded this race sponsored by the Virginia Happy Trails Running Club. For many years, he said a prayer for Martha before sending participants to run one of the most grueling races in Virginia. I cannot fathom how a forty-five-year-old woman with no athletic training and a pretty little pair of shoes could have made this ascent in a snowstorm and not for the first time. "Over the Mountain Steep" was my attempt at imagining her story and making sense of either her courage or foolishness.

I lived in the province of Friuli-Venezia-Giulia in Italy from the mid-90s to 2001. I took inspiration for the character of Eddi in "Last of the Viking Seals" from a number of women in my acquaintance who were always frank, offering their voluble opinions regardless of their reception. At the time, national fear of both Romani and Albanians was rampant. I heard stories of nocturnal thieves who despoiled victims sedated by hoses of sleeping gas inserted through vents and open windows. The train conductor's suspicion of Matteo's mother stems from these widespread beliefs.

283

Finally, I wish to address my dedication to A. in "The Words of All Our Fires." I wrote "The Boy and the Bear" for my eldest son Philippe, who, like Oliver, was a runner and swimmer in high school. There the resemblances end. I am not Sylvie and he is not Oliver, though I felt deeply the hardship of letting go of a child on the cusp of manhood and independence. Four years after this story's publication, one of my son's longtime friends left this world far too early. His death marked me in profound ways, and I still think of him often. He was a gifted athlete, a true leader. Watching him swim a sprint, a medley, a team relay, or a long 500-meter freestyle left us spectators in awe. He was intelligent, curious, spontaneously funny, and always sensitive to the needs of others. He was the kind of teenager who could talk to adults as effortlessly as he talked to his peers. Again, there the resemblances to Oliver end. A. is not Oliver and Sylvie is not A.'s mother, one of the loveliest women I have ever met. The circumstances, characters, and settings of the story are purely my own. I wrote this short story during the course of three days in September 2020. The writing flowed from somewhere deep within me, from a place I can only describe as a wellspring of grief. "The Words of All Our Fires" was accepted for publication (at *Storgy Magazine UK*) faster than any other story I have written.

Anders, you are never forgotten.

Publishing Credits

The stories in *The Kindness of Terrible People* appeared in slightly different form in the following magazines:

"To Lie Engulfed in the Waves of the Sea" (as "Manon, Christophe, and the Sea") in *Maryland Literary Review*.

"The Ethics of Keeping Company with Strangers" (as "Small Signals") in the anthology *Muddy Backroads: Stories from Off the Beaten Path*.

"Madeleine Bouletier, She-Wolf of Crozon" in *Orca: A Literary Journal*.

"Love Among the Orange Groves of Old Hollywood" (as "Jude and Mary's House of Love," 2017), "The Boy and the Bear" (2015), "Over the Mountain Steep" (2018), "Godfrey Green" (2022), and "The Beast Who Knew the Songs of Billie Holiday" (as "Lost & Found," 2020) in *The Northern Virginia Review*.

"A Baby of the Ganges" in *Fiction International*.

"The Kindness of Terrible People" in *Griffel*.

"What Came After the Harvest" (as "Yields of Harvest") in *Broad River Review*.

"Olympic Hopeful, 19, Dies After Winning U.S. Figure Skating Championships" (as "Slaked") in *Cerasus Magazine*.

"The Words of All Our Fires" in *Storgy Magazine*.
"Boys and Girls Swimming Like Dolphins" (as "The Shape of Dolphins") in *Stonecoast Review*.

Acknowledgments

I give a thousand thanks to mentors, editors, and friends who read early versions of some stories and provided invaluable feedback: Richard Bausch, Maria Browning, Whitney Bryant, Lucy Corin, Walter Cummins, Mark Facknitz, Steve Goodwin, David Grand, René Steinke, Michael Strzelecki, Tom Zoellner.

Jennifer Buxton Haupt read the entirety of this collection in its first iteration, and her thoughtful comments informed the initial order of these stories. I am thankful for her time and dedication.

I send my gratitude heavenward to the wisest counselor and keenest editor, the late Robert Bausch. When introducing me, Bob liked to say, "I taught her everything she knows!" He did teach me much about the writing craft—but even more so about generosity and compassion.

Bob, I wrote my way to the end, just as you said I would.

I am indebted to "Wild Bill" Taylor, my A.P. Literature teacher at Ogden High School, for not only praising the first personal essay I wrote in English, but also believing I had talent. I trusted my writing abilities because you did. You were one hell of a teacher.

Jeffery Renard Allen generously endorsed this book, and I am forever grateful for his support.

For motivation and writerly conversations, I must thank the following individuals: Renée Ashley, Denny Bausch, LeAnn Bednar, Chloe Biggs, Coe Booth, Ashley Bradbury, Cameron Campbell, Rebecca Chace, Emily Chiles, Kelly Cochran-Yzquierdo, David Daniel, Ruth D'Eredita, Annick Dupal, Emmanuelle Dupal, Françoise Dupal, Patricia Dupal, Andrew Felsher, Brian Fence, Connie May Fowler, Donna Freitas, Erin Hill-Dowdle, Harvey Hix, Jo Houston, Shannon Jackson, Faye Jones, Jill McCorkle, Nicole Melleby, Marcella Amaya Musman, Dac Nelson, Lise Olsen, Ray Orkwis, Nathan Reilly, Rosie Schaap, Eliot Schrefer, LeeAnn Thomas, Padma Viswanathan, Ellen Graham Weeren, Kevin Winfrey.

These stories were written over the course of twenty-six years, with false starts and breaks, but the collection took shape while I was a graduate student at Fairleigh Dickinson University. There I received scholarships affording me time to write, and I wish to thank my benefactors from the bottom of my heart.

First and foremost, my deepest gratitude to Daniel C. and Martina Lewis: I could not have completed my studies without your financial assistance. I hope to pay it forward and to thank you in person someday. I also thank the J. Michael Adams family, the FDU Alumni Association, and Minna Zallman Proctor, sparkling director, for giving me an editorial assistantship with *The Literary Review*. René Steinke directed the program for a decade, and she was a dedicated and encouraging steward, a beautiful writer and friend. Both women supported my efforts, for which I am immensely grateful. Likewise, I must thank the fearless Gracelyn Weaver for helping me in countless ways.

At Wroxton College in Oxfordshire, where I composed parts of and edited many of these stories, my thanks go to Dr. Nicholas Baldwin, Sue Clempson, Robert Denton, Carol and Susan Harrison, John Hitchman, Amanda Mabbitt, Mavis Maloney, Sam Morris, Martine Perrett, Andrew Rose, and the entire housekeeping and kitchen staff.

My sincerest appreciation goes to my extended family members, by birth or marriage, my classmates in the MFA program, and all my colleagues at NVCC. I am sorry not to name you all here. Likewise, to my students, past and present, thanks for going along with the unorthodox assignments I created for you.

For my Fall 2023 Presidential Sabbatical, awarded by Northern Virginia Community College, I thank Dr. Anne Kress, Dr. Donna Minnich, the Board of Trustees, the College Personnel Board, and my Woodbridge Campus team: Maddie Coradin, David Epstein, Stephanie Harm, Dr. Richmond Hill, and Dr. Julie Quinn.

At *The Northern Virginia Review*, Adam Chiles, Ruth Stewart, and the entire editorial board, old and new: you championed my work over many years, for which I am so thankful. I am indebted to the following editors for selecting my stories: At *Broad River Review*,

Claire Allen, Reagan Davis, Anna Grace Jones, Victoria Price, and guest judge Crystal Wilkinson for choosing my story "Yields of Harvest" as runner-up for the Rash Award in Fiction (named for Ron Rash); at *Cerasus Magazine* (UK), Ashley Sapp and John Wilks; at *Fiction International*, Harold Jaffe and Laura Mazzenga; at *Griffel* (Norway), Milica Derocher and Liam Oliver; at *Maryland Literary Review*, Nathan Leslie; at *Orca: A Literary Journal*, Renee Jackson, Zac Kellian, and Joe Ponepinto; at *Stonecoast Review*, Shannon Bowring, Aimee DeGroat, and Katrina Ray-Saulis; and at *Storgy Magazine* (UK), Anthony Self.

The story "The Ethics of Keeping Company with Strangers" (as "Small Signals") was published in the anthology *Muddy Backroads: Stories from Off the Beaten Path* (MadVille Publishing, 2022). I thank publisher Kim Davis and editors Bonnie Jo Campbell and Luanne Smith. Luanne's generosity toward me and the writing community is unmatched. She is a true champion of women in the arts, and I am lucky to call her a friend.

My cosmic thanks go to Laurin Bellg, my soulful sister-in-writing, who belongs in just about every paragraph of these acknowledgments. You, Albert, Katie, and Kara, welcomed me in Door County when I needed it most. You taught me the arts of reframing situations, trusting my own instincts, and choosing empowerment, which allowed this volume to find a rightful home. Much gratitude to the Swan Abbey Editorial Board, Nikki

Kallio, Janet McIntyre, and Katie O'Connor, for accepting my submission for publication. And my thanks go to Dinah Drazin for designing the cover and typesetting the interior of this book. Her work is superb and elegant.

It takes a village, and I am fortunate to have the loveliest, wayfaring villagers with me.

My children Philippe, Drake, Luke, Mason, and Maia are the stars of our stage: thanks for being the greatest of players and accepting the many roles your dad and I assign you. I love you so very much.

Last but not least, my village has but one chieftain: my husband Travis, who makes all things possible. Love, let's build a hut on the coast of a boisterous sea and forever live like hermits. I love you mosterest.

*　　*　　*

Should you choose *The Kindness of Terrible People* for your book club, please register on my website, www.stephaniedupal.com, for a virtual discussion with me. I would be honored to spend time with you and to answer any questions you may have about these stories, the craft of writing, or the publishing process.